I0611001

Playboy in a Kilt

An Opposites Attract, Fake Engagement, Small Town Scottish Romance

Kilted Hearts

Book Three

Kait Nolan

Take The Leap Publishing

Copyright © 2023 by Kait Nolan

Cover Design by Lori Jackson

All rights reserved.

No part of this book may be reproduced in any form or by any electronic or mechanical means, including information storage and retrieval systems, without written permission from the author, except for the use of brief quotations in a book review.

ONE

"She didnae even try to deny it."

Connor MacKean took one look at Hamish Colquhoun's face and opened the door of his Airbnb wider. After seeing his best friend's wife out at a club in another guy's arms, he'd expected this visit.

Hamish stepped inside, prowling over to the window that afforded a glimpse of Edinburgh Castle—if you angled just right. Not that Connor thought his friend was admiring the view.

He shut the door. "Did you expect her to?"

"I dinna bloody ken. It's no' like there's a manual for how to confront your wife about having an affair." Temper had him sliding from his usual perfect diction back into the Highland Scots accent that had largely faded over his many years as a lawyer in Edinburgh.

Connor winced and wondered for the hundredth time if he'd done the right thing in telling Hamish what he'd seen at the club last night.

As he had for many years, he'd come to the city to celebrate New Year's Eve, expecting to break his eight-month hiatus from women and find an interesting companion to share his bed for the night. Instead, he'd turned down an offer from one of his charming former flings with an off-the-cuff lie about being engaged. To Sophie Cameron, his sister Kyla's best friend, of all people. Realizing he wasn't at all in the right headspace for the games he'd once been so damned good at, he'd turned to leave and spotted Dayna on the dance floor, snogging Kyla's ex.

How could he keep his mouth shut about *that?*

Not knowing what else to do, Connor crossed to the kitchen of the apartment and poured a glass of Glen Moray single-malt whisky. Then, figuring this wouldn't be an easy conversation, he poured himself one as well and carried them both to the window.

"I'm sorry. I ken I've basically blown up your life. But I just couldn't go on knowing what she'd done and let you continue your marriage as if everything was fine."

Surprise momentarily blanked out the misery on Hamish's face as he accepted the glass. "You weren't the one who blew up my life, mate. I've been doing a damned fine job of that all on my own."

"What are you talking about?"

Hamish took a long sip of whisky and closed his eyes. "Things havenae been right with Dayna for a long time. They were maybe never right, but I couldnae admit that to myself. Especially not once we had Freya. Not when I couldnae have..." He trailed off and drank again.

Connor frowned, wondering where all this was coming from. "Not when you couldnae have what?"

Hamish stared at the floor, his throat working. Guilt was etched in every line of his body when he met Connor's gaze again. "Afton."

Stunned to the marrow, Connor could only stare.

Afton Lennox had been part of their band of friends since childhood. And because of a three-hundred-year-old marriage pact between the MacKean and the Lennox families that held the fate of their respective estates hostage, she'd been Connor's intended bride from the moment she'd been born. Connor had long since resigned himself to his familial duty, and he'd made it a point to be friends with the woman he'd expected to spend the rest of his life with. But he'd deliberately avoided romantic entanglements with her, figuring it was better to enjoy his freedom while he had it, as he had no intention of breaking his vows once he took them.

How could he not know that Hamish had feelings for her? What kind of selfish prick was he not to have seen?

But he started thinking back to how Hamish had behaved around Afton. He'd always been a little more formal with her. Less physically comfortable and affectionate than he was with the rest of their group. So far as Connor knew, they'd never really hung out on their own. He'd just assumed they had little in common, but maybe it had been something else entirely. Maybe it had been about maintaining a strict propriety because, so far as Hamish was concerned, she'd been taken. He couldn't have pursued anything with her because she was meant to marry Connor.

"I dinna ken what to say."

"There's more."

Realizing his friend was determined to unburden himself, Connor took a bracing sip of his own drink. "All right."

"I kissed her."

"When?"

He hesitated. "The day before she disappeared."

"Oh." Probably he ought to say more than that, but it was all he could manage through the shock. That had been just a week before the wedding that wasn't.

"I didnae plan on it. And I never set out to betray you. I swear it."

Seeing Hamish's knuckles going white, Connor gripped his shoulder. "You didnae betray me. I was never in love with Afton. You ken that well enough."

"It's not just that." Misery bowed his shoulders as he dropped into a nearby chair. "I'm the one who told her about the loophole. That she could gamble away the estate."

"Oh." Connor knew he was beginning to sound like a broken record, but none of this was what he'd expected in the wake of Hamish confronting Dayna about her infidelity.

"I never wanted to hurt anyone. But I saw how much Afton was struggling with your impending wedding and being trapped in an arranged marriage, and I couldnae *not* tell her. Even though I knew it could mean that you and Kyla would lose Ardinmuir."

Connor thought back to what Hamish had said to him at the "engagement" party the day the final banns had been read. That he hadn't been doing right by Afton. And he'd been correct. Connor had been all caught up in his own feelings about their imminent marriage and had given up on the idea of ever getting out of it. Hamish had spent most of his career as a lawyer searching for a way and finding nothing.

Another piece clicked into place.

"So, all those years you hunted for a way to dissolve the marriage pact...?"

Hamish nodded. "It was the reason I went into law. I'd likely have done it just for you, either way. But I hoped I'd find something that would free you both. And I did. But when I told her, I never dreamed she'd actually go through with it."

Instead, Afton had surprised them all, sneaking out of town and heading to Las Vegas, where she'd gambled the entirety of her estate, Lochmara, to an American cowboy. The one his sister Kyla had ended up marrying seven months ago, thus resolving the pact and saving their ancestral home from the longest-standing threat they faced.

"I think you can stop beating yourself up over that. Because Kyla and Raleigh are perfect for each other, and you saved me from a loveless marriage. In the end, it all worked out for the best. At least regarding us. If you need my forgiveness, you have it."

"Thanks for that." Hamish drained the last of his glass.

Understanding that his friend's honor might need a little more, Connor pressed further. "And if you think you need my permission to pursue Afton, you dinna. She was never mine. Not in any real way."

"It's a non-issue, as she's dropped off the face of the earth since she went to the States."

A detective had tracked her as far as Vegas. Once Raleigh had come to claim Lochmara, they'd let the search drop, expecting her to return home eventually, at least to collect her things.

"She hasnae been in contact with you, either?" Connor asked.

"I'd have told you if she had. And anyway, I'm still not free. Not yet, anyway."

Connor settled back in his chair. "So that's it, then? No attempt at counseling or whatever?"

"There's no point. Dayna and I have been having problems for a while. This was just the final nail in the coffin. At least we willnae have to deal with the full year of separation. I think maybe that's why she had the affair. She wanted out."

"It's a bloody terrible way of going about it."

"I dinna disagree. But I think we're both relieved at the prospect of being done. Our marriage has become a farce. So, yes, I'll start divorce proceedings this week."

"And then what?"

Hamish loosed another long sigh, rolling the glass between his fingers. "That'll depend on what custody arrangements are agreed on. I want to move home to Glenlaig, and I want to bring Freya. I have no idea if Dayna will fight me on that."

"Well, of course, you can both come and stay at Ardinmuir while you get back on your feet, so you're not tucked up in your parents' spare room." What was the point of living in a massive, six-hundred-year-old castle if you couldn't provide space to friends?

"It'll be a while before we get to that point. But thanks for the offer."

Connor retrieved the bottle of whisky and poured them each another glass. "Well, for better or worse, it'll be good to have you home. In the meantime, is there anything else I can do to help?"

Hamish drained the second glass. "Just keep the whisky coming."

———

"I thank ye so much for staying open late for me today."

Sophie Cameron beamed a smile at the elderly gentleman on the other side of the counter. "Of course, Mr. Fraser. I'm just relieved everything turned out all right at your doctor's appointment."

William narrowed faded blue eyes and grimaced. "Bunch o' bother and nonsense. I'm healthy as a horse. But the missus insists they do the tests to prove it."

"As well she should. You're a catch. She'd never find the like of you again."

Her elderly customer blushed up to the tips of his ears.

At eighty-two-years young, William Fraser had been married to his wife, Hettie, for sixty-one years. The two of them still had regular date nights in the village and could frequently be seen walking the high street hand-in-hand. Every week, like clockwork, William stopped at Sophie's flower shop and bought a bouquet of Hettie's favorite blooms. As far as Sophie was concerned, the pair of them were #relationshipgoals, and she adored having the privilege of helping him bring a little brightness and love to his wife. It was the least she could do for the man who'd been her most regular customer since she'd bought Village Blume from her boss, Agnes McNeary, years before.

She handed over this week's clutch of hothouse tulips in a vibrant shade of pink. "These are sure to help combat the dreary skies."

"Aye, that they will. See you next week, lass."

"I look forward to it, as always. Tell Mrs. Fraser I said hello."

"I'll do that."

After seeing Mr. Fraser off, Sophie finally turned the sign in the front window to *Closed* and went through the usual routine to lock up for the night. It didn't take long. She'd already cleared her workstations in the back while she'd been waiting for William to arrive, so she only needed to shut down the POS system and review tomorrow's list of arrangements. After checking one last time to make certain the cooler where she kept her stock was closed, she locked the door. For a fleeting moment, she considered walking up to The Stag's Head pub for supper. She was exhausted. But she still had a few hours' work to do for her second job, so she opted to head home and put together a sandwich and cuppa soup to eat at her computer.

Darkness fell so early in the Highlands this time of year. Not that it stopped the residents of Glenlaig from getting out and about. Sophie nodded in greeting to the many familiar faces she passed on the walk home. She loved that. Loved living in a village small enough to know most everyone. Or feel like she did, at least. It meant that she was witness to all the joys of her friends and neighbors. The births, the weddings, the anniversaries, the celebrations. And she was there to pay respects at the tragedies. The deaths. The illnesses. Flowers had the power to mark all of it. It was a big part of why she loved them. Why she'd chosen them as a career. There was too much ugliness in the world, and she wanted to combat that with joy.

Of course, having a flower shop in a small Highland village didn't exactly make her flush with cash. Which was why she still lived at home with her stepmother. And also why she and her best friend, Kyla MacKean, had started an event planning business around Kyla's home estate of Ardinmuir. A centuries-old castle made for a hell of a backdrop for weddings. They'd even hosted a couple of retirement parties and a bat mitzvah so far. The business had gotten off to a bumpy start, but they were finally in the black. Not enough to make a huge difference to her personal bottom line. Not yet. But they'd been able to expand enough to hire some part-time staff, which was necessary to keep them both sane.

Chilled through by the end of the half-mile walk to the house, Sophie was looking forward to that soup. And maybe even a long, hot bath, if there was time before settling in for work and a cuddle with Cori, her ancient Grand Dame of a cat. She carefully stomped the snow off her shoes before letting herself inside. Out of long habit, she slipped the shoes off and put them in the drip tray.

"Sophie? Is that you?"

Lorraine's voice called out from the lounge, and Sophie knew by the wheedling, faux-frail tone that her plans for the evening had just gone up in smoke.

Tension lodged itself between her shoulders. *Of course it's me. Who the bloody hell else has a key?*

Breathing through the frustration, she modulated her tone. "Yes, Mum."

"Come here."

Never a "please." Just a demand.

Sophie flexed her hands into fists, then released them again as she went to see what her stepmother wanted.

Lorraine was sprawled out on the sofa in what Sophie privately thought of as her Fainting Couch pose. She looked like the heroine in some old silver screen movie, stretched out with a forearm draped across her brow. A blanket was draped over her lap, and a plate with the remains of whatever her dinner had been sat on the coffee table, next to an assortment of glasses and evidence of multiple snacks. Evidently, she'd been camped out here for a while.

"Be a dear and clear all this away, and make me a cuppa tea. I just canna make it to the kitchen again."

Sophie wondered what today's ailment was. So many of them felt performative. She'd never called Lorraine on any of it. She didn't live in the other woman's body or head. Perhaps she was wrong. Perhaps her stepmother did actually suffer from a myriad of chronic illnesses and deserved the disability check she got from the government every month, though Sophie had never seen any medical documentation to that effect. Still, she'd made a deathbed promise to her father to take care of Lorraine, and that's what she'd done all these years.

Thinking of him and his big, booming laugh, and the hugs that had made her feel safe, no matter what was going on in her world, Sophie gathered up the dishes and headed for the kitchen. She stopped dead at the sight of it. No wonder Lorraine couldn't make it to the kitchen again. It appeared that whatever she'd made had required the dirtying of every pot, pan, and dish in the house. The stove, the table, and every counter were covered. And there was Coriander, crouched over a dish, tan tabby-striped tail twitching as she licked.

Sophie leapt forward, scooping her baby up and out of prospective harm's way. *Please let her not have eaten something that will make her sick.*

Cori yowled in protest at being kept from her feast.

"You know you're not supposed to be on the counters or table."

Her yellow-green eyes narrowed in displeasure as if to say, "It's hardly my fault Lorraine left all this temptation in my path."

As if hearing the thought, Lorraine called, "Oh, and do the washing up while you're in there."

Sophie fought not to grind her teeth. Her stepmother always had the energy to make the messes but never to clean them. But she bit back the bitterness, knowing it would do no good to express her frustrations. Opening a tin of Cori's proper food, she set her beloved girl on the floor and went to put on the kettle. This mess would have to be sorted before she could even fix her own supper. But perhaps there'd be some sort of leftovers in the fridge from this grand kitchen disaster. Tugging open the door, she found none. How on earth had Lorraine dirtied up so many dishes for something with only enough for her to eat? Disgusted and even more exhausted, Sophie doused a tea bag in boiling water and rolled up her sleeves to load the dishwasher. After a brief pause to deliver the tea, she dove into the rest.

It took nearly an hour to get through the pile, washing and drying and putting away, during which Cori finished only a few bites of her own food before disappearing in a feline huff. Frustration and resentments simmered with every piece of cookery equipment Sophie returned to its rightful place. By the time she'd finished, she didn't even have the energy to assemble a sandwich. Grabbing an apple from a bowl on the counter and a granola bar from the cupboard, she quietly made her way upstairs to dive into work. Pulling up the email for Ardinmuir Event Planning, she responded to a few brides with updated floral design suggestions; revised a seating chart in accordance with the news that an upcoming groom's mother had remarried, and he was afraid she'd make a scene with her new, younger, trophy husband; and updated some spreadsheets based on vendor quotes. Cori wandered over and circled in her lap twice before settling in, half on the edge of the laptop. Wiggling the computer a little, Sophie managed to toggle over to the website and answer a new query from an American bride about booking a consultation for a destination wedding. By the time she'd gotten through all of that, her brain was fuzzy with fatigue. Everything else would have to wait until tomorrow. Maybe she could carve out a little time to work at the shop once she'd finished prepping the arrangements for the day.

Before logging out, she opened up her personal spreadsheet, entering the daily income totals and expenses for Village Blume and checking the column that auto-calculated exactly how long it would be until she could afford rent and living expenses on top of the rent for the shop itself. The goal was closer than it had ever been. Another six months. Nine, maybe, depending on how the event planning business went. Then she'd finally have the chance to be out on her own.

She'd been working her ass off toward this for years now, and seeing the progress she'd made left her with a deep sense of satisfaction beneath the exhaustion. She wondered if she could sneak downstairs for a glass of wine before bed. That seemed a fitting, small celebration.

But before she could even shut the laptop for the night, she heard Lorraine calling her name again.

Fighting down the frustration, she took a half-dozen slow, deep breaths.

Just six more months. I've done this for fourteen years now. I can do it for six more months.

Fixing a neutral smile in place, she set Cori aside and got up to see what her stepmonster wanted now.

Two

Connor eyed his great uncle across the expanse of the kitchen island. "Explain to me why you're making a dessert to go on top of the dessert?"

Angus didn't lift his gaze as he continued to pipe buttercream frosting onto one half of the wee macarons he'd made. "Because if I get a callback, I want to be able to show multiple skills in a single bake. And I think the macarons will provide a lovely bit of texture against the creme pâtissière and fruit of the tart."

At nearly seventy-eight-years old, Angus had finally submitted his application to be a contestant on *The Great British Bake Off*. He'd always baked, but he'd been practicing in earnest for the past five years, which Connor, and everyone else they knew, had benefitted from on the regular. Which made Connor grateful for the fact that he had an active occupation to work off all the delights.

Munro Sinclair turned from the hob to peer over his shoulder. "It'll look stunning."

Angus's lips curved, and his cheeks pinked at the praise, though his rhythm on the icing didn't falter. The two men had been lifelong friends and had once been something much more. Connor didn't know what their fallout years ago had been about, but Munro had popped back up after Angus's heart attack last year. Since then, it seemed they'd sorted out their differences. Connor was thrilled to see it. His great uncle had devoted so much of his life to him and Kyla since their parents' death. It was long past time Angus found his own happiness.

"Do you need any help? Everyone should be arriving soon."

Angus waved the offer off. "I'll be finished. It's all about assembly from here on out."

As if summoned by his words, the kitchen door opened, and Kyla strode in, followed by her husband. Even after all these months, Connor hadn't quite gotten used to seeing a cowboy walk through his door. But though Raleigh Beaumont had moved across the world from Texas, he hadn't changed his attire one iota. Connor appreciated that he was that comfortable in his own skin, and Raleigh had more than proved he was good people in how he'd taken to stewardship over Lochmara and all its tenants. Not to mention how he absolutely doted on Kyla. Connor had never seen his sister smile at her ex, David, like that.

The thought had him circling back to the reason he'd asked her to come a little early to their bi-weekly family dinner, and he felt a low pulse of dread. He wasn't exactly sure *how* she'd take the news of the affair.

"Something smells divine." Kyla crossed the room to hug Angus before moving to Munro to do the same.

"Cottage pie with something magnificent for dessert, courtesy of himself."

"Mmm. That sounds wonderful."

Connor jerked his head toward the hall. "Talk to you for a bit?"

Raleigh removed his ever-present black Stetson and hung it on a hook by the door. "Is this a siblings-only conversation, or you want me, too?"

"You might as well come on."

Connor hated the way the color leeched out of Kyla's cheeks at his words. So much of the burden of Ardinmuir had fallen on her over the years. He'd had his duty to wed, and for more than a decade, he'd left most of the rest to her. Only after she'd been the one to resolve the marriage pact had he discovered the true extent of what she'd been navigating on her own. Connor had been working his arse off to make up for that ever since.

The moment he closed the door to the family lounge, Kyla reached for Raleigh's hand. "What's wrong?"

"Nothing. At least, not like you're imagining. I'll be telling the others when they arrive. I just wanted to tell you first."

"Tell me what?"

Connor took a breath. "Hamish is getting a divorce."

His sister blinked the blue eyes that were so like his. "What? What happened?"

"He found out Dayna was having an affair. With David."

Raleigh tugged Kyla into the shelter of his arm. "David? As in David Murray?"

"As in the David she threw over for you, aye."

Her mouth dropped open. "Holy shite. How did he find out?"

Of course she'd ask that.

"Because of me, actually. I saw them out together when I was in Edinburgh for New Year's Eve."

"Are you sure?"

"It's pretty hard to mistake the meaning of them having their tongues down each other's throats."

Her head kicked back. "Aye. Right. That's... Jesus. Poor Hamish. Poor Freya."

Raleigh squeezed her tighter. "What's gonna happen now?"

"Hamish wants to move home and bring Freya with him, but it'll depend on what sort of custody arrangement he and Dayna manage to set up."

Kyla winced in sympathy. "How's he taking it?"

Connor thought of what Hamish had admitted about his feelings for Afton. That definitely didn't feel like his news to share. "To be honest, I think he's a little relieved. He said things havenae been good with them for a while. So, I suppose in a way it's a good thing."

"I don't get it," Raleigh remarked. "I mean, obviously, I don't have the best impression of David, but why the hell would she choose *him* over Hamish? He's just so... bland."

Kyla reached up to toy with the ends of her red hair, an old gesture that told Connor she was thinking. "They're both city people, through and through. They don't understand the way of life up here in the Highlands. David never understood my attachment to this place and my willingness to do anything to save it. Honestly, I think Dayna's much the same. She gave Hamish a lot of grief over the years for his allegiance to us as friends and all the efforts he put into trying to find a way out of the marriage pact. She resented us. She tried to hide it, but I knew. So, in that sense, frankly, good riddance. I hope Hamish can come home. It'd be better for him."

"That's the bloody truth," Connor agreed.

"Was that it, then? I mean, not that it's a small thing," Kyla amended, "but you could've just told us with everyone else."

"I know. I just thought the news might bring something up for you, and I wanted to give you the chance to react in private, just in case."

Her lips curved, and she stepped into him for a hug. "That's thoughtful of you, Con, but I'm more than at peace with my choice. David was wrong for me on every level."

"I wonder how long this thing with Dayna's been going on," Raleigh murmured.

"That I dinna ken. I have no idea whether it's new or... er... longer standing."

Kyla shuddered. "Well, that's a sobering thought. I wouldn't have believed David would cheat on me, but then I'd never have thought he'd get involved with a friend's wife, either. Water under the bridge, at this point."

"I say we wipe the nasty taste of the whole thing out of our mouths with the dinner that seemed just about ready when we got here," Raleigh suggested.

"I can definitely get behind that." Connor led the way back to the big stone kitchen.

Most of the rest of the guests had arrived. Charlotte Vasquez, Raleigh's stand-in mother, was shoulder-to-shoulder with Munro, peering at the cottage pie resting on the hob. Her partner, Malcolm Niall, the estate manager at Lochmara, was filling glasses with ice. Gavin, the thirteen-year-old runaway who'd brought the two of them together, was helping Angus assemble the macarons. A sign of high praise, as Angus rarely let anyone help with his bakes. Ciara McBride, one of Connor and Kyla's cousins, was washing berries at the sink. Her big brother, Ewan, who owned The Stag's Head Pub in Glenlaig, was bent over at the fridge, shoving a six-pack inside.

Even as Connor took inventory, their final guest opened the door. Sophie slipped into the cheerful chaos of the kitchen like a shadow, her arms full of flowers. Greetings were tossed out, and though Sophie smiled and returned them, he could tell something was off. A tightness dimmed her smile and darkened her pretty grey eyes. As he took in the rest of her, he could see the tension in her shoulders and the too-tight clench of her hands around the flowers. From years of observation, he knew she'd had some kind of run-in with her stepmother.

So, as she slipped out to take the flowers to the dining room, he broke away to follow.

———

Sophie took advantage of the usual chaos of the family of her heart to escape. Putting together arrangements for a tablescape would afford her just enough time to recalibrate and shake off the encounter that had cast a pall over her day. She laid the bundles of flowers on the big dining room table and went to retrieve some containers from the breakfront cabinet that dominated one end of the room. When she swung around, she spotted Connor in the doorway and jolted, clutching the trio of vases to her chest before they could slip to the floor and break.

"Connor! You startled me."

He stepped into the room, sharp blue eyes fixed on her. "Are you okay?"

In point of fact, she wasn't okay. She was annoyed and frustrated and struggling to hold back a resentment toward her stepmother that seemed to grow by the day. But none of that fit with the woman she wanted to be, so she didn't see the point in giving it voice.

"I'm fine." So saying, she moved toward the table and began arranging the flowers. The movements were familiar and soothing.

Sophie felt the weight of Connor's gaze on her as he crossed to grab the placemats, napkins, and silverware. He said nothing as he laid everything out, until he finally stopped directly in front of her, on the opposite side of the table.

"You ken it's okay if you're no' fine, right?"

Surprised, she lifted her eyes to his. That familiar face was full of concern and a look of knowing that left her unsettled. Connor MacKean had never been a serious man. From the time he'd learned to toddle, he'd left that role to his sister and taken on the guise of a clown. For years, Kyla had lamented his inability to settle down and focus on anything real, but Sophie had seen what he'd really been doing—trying to emotionally lighten her load in the only way he knew how. By making her laugh. But there was nothing of the jester now.

She realized that, since Afton's defection and the resolution of the marriage pact, he'd been far less the carefree playboy she'd known all these years. For the first time, she wondered what exactly it meant for him that the duty he'd been raised to carry out had been taken on by Kyla. How did that change things for him, beyond the obvious that he was no longer bound to marry someone he didn't choose himself? And what did it say about her as a friend that it hadn't occurred to her to ask until now? Did his question stem purely from concern for her, or from a deeper place of not being all right himself?

Sophie didn't have a chance to ask because the others began spilling into the room carrying plates and dishes of food.

She quickly finished with the flowers and took her customary seat beside Kyla at the head of the table. Plates were passed and filled, family-style. The breadbasket made the rounds. Wine was poured for the adults present. Conversation flew fast and furious, saving Sophie from the need to add to it herself. She soaked in the atmosphere of love and affection in the room, feeling the rough edges smooth out as they talked about Gavin's first week back at school after a term off, and discussed Angus's chances at getting a callback for *The Great British Bake Off*. This was home, and these were the people she'd chosen as hers.

"Well, I for one am delighted to be done with uni and home so I can take advantage of all your practice," Ciara announced, dipping a dinner roll in the gravy from the cottage pie with dramatic flare.

"And we're glad you're home and said yes to the job offer," Kyla added.

"It's good experience and gives me a way to build my skill set beyond just strapping on an apron to help himself here at the pub."

Ewan sent her a bland stare over a bite of cottage pie. "Nobody made you sign on to be a server or offered you apartment space as part of the bargain."

She batted long-lashed eyes at him. "I love you, big brother."

"That's what I thought."

"I confess, I didn't expect the event planning assistant job to come with a massive game of canine hide-and-seek," Ciara admitted.

The puppy Raleigh had gifted Kyla for Christmas was adorable and more than a handful.

"You and me both," Kyla said. "The poor wee pup was

howling for near to half an hour before we tracked him down under one of the beds upstairs."

Raleigh picked up the story. "His collar had gotten stuck on the bed frame, and he couldn't get out. Needless to say, we're keeping doors shut right now so Dugal can't get into any *more* trouble."

Charlotte laughed. "I expect he's got a ways to go before he's free of that. Don't you remember how long Pickles got into stuff when you were a boy?"

"Pickles?" Angus asked.

"He was my dog when I was a kid," Raleigh explained. "Got him when I was about eight. Also a Christmas puppy. I loved that dog so damned much, but Lord, if he didn't manage to seek out and roll in the smelliest thing he could find on at least a weekly basis. Given we lived on a cattle ranch, you can imagine there was ample opportunity."

"That sounds right manky," Ewan observed.

"If that means disgusting, you're right," Charlotte confirmed. "It only took a few months before Lily declared he was permanently an outside and barn dog. Not that the declaration stopped Raleigh from sneaking him into the house on the regular."

"He was my best boy. And when he got old, he liked to soak in a warm bath to ease his bones. What was I supposed to do?"

"Such a softie." Kyla leaned over to kiss Raleigh with clear affection.

The way his big hand came up to cup her cheek made Sophie sigh. After everything Kyla had been through, she deserved every moment of wedded bliss with her perfect cowboy. But there was a little pinch around Sophie's heart. Not envy. Never that. She didn't begrudge her friend a thing. But a yearning to find the same. A real relationship was something she'd filed in the "Someday" category, along with moving out on her own. Perhaps a part of her had expected to have found someone to merge her life with by now. Someone who'd help take her away from the parts of her life she didn't like. But Sophie wasn't a woman waiting around for a hypothetical prince to fix her problems. She was more than capable of saving herself. It just might take a little longer.

As dinner shifted to dessert, Sophie leapt up to help Angus pass out servings of his truly beautiful blueberry tart. She slid a plate in front of Kyla and noted the still full wine glass.

"Are you feeling all right? It's not like you to skip the wine after the busy week we just had."

In the moment's hesitation, when Kyla looked to Raleigh, Sophie knew.

"Oh, my God. You're not drinking your wine. Are you—?"

Her smile lit up like the sun. "Pregnant."

"Oh my God!" Sophie hastily set the rest of the plates she was carrying down and bent to wrap her friend in the tightest squeeze. "I'm going to be an aunt! Holy crap!"

There followed a cheerful and tearful—on Charlotte's part—cacophony of congratulations as everyone present hugged the mum-to-be and pumped Raleigh's hand. Angus declared they needed to toast and promptly disappeared to find some fizzy juice for Kyla.

Connor was the one who lifted the first glass. "To my sister, for bringing along the next generation. I promise to be the favorite uncle and never to get my new niece or nephew into *too* much trouble. And to Raleigh. I'm glad she chose you, mate. I dinna think anyone could love her better."

Damn if that didn't hit Sophie right in the feels. Kyla pressed a hand to her heart. Charlotte, predictably, burst into a fresh bout of happy tears. Even Raleigh seemed a little shiny in the eyes as he reached for his wife's hand.

By the time toasts made it around to Sophie, she'd gotten herself under control. "To Kyla and Raleigh. Thanks for giving me #relationshipgoals. I definitely won't settle for anything less than what you two have found together. And I can't wait until this wee one arrives so I can spoil him or her absolutely rotten. When are you due?"

"Toward the end of July."

Which would be peak wedding season if everything went according to the business plan they'd drafted. Sophie instantly began thinking about what they'd need to do to accommodate if Kyla got put on bedrest and, at the very least, how they'd do without her while she was on maternity leave.

Kyla flashed an indulgent smile. "I can see your planner wheels turning. We'll sort things out. Ciara will be fully trained up by then, and, with luck, we'll be able to hire some more staff. There's time."

Not nearly as much as Kyla thought, but Sophie kept that to herself. Tonight was about celebration. "One point of business before we move to dessert. I booked a consultation with an American bride for the day after tomorrow at two. Will you be able to join?"

"Oh, damn. We're going to be in Inverness at the doctor's office for my first checkup."

Sophie shifted gears. "It's no trouble. I can go over our basic packages and get a sense of what she's looking for and whether she's really serious about considering us for a venue. If she is, we'll work up the pitch together, as usual."

"Sounds like a plan."

"No more business," Angus declared. "This tart isnae going to eat itself."

"I volunteer as tribute!" Gavin announced.

On a chorus of laughter, they all dug in.

Three

Shoulder to shoulder with Fergus Hughes, Connor eyed what remained of the stone cottage—one of many on the estate that they were renovating. The roof had caved in some time ago, judging by the flora that had sprouted up from debris on the floor and evidence of the fauna that had taken refuge within its walls. Fallen snow coated everything, adding to the abandoned air.

Fergus uncrossed one massive arm and scratched at his ginger beard. "We've got our work cut out with this one. Chimney likely needs rebuilding, which canna be done 'til spring. New windows. New beams and roof. And all that before we can even think about sorting out an interior layout."

"I didnae realize it had gotten this bad." And as estate manager for Ardinmuir, Connor should have kept up with the condition of the crofter's cottages on the property. But like so many things, this was something else that had slid when their parents had been killed in a plane crash more than ten years ago.

At eighteen, Connor had taken over the handling of the tenants and stock, while Kyla had done everything else, managing the books and business of the estate. He'd learned on the job, helped out from time to time by Malcolm, who served the same function for Lochmara. They'd kept their heads above water. Barely. But in modern times, it had become more and more difficult for crofters to make a living farming the five- to twelve-acre parcels without some form of supplemental income, so many tenants had let their leases go. It was the end of an era and a way of life. Some of those families had worked the land on Ardinmuir for generations.

As Highland farmers faced the same challenges as the rest of the UK, finding new tenants had been incredibly difficult. When they hadn't been replaced, the estate had been forced to let go of staff, and the upkeep of those empty houses had taken lower priority. It took money and hands they didn't have. That had gone on so long, Connor and Kyla had straight up forgotten about some of the cabins. Out of sight, out of mind. Then last summer, Raleigh had proposed renovating them for use as vacation rentals. It was a form of diversification that hadn't crossed their minds, and they'd thrown themselves into repairing and updating the cottages in the best shape.

Those Airbnb and VRBO rentals had saved their arses in a big way by covering the massive balloon payment that had come due on the biggest loan taken out against the estate. It was a debt Connor hadn't even been aware of until Kyla had married Raleigh, leaving the books behind at the castle. There'd been so much fallout from the gambling addiction their father had hidden. He'd wiped out most of the money that had been meant to run the estate for the next two generations. If not for Raleigh's brainstorm, they would have been, in a word, fucked.

Feeling incredibly guilty for everything his sister had been handling all on her own, Connor had thrown himself into the renovations alongside Fergus, Malcolm, and Raleigh, along with a handful of other helpers whenever they joined the effort. Charlotte was handling the interior design, using charity shop finds and the vast stores of furniture that had cluttered up chunks of the castle to furnish them. Sophie had put her green thumb to work on the landscaping for each. Kyla had designed the website, which dovetailed nicely with the event planning business, as those who opted to get married at Ardinmuir needed somewhere for themselves and their guests to stay. At this point, there were nearly twenty functional rentals across the two estates, with more than a dozen to go that needed a lot more work.

Fergus didn't take his gaze off the cottage. "Do we have the budget for this?"

"Now that the big loan payment has been made, we've got a wee bit of breathing room. We knew we'd have to put more of the profits toward renovation to get these last cottages in proper shape. They'll end up paying for themselves once we're done."

"If you say so. You sure you want to tackle this one next?"

"Obviously, we willnae be able to complete it until warmer weather, but we've got to clear the mess before we can decide what needs addressing first. Once we have that blank canvas, we can talk layout with Charlotte and order in the materials. That'll take some time to get here, and we can work on clearing the others in the meantime."

"Right enough."

They tugged on their gloves and got to work, hauling out the remains of the original roof and the splintered beams. It was mindless work that gave him ample opportunity to think about his other efforts to contribute to the estate coffers. He'd done a multitude of side jobs over the years. Running custom tours of the Highlands. Working odd jobs around the village. A monetized social media presence capitalizing on the world-wide obsession with all things Scottish since Diana Gabaldon's *Outlander* had become a phenomenon. But the thing that had turned out to be the most gratifying was a sideline not even his family knew about.

Well, Raleigh had stumbled across it during his evaluation of the estate last year. But he'd promised to keep his mouth shut, so long as Connor told Kyla about it himself. But Connor didn't know how. Deep down, he believed his hobby had the potential to be truly profitable. The extra chunks he'd been able to winnow off their loans were proof of that. But he hadn't figured out all the details yet, and until he did, he wasn't telling her or anyone else. He didn't have her gift for the business side of things, and he didn't want to risk being told his passion was a fool-hardy pursuit at best, or a waste of time and money at worst.

By one o'clock, they'd managed to move the bulk of the debris out of the cottage, leaving a more or less empty shell. Over thermoses of hot tea, they discussed prospective layouts. With several of the interior walls having rotted away, they could change the floor plan to a more open concept. They'd gone that direction with the smaller cottages, but this one had enough space for three bedrooms.

"There are families that need more room than the one- and two-bedrooms provide," Connor argued.

"But do you want to get into letting to families?"

"Their money spends as well as anyone else's."

Fergus crossed his arms. "Aye, but kids can be verra destructive."

"That's what rental deposits are for. Let's measure for a three and calculate the cost of materials. Kyla will run the numbers to see what makes the most sense, and we'll go from there."

In agreement, they took down the dimensions needed. By the time they'd finished, fresh snow was falling.

Connor dusted the powder from his hair. "I think we're done for the day."

"Just as well. Light'll be gone in only a couple more hours, and I've got some errands to run in the village. I'll draw up some base plans and email them to everyone. It'll probably be tomorrow afternoon."

That would give Connor some time to spend on his own projects. "Works for me."

After Fergus drove off with a wave, Connor climbed into his own 4x4 and headed back to the castle. It was well past time for lunch, and he was starving. He'd raid the kitchen, then head up to his hideaway.

As he rolled up the long castle drive, he spotted Sophie's little blue Fiat parked out front. Of course she'd elect to have her client meeting here. The better to show off the castle. He pulled his 4x4 around to the kitchen entrance and parked. As he got out, another unfamiliar car crunched up the drive. Probably Sophie's clients. That supposition seemed to be correct as two women parked behind the Fiat and stepped out of their car. Connor frowned as they made their way toward the front door. There was something familiar about the brunette and the way she moved. As she turned her head to laugh at something her companion said, he caught a flash of her profile and recognition dawned.

Oh, no. Oh shite.

Even as the thought crossed his mind, the door opened, and the women stepped inside.

Connor pocketed his keys and bolted for the nearest door.

———

"Welcome to Ardinmuir Castle!" Sophie knew her voice was just a shade too bright as she greeted her clients, but something about these women intimidated her. They looked posh and put together. And judging by the designer shoes gracing their feet, they were likely working with the sort of budget that meant they had plenty of options for a destination wedding venue. She needed to nail this presentation. "Please, come in out of the cold. I'm Sophie Cameron."

The brunette beamed and shook her hand. "I'm Swayze Parish, the maid of honor. And this is Alyssa Wang, my ride-or-die bestie. She's our bride." The American South dripped from Swayze's voice, though it was a slightly different accent than Raleigh's.

Alyssa offered a tranquil smile that warmed her deep brown eyes. "Great to meet you. I've been studying the photos on the website, and this place is just amazing."

"We like to think so." Sophie waved them inside. "Please,

come this way." She began to lead them through the labyrinthine halls of the castle.

"It definitely lives up to the hype," Swayze gushed. "I understand it's six-hundred years old?"

"The oldest part of the structure that's still standing is, aye. There was an even older one on the site that dated back to the twelfth century, but it was destroyed in a siege between clans." As they walked, Sophie reeled off the history she'd soaked up about the castle over a lifetime, explaining the pieces that had been added on by different MacKean ancestors over the centuries. Her running commentary left little room for comment. It was a nervous habit she couldn't quite quell in the moment. This was Kyla's place, and though Sophie had run tame in this home all her life and knew the history almost as well as her friend did, she felt a little like a fraud. By the time they got to the formal parlor, she'd run out of words and was grateful to be able to switch into hostess mode and offer them tea or coffee from the service she'd set up in anticipation of the meeting.

"Oh, coffee would be lovely," Alyssa said. "It's a lot colder here than home."

"Of course. How do you take it?"

"Just a little milk or cream."

"And you, Swayze?"

"I like my coffee like I like my men—sweet and blond. Two sugars, please."

Happy to have something to occupy her hands, Sophie prepared the coffee as the two women wandered the room, admiring the collection of antiques.

"So where is home?" Sophie asked.

"Atlanta, Georgia," Alyssa explained.

"What about you, Swayze?"

"Originally from a little town in north Georgia. Alyssa and I were college roommates. Atlanta is technically my base, but my work takes me all over the place. Which suits me fine, as I like to travel."

Sophie carried the cups over, pleased when they didn't rattle in the saucers. "Here we go."

As Swayze took her cup, she beamed. "I just want to say it's so incredibly nice to meet you, Sophie."

Hadn't they already done this part? But she returned the smile. "Thank you."

"You're a very lucky woman."

"Oh?" What were they talking about?

"Of course you are." Connor strode in, as if he'd been a part of the conversation from the beginning.

Before she could ask what he was doing here, his long-legged stride ate up the distance between them, and he reached for her. She barely had time for more than a gasp before he'd drawn her flush against him and lowered his mouth to hers.

Sophie wasn't the sort of woman who made a scene. Quiet and reserved, she preferred to fade into the background and observe. For two long, humming beats, she felt outside herself as Connor MacKean, her best friend's little brother, lost his bloody mind and kissed her. Then sensation caught up with her, and every single brain cell short-circuited. Her body went up in flames, instinctively leaning into him, seeking more. Because, holy hell, there was absolutely nothing little about him now, and the man could *kiss*.

Christ, that mouth. She'd seen it puckish. Curved with insouciance. Grim with purpose. Twisted in grief. But she'd never known he could do *this*. With every moment that passed, she sank deeper and wanted more.

By the time he pulled back, her head was reeling. She'd lost all sense of time and place, with no idea whether the kiss had lasted for seconds or minutes. Her hands were fisted in his jacket.

Connor's eyes, so very blue and intense, stayed on hers. "Swayze, I see you've met my Sophie."

His Sophie?

Belatedly remembering their audience, Sophie's face flushed. Oh, God. This was the height of unprofessionalism. Before she could pull away, he slid an arm around her, curving a possessive hand on her hip.

Swayze grinned. "I have. She's lovely."

"She is that," Connor agreed.

Sophie had no idea what was happening, and that hand on her hip felt like a brand.

"Swayze is a social media influencer and a friend of mine," Connor explained. "I ran into her New Year's Eve, when I was down in Edinburgh, and told her about the event planning business. I'm glad you took me up on my suggestion to check it out."

With a little laugh, Swayze sipped at her coffee. "Not gonna lie. I was disappointed to find out you're engaged, but it's worth it to find out about this place. Don't you just love it, Alyssa?"

Engaged?

Sophie looked at Connor. Because she'd known him all his life, she read the plea beneath his affable expression. *Please, just go along with this.*

She had no idea what he was on about, but it would hardly make a good impression to call him out on it now, so she wrapped an arm around his waist to further sell this ludicrous fiction and felt the vibrating tension in his frame. "Was there something you needed, love? I've got a lot to go over with Alyssa and Swayze."

Because she was pressed up against him, she felt some of the stiffness leech out of his body. Good God, how had she not realized how leanly muscled he was?

"No. Just wanted to steal a kiss on my break and say hello. I'll get out of your way so you can get down to business." He released her, and Sophie felt oddly bereft as he stepped back.

"I'll come find you when we're finished." Translation: You will give me a detailed explanation of this lunacy.

Connor jerked a nod. "I'll be in the kitchen, having a late lunch. Swayze, good to see you again. Alyssa, nice to meet you. I hope you find Ardinmuir suitable for your needs."

They all watched as he strode out of the room.

"Yep, very lucky woman," Swayze murmured.

Alyssa hummed in agreement.

Belatedly, Sophie realized Swayze must've been one of *those* "friends"—a.k.a. one of Connor's many former flings. Like everyone, she knew he was something of a playboy. He'd never made a secret of the fact that he enjoyed women, and he was a natural flirt. He'd been meant for an arranged marriage, so who was she to judge? Most of the time, she simply forgot about it, because he didn't seek out such companionship at home, and certainly he'd never turned such attentions her way. But as she faced off with this woman he'd probably taken to his bed, Sophie struggled with a wholly unfamiliar jealousy.

This was *Connor*. Kyla's brother. The man who'd always been as much sibling as friend. She'd never looked at him as anything else. She'd never once thought of kissing him. Well, maybe once or twice in a purely academic sense, given he was supposed to be quiet adept at it. But never *seriously*.

Now that she knew the taste of him, the feel of his body wrapped around hers, and she wasn't at all sure she'd be able to forget it.

Sophie wasn't sure what to do with that.

For now, she needed to put it out of her mind. They needed to land this contract, and that meant she needed to switch back into business mode.

"Right. I apologize for that interruption." She poured herself a cup of tea from the carafe she'd prepared and gestured for the two women to take a seat. "Why don't you tell me a little more about what sort of vision you have for your wedding?"

Four

Despite what he'd told Sophie, Connor bypassed the kitchen and headed straight outside into the snow. He needed the cold, needed to move to expel the heat and energy pumping through him after that kiss.

In his heart of hearts, he knew such a blatantly public display of affection hadn't been strictly necessary. He could have done some fast talking, and Sophie probably would have rolled with it and asked questions later, rather than make a scene in front of clients. But when he'd walked in and seen her, dressed to impress and playing the consummate hostess in *his* home, kissing her had felt imperative.

He hadn't meant for it to be more than a peck, a gesture intended to make a point and sell the lie he'd told Swayze at New Year's. Then he'd gotten his hands on her, tasted that single, delicious gasp of surprise, and he hadn't been able to stop himself from giving in to the fantasy and kissing her as he'd wanted to kiss her for years. A part of him had done it to answer whether his attraction to her was driven by her complete unattainability. But there was no question the chemistry wasn't one-sided. Despite the fact that he'd taken her completely by surprise, she'd kissed him back.

Before Swayze had spouted off about the engagement. Before she'd had any inkling why he was doing it. Sophie had kissed him back, pressing against him for more. And it had been glorious. So glorious, he'd nearly lost himself, forgetting why he'd started it in the first place. The arousal and attraction in those striking grey eyes had felt like a victory.

But she'd demand answers. And rightly so. He had to figure out what the hell to tell her.

Because he had Sophie on the brain, his feet carried him to the one place on the estate that always made him think of her. The old Victorian-era greenhouse had once been a showpiece of iron and glass. But it had fallen into disrepair decades before either of them had been born. They'd all played here as children, at least until he and Hamish had a narrowly escaped injury when one of the panels of glass had crashed down from above. After that, his parents had banned them all from setting foot inside it.

But Sophie had always loved this place and dreamed of eventually seeing it restored. Connor had long ago vowed to find a way to give her that dream. That was what had driven him to take the blacksmithing class a few years ago. He'd thought perhaps, if he learned the basics, he could take on some of the labor of replacing the damaged parts of the frame. He hadn't known he'd fall in love with the process. Hadn't known he'd have an aptitude for the art. The whole project had been his secret. The greenhouse sat far enough away from the castle proper that no one had noticed the progress he'd made. There was a veritable wall of overgrown forest blocking the view, so unless someone came hunting on purpose, his secret project was safe. He'd worked on it in fits and starts, as he'd been able to afford materials. If Sophie had her own greenhouse, she could grow some of her own flowers, which would not only bring her joy, it would offset some of the costs for her inventory. That meant she'd have more to put toward moving out of her stepmother's house.

Connor wanted to give her *that* more than anything.

For years, he'd watched her suffer at the hands of that woman.

Lorraine Cameron was nothing like Sophie's mother. He had fond memories of Naya, who'd brought color and spice to all their lives with the food and stories from her native India. She'd been a gentle soul, much like her daughter. Robert Cameron had been utterly devoted to her. They'd all been devastated when she'd died. That Robert had remarried so soon after had been a shock. Connor's own mother had opined that some people didn't know how to be alone. Sophie had only wanted her father to be happy. And maybe he had been. It was hard to say, as he'd died himself of a heart attack barely six months later.

That was when Lorraine's true colors had begun to show. She'd never been overtly abusive to Sophie—at least, not to Connor's knowledge. But her bigoted attitudes and racist leanings were clear enough. She didn't look at Sophie and see a daughter. She saw a servant. Someone lesser.

Connor had never understood why Sophie had stayed a moment past the point she turned eighteen. He and Kyla had made repeated offers for her to move into the castle. They were always shot down. She'd made it clear the issue was off-limits. Beneath that quiet determination, she was stubborn as a mule, determined to rescue herself. Sophie was a strong, capable woman. Connor knew she'd manage somehow. But it didn't change the fact that he wanted to be the one to help her. So he'd done what he could to lighten her load, making her laugh, taking her mind off her problems. It wasn't enough, and not nearly as much as he wanted to do. But it was what she'd allowed. He'd been forced to live with that.

As he took in the remaining work to be done, he realized that if he pushed himself, he could probably knock the rest of this out in the next few months. Of course, that depended upon the rest of his workload and the availability of materials.

And then what? Are you planning to present it to her, hoping she'll fall at your feet?

No. He absolutely never wanted to see Sophie on her knees like some kind of servant. If she elected to assume that position to torture him, that was a different matter entirely. As the image planted itself in his head, his cock stiffened. Again.

Getting well ahead of yourself, MacKean.

The fact of the matter was that he wanted Sophie. Now, perhaps, more than ever. He wouldn't forget how she felt beneath his hands, how her mouth had moved against his.

Connor was no stranger to want. He enjoyed women. He saw no sense in apologizing for that, especially when everyone involved had always been on the same page. But there was just something about Sophie that pulled at him as no one else ever had. He wanted more with her, and with the marriage pact satisfied, he was finally free to pursue it. In theory.

Would the kiss change anything? If it did, how would his sister react? Those were, he decided, questions for Future Connor. Present Connor needed to get food and figure out what the hell he was going to say to Sophie when she came for the answers she rightly deserved.

He still hadn't figured it out by the time she tracked him down in the kitchen more than an hour later. She crossed to the sink, setting down the tray of tea and coffee she'd had set up in the parlor. Connor stayed where he was at the table, lest he give into the urge to grab her and pick up where he'd left off.

"There's cake, if you want some."

"Mmm." With precise movements, she loaded the cups into the dishwasher and began to rinse out the coffee carafe and teapot. Then she leaned back against the counter and crossed her arms. "I think you owe me an explanation."

Connor searched her face. If she was angry, she didn't show it. Whatever emotion she felt was locked down tight. Feeling as if he was flying blind, he dove in.

"Swayze and I were a thing for a weekend a couple of years ago. As I mentioned, I ran into her in Edinburgh over New Year's. We caught up a bit. She mentioned she was in Scotland helping screen potential venues for her friend, so I told her about the event planning business. When she expressed... um...

interest in picking things up where we'd left off, I wasnae on the same page. But I didnae want to hurt her feelings, so I blurted out I was engaged. It's something I've done over the years. A convenient excuse while the pact was still in place. But since Afton's gone, it felt weird to say her name when Swayze asked."

Sophie's brows drew together, black slashes of punctuation against those striking grey eyes. "So you said mine instead?"

He rubbed at the heat that crawled up the back of his neck. "You were the first person I thought of."

"Why?"

She looked so truly baffled that for a few moments he considered coming clean about the fact that he'd had a thing for her for years. But she only saw him as Kyla's brother. As a player. Never mind that he hadn't had a single date or other entanglement since Afton disappeared. If he wanted a real shot with her—and if the past couple of hours had proved anything to him, he did—he needed to prove he was more than that. Better than that.

"You've always been there." That was part of the appeal, wasn't it? She was someone who'd known him all his life. She understood him in a way few people did. Why that was different from Afton, he wasn't sure, other than that none of it was mandated.

Something flickered over her face at that. "I see."

He wasn't sure she did. But he needed to get on with this. "Anyway, I apologize for putting you in an awkward and uncomfortable position. That really wasnae fair to you." *No matter how much I enjoyed getting my mouth on you.*

He waited for her reaction, wondering if this would finally be the thing that roused her temper enough to rake him over the coals.

But that wouldn't have been his Sophie.

Instead, she sighed. "Well, no harm done, I suppose."

"Things weren't weird at your meeting after I left?"

She hesitated. "No."

He wasn't sure he believed her, but before he could say so, she straightened.

"I need to get to work on putting together a proposal for them. I'll see you later, Connor."

As she strode out, he found himself regretting that their brief, fake engagement was over. Because it just might have been the closest he'd ever got to Sophie Cameron.

"Alyssa comes from old money, or so Swayze said. She and her fiancé want to escape all the pomp and circumstance that would go along with that back home, so they've decided on a destination wedding," Sophie explained.

"So, are we looking at a small-scale elopement, intimate family wedding, or something larger?" Kyla asked.

Sophie checked her notes. "Ten in the wedding party, counting the maid of honor and best man. Approximately seventy-five guests."

"That's not exactly intimate."

"Evidently, if they got married in Atlanta, it would be closer to five hundred, so by comparison, this is small and manageable."

"Do they have a specific date in mind?"

"They're somewhat flexible, but they're aiming for the end of March or early April."

"That soon?"

"It's a short turnaround, but we've got availability, and she made it clear money was no object. If we need to hire extra staff to pull it off, we can pass that cost along, and I dinna think she'll blink."

Kyla still looked uncertain.

"Did I mention how the maid of honor is a big social media influencer? If we get this contract and wow them, it's possible she could put the word out. That kind of word of mouth could be worth its weight in gold. Or stress, as the case may be."

Of course, that got Sophie thinking about Connor and that kiss again. Not that she'd stopped for longer than thirty seconds at a time over the past two days. Should she tell Kyla what had happened? About Connor announcing her as his fiancée?

Chances were, the idea of it would send Kyla to the floor, rolling with laughter. Sophie didn't feel much like laughing because that kiss had been... Wow. No one had ever kissed her like that. A part of her chalked the whole thing up to the fact that he was something of a Casanova. He'd had a lot of experience, so it only made sense that he knew how to kiss a woman. Sophie couldn't stop herself from taking that thought to its inevitable conclusion, wondering how well he did everything else that went along with that reputation.

What the hell was wrong with her? This was *Connor*. Her best friend's little brother. She'd never looked at him as an actual man before. Never mind the fact that he'd towered over her for years now. A part of her had still seen the impish school boy who'd played pranks on her and Kyla. But now, she didn't think she'd ever be able to look at him and not remember the shape of those long, lean muscles beneath her hands or the feel of his hands on her.

"Are you okay? You look awfully flushed."

Sophie stopped herself from pressing both palms to her flaming cheeks. She couldn't mention this to Kyla. It was too weird. Too personal. As she racked her brain for another excuse, the door to the shop opened. Thrilled with the timely interruption, she shot to her feet.

"Welcome to Village Blume. How can I help... you?" The enthusiasm waned as she spotted her landlord, Mr. Milligan.

"I just wanted to drop off the new lease." He slapped an envelope on the counter.

Sophie automatically opened it, intending to sign on the spot to renew. But the number written in for the amount of rent due monthly had the blood draining from her face. "This is forty percent more than I'm paying now."

"Aye. It's prime real estate. I can make more. If you canna pay it, someone else will."

Livid and horrified, Sophie struggled to think of a response that wouldn't antagonize the man.

Kyla straightened from her chair. "Are you planning to make actual repairs on the place, or do you continue to expect to charge a premium for one step above a hovel?"

The old man's face turned beet red.

Milligan had always been a shitty landlord, doing less than the bare minimum of maintenance, and even going so far as to refuse to allow Sophie to make repairs herself out of her own pocket. It was a particular sore spot with Kyla, who felt Sophie had been taken advantage of. But this was not the answer.

"Not helping," Sophie murmured.

"Ungrateful... I'll no' be spoken to in such a manner on my property," he sputtered.

Sophie rushed to intervene. "She's not your tenant, Mr. Milligan. I am."

He growled, slapping the envelope again. "Those are the terms. If you dinna accept them, you'll be expected out at the end of next month. I've already got a waiting list."

Without waiting for a reply, he stalked out of the shop, slamming the door behind him.

Was that actually true? Or was it simply a strong-arm tactic meant to keep her in line?

"You're not signing that lease," Kyla insisted. "You have to find some other space."

Sophie was so tired of this argument. "There is no other space in the village. At least, not one I can afford." In all honesty, she wasn't entirely sure how she'd swing this rate increase as it was. She'd have to dip into her move out fund to do it, which delayed her getting away from her stepmother. That was its own crushing blow.

But she was determined that she'd make it on her own. Eventually. She needed to do it that way, without depending on someone else.

"Then, at the very least, save yourself the stress and move out. You know there's ample room at Ardinmuir. Lochmara, too. Or you could take one of the cottages on either estate. There are options, Soph."

"No." She didn't want charity. It was no one's responsibility to bail her out of her life circumstances. No one's but her own.

Kyla's blue eyes glimmered with familiar disappointment, as they did every time she made this offer, and Sophie rejected it. She sighed. "It's your choice." But her tone said, *It's your funeral.*

Tired of this argument and entrenched in her position, Sophie returned to her notes. "Let's get back to work."

"Fine. But will you please have Hamish look the lease over to make sure that asshat isn't trying to put anything else over on you?"

"I hate to bother him right now. He's got his hands full with the divorce."

"Sophie. It'll take him ten minutes to read the thing. You know he'd be angry if you signed it and locked yourself into even worse terms, if he could've saved you from further heartache."

Knowing Kyla was right, she relented. "Fine. I'll send it to him tonight. For right now, we need to put together this quote. I've been running some preliminary numbers on flowers and catering..."

Five

The bar of steel glowed orange as Connor used a pair of thick, flat-jaw tongs to pull it from the fire. Resting it against the top of his anvil, he snagged a nearby hammer and began to pound, slowly elongating the shape. The vibration of every strike sang up his arm, a satisfying reminder of the effort going into the piece, and a cathartic release of all his pent-up frustrations. As the metal cooled, he returned it to the fire, waiting for that telltale glow.

It had been five days since The Kiss. Five days since Sophie had shrugged it off as no big deal. Five days since he'd seen her.

Connor didn't know if she was avoiding him on purpose. Given everything on her plate between running two businesses and juggling the demands of her stepmother, it wasn't unusual for him to go several days without seeing her. But that had been before.

Worry bubbled at the back of his brain as he pulled the iron from the fire and repeated the process, using heat and muscle to flatten the metal before returning it to the forge. He was many hours away from the finished product, but in his mind, he could already see the final angles of the blade.

What if he'd made things permanently weird between them?

They'd been friends for years. Family, of a sort. She mattered to him. Ardinmuir had always been a safe space for her—something that had been especially important in the years since her father passed. Connor didn't think he could live with his reckless action somehow ruining that for her.

Absently, he closed the tongs around what would become the tang, drawing it from the fire. The heated metal began to slip, and his hand jerked, bumping against the edge of the forge. Hissing in pain, he dropped the blade and the tongs, and rushed outside to shove his hand into one of the drifts of snow that had built up against the side of the cottage. Swearing a blue streak, he packed more snow around it, already feeling the burn deep in his skin. He knew better than to approach any of this work without having his brain fully on the job at hand. Anything less opened the door to serious injury.

The skin was already blistering when he pulled it from the snow.

"Eejit."

Back inside the cottage, he dug around in the cabinet for burn cream. This wasn't the first burn he'd sustained, and certainly wouldn't be the last, so he kept a well-stocked first-aid kit on hand. He'd just smeared a generous amount of lavender salve on the angry welt when someone knocked at the cottage door.

Connor tensed. No one came here but him. Nobody even knew he'd set up his forge at this old crofter's cottage. Except for one person.

When Raleigh shoved open the door, Connor loosed a breath. "It's you."

"Hey, man." His gaze dropped to the open first aid kit. "You hurt yourself?"

"I'm fine. Just a wee burn." No reason to mention it hurt like a son of a bitch. He laid on a square of gauze and taped it in place. "What are you doing here?"

"Went by the castle, and when I didn't find you, I figured you were either at one of the renovation sites or out here."

Tugging on heat-proof gloves, Connor bent to retrieve the tongs and fallen blade. "Did you need something?" He struggled to keep the edge out of his tone. This was his private sanctuary. He didn't like having others in it.

Instead of answering the question, Raleigh peered with interest at the partly formed knife. "What are you working on?"

"A bowie knife."

Interest lit his brother-in-law's gold-brown eyes. "You can do that?"

"Aye. This one's a custom order job." Which was the only reason Connor was working on it instead of more supports for the greenhouse. He needed the paying jobs to cover all the materials for the restoration.

"How's that work? Do you have a website or something?"

"No. I operate mostly by word of mouth."

"Is it all blades?"

"Not entirely. I split my time between those and architectural blacksmithing."

"What's that? Like railings and gates and shit?"

"Among other things." Realizing Raleigh wouldn't be rushed, Connor indulged him a little. He nodded toward the opposite end of the room. "You can see some of the finished work over there."

Raleigh strode over and examined the assortment of blades. With a gasp of delight, he lifted a viking axe off the rack and examined the ornate knotwork etched into the head. "You made this?"

"Aye." He was damned proud of it, too. That sort of artistry was the kind of work that he'd fallen in love with. The side hustle he really wanted to turn into a true business. But the architectural side was easier to justify. The greenhouse wasn't the only part of the estate he could help restore with this skill set. It was part of the stewardship of a property this old, maintaining the historical integrity of the place.

"Damned cool. You're clearly good at all this, so why haven't you told Kyla yet?"

Taking a page out of his brother-in-law's book, Connor answered the question with another question. "Where is she, anyway?"

"Over at Ardinmuir. She and Sophie have a pitch meeting today."

So maybe Sophie wasn't actually avoiding him. Their business picking up was a good thing.

"Don't think I don't see what you're doing. When are you gonna tell your sister?"

Connor twitched his shoulders. "I dinna ken."

"It's been months, man. I'm tired of keeping this secret. What is it you're so afraid of?"

So many things.

Not being taken seriously, or worse, being laughed at. Being told he was wasting his time and ought to give the whole thing up. Being told he wasn't good enough. Because he'd never been good enough at anything. Kyla was the overachiever. He was the screw-up. And that had been okay because he'd faced his duty to marry without complaint, even though Afton hadn't wanted him. He hadn't wanted her, either. Not like that. But the marriage pact was the thing he couldn't screw up. And then she'd gone and gambled Lochmara away and that, too, had fallen to Kyla.

Connor was desperate to make a difference. To make up for all those years that he'd let her carry everything. He had no idea whether his blacksmithing could do that, but he had promised Raleigh he'd tell Kyla. In truth, he was lucky his brother-in-law had given him this long a grace period and hadn't just invoked spousal privilege and told her himself. That grace period was up.

Adjusting some settings on the forge, he put the blade back in to heat. "I'll tell her and everyone else at the next family dinner." That gave him a week to figure out how he'd reveal the whole endeavor and make this seem like a worthwhile pursuit.

"Good. Because when I say, 'if you don't, I will,' this time, I actually mean it."

Connor resisted the urge to growl. He hated being backed

into a corner.

Raleigh moved toward the door but paused to clap him on the shoulder. "She's not gonna react like you think, brother. Have some faith."

He had all the faith in the world in his sister. It was himself he was worried about.

———

Sophie eyed the clock on the dash of her car. She was cutting it awfully close, waiting this late to leave for the castle. But she'd spent extra time at the shop, pulling together some bouquet concepts she hoped would really impress Alyssa. At least, that was what she was telling herself. The additional work of bringing the bouquets to life hadn't been necessary. She and Kyla had polished their presentation last night. But since this pitch meeting was happening in person, rather than via a Zoom call or email, she'd wanted to go the extra mile.

And she was avoiding Connor.

Which was stupid. He was a regular part of her life. A friend.

But she wasn't having heated dreams about any of her *other* friends. Wasn't imagining any of *them* coming into her shop, setting her on the counter, and sliding their hands into her hair before kissing her senseless. The multiple plasters on her fingers were evidence of how often she'd been falling into that daydream, so, right now, she didn't know how to even look at Connor without blushing deeper than one of her roses. But she was out of excuses to stay away.

Professionally, she needed this meeting with Alyssa and Swayze to go well. Landing the contract would go a long way toward covering the next several months of increased rent on her shop—because, despite what she'd promised Kyla, she'd signed the lease without bothering poor Hamish. There were no other viable options for space in Glenlaig. So this pitch was imperative, and she couldn't afford for the whole thing to become some sort of cock-up because of her nerves about Connor. Then there was the added fear that Swayze would mention Sophie's so-called "engagement." Connor certainly hadn't told his sister, because Kyla hadn't brought it up to her. But as she neared the estate, Sophie wondered if she ought to tell Kyla herself, just so she didn't make a thing of it, should the topic arise.

The idea of it was about as appealing as a corpse flower in full bloom.

When Sophie pulled into the drive, she was relieved not to see any sign of their clients or Connor's 4x4. She let herself in through the kitchen door, juggling the bouquets as she headed for the parlor.

Angus looked up from the counter, where he was putting the finishing touches on a dozen cupcakes that appeared to have an orange blossom and bumblebee theme. "Hello, lass. Can I help you with those?"

Because her arms were straining, she offered a couple of the bouquets. "You're a lifesaver, Angus."

"Anything for one of my girls. Kyla's already set up." They wound their way toward the parlor. "You've been a ghost around here lately."

Great. Even Angus had noticed her abnormal behavior. "It's been a busy week getting everything together for this proposal."

"You're going to nail it." His adamant confidence gave Sophie a needed boost.

At the foot of the stairs, she paused to press a kiss to his papery cheek. "Thank you. I needed that."

"Have faith, lass."

Hers was feeling a little shaky at the moment.

Kyla apparently had no such issue. She was fairly vibrating with excitement when they arrived at the parlor. Of the two of them, Kyla was the one who actually enjoyed working with people. Sophie preferred being the organizing force in the background, so she was happy to leave much of the actual interfacing to her partner.

"Sorry I'm late. I decided pictures weren't good enough."

Kyla's eyes widened at all the bouquets. "So I see."

"Overkill?"

"They're utterly gorgeous. If Alyssa doesn't love them, she's not the right client for us."

"I'm not sure that's how this is supposed to work, but I appreciate the vote of confidence. Thanks for helping carry them, Angus."

"Anything for you, love. I'm back to my cupcakes. There'll be some waiting for you both when you're finished."

Sophie didn't think she could eat a thing, but she smiled, nonetheless. After he'd gone, she busied herself arranging the bouquets to best display them and trying to find the right words.

"There's something I really need to tell you."

Kyla stopped her frenetic pacing. "Oh?"

"I—"

The doorbell rang.

"Hold that thought. We've got a meeting to get through."

Sophie bit back a curse. *Too late now.*

As she followed Kyla to the front door, she sent up silent prayers that all would go well.

"Welcome to Ardinmuir Castle! You must be Alyssa and Swayze. I'm Kyla MacKean, Sophie's business partner." Kyla shook each of their hands. "Thank you so much for being willing to come back for an in-person presentation."

"We're thrilled to come back. This place is just so gorgeous. I texted my fiancé all about it," Alyssa gushed. "I won't lie. I've got high hopes for what you're showing us today."

"We've been hard at work since you met with Sophie last week, so I think you'll be pleased."

"Can't wait," Swayze enthused. "Sophie, great to see you again."

Her mouth felt dry as dust, but she managed a nod and murmured, "And you, as well."

"Come on back to the parlor." Kyla shut the door and led the way.

Once they'd been settled with coffee and some of Angus's brandy snaps, Kyla launched into their presentation. Their two guests listened with rapt attention to the proposed options for color schemes, decorations, and menus. Sophie barely heard a word as she waited on pins and needles, expecting them to say something about the engagement at any moment. When Kyla had finished her portion, Sophie took over explanations for the flowers. Both women ooed and ahed over the bouquets she'd put together, and when Alyssa's eyes went misty at the cascading arrangement in purples, blues, and winter whites, she knew she'd made the right call going with something she could hold.

"These arrangements are silk, which makes for wonderful post-wedding keepsakes. But any bouquet can be done in live blooms, if that's your preference."

"And if you choose Ardinmuir, we are more than happy to work with you on any details that aren't quite what you're looking for. These are just starter concepts," Kyla explained.

The two women looked at each other, exchanging some silent communication before nodding at each other.

"We love it," Alyssa announced. "This is where I want my wedding."

"Wonderful! When are you looking to book?"

"Well, that's a bit a of a thing. Can you pull this off in eight weeks?" She named a date the last weekend of March.

They'd prepared for this. "It's a tight turnaround, so we'd need to hire some extra staff to do it. We've put together a second quote accounting for that." Sophie passed over both estimates. "Take a little time to look them over and decide—"

Alyssa glanced at the bottom line of each. "Done."

"Just like that?" Kyla asked.

"Just like that. I want to get married here. Ryan isn't going to fuss. He's just so thrilled we're not doing the country club thing back home."

"Well, okay. In that case, I have contracts right here." Kyla pulled them out and went over the pertinent details before offering a pen.

Alyssa signed with a flourish and beamed. "Swayze, you good with sticking around in Scotland until the wedding?"

Wait, what?

"You know it! In my capacity as maid of honor, I'll be around to help y'all with anything you need. We're planning to document the whole experience via social media, so long as y'all are okay with it."

Sophie and Kyla exchanged their own look, both fighting back the urge to whoop. They knew what kind of impact this could have on their business if everything went well.

"Excellent! This is going to be awesome. There's so much more in the area I didn't get to see last time I was here. I know Connor knows all the best places."

Sophie tensed as Kyla's brows arched. "You know my brother?"

"Oh, I took one of his tours a couple of years ago. It was a really memorable experience."

Aye, I bet it was.

The bolt of jealousy was swift and potent. Sophie fought to relax the hands that had balled into fists.

Oblivious to her reaction, Kyla continued. "Well, I'm sure if you've a mind to see more of the country while you're here, he'd be happy to put together an itinerary."

Sophie stayed silent. She didn't want him putting together itineraries or anything else for this woman. And that was ridiculous. She had no hold over him. They weren't really involved. There was zero reason he couldn't pursue something with Swayze, beyond the fact that he'd claimed he didn't want to.

Realizing the two women were rising, Sophie stood, dragging her attention back to the present to walk them out.

At the door, they shook hands again.

"Oh, Swayze, if you're looking for lodging while you're here, we've got several cottages on the estate. We usually rent them out by the day on Airbnb, but we can arrange for a price-break on a longer-term lease."

Oh, shite.

"That would be absolutely amazing. Having an actual base of operations would be ideal. Would you have something available starting next week?"

"I need to check with our property manager, but I feel certain we can accommodate you. I'll email you with details."

They said their final goodbyes. Then Kyla shut the door and turned to take Sophie's hands.

Her bright blue eyes sparkled, and her smile was absolutely radiant. "We did it!"

Sophie blew out a breath. "We did it."

Kyla frowned, searching her face. "You don't seem as excited as I thought you'd be. Everything okay?"

It definitely wasn't. She was too busy thinking about the ramifications of Swayze actually being on site for the next two months. That could get very sticky, very fast.

"I'm just thinking about details. We'll pull it off. We've run the numbers. It's just a big undertaking."

"A big undertaking that stands to explode our business in the best possible way," Kyla reminded her.

Assuming Connor's little white lie didn't blow up in their faces.

"God willing."

"Let's go have a celebratory cupcake."

Sophie automatically fell into step with her friend as they headed toward the kitchen.

"Oh, you'd said there was something you needed to tell me before they got here."

Right. That.

She still needed to tell Kyla, but there was more information to gather.

"It can wait. I've got something I need to do first."

Six

Connor turned off the belt grinder and shoved up his safety glasses to examine the edge of the bowie knife. It would cut at this stage, but it wasn't quite where it needed to be. He reached toward the power switch on the grinder and felt the phone in his pocket vibrate with a text. Tugging it out, he glanced at the screen, and his pulse jittered with a mix of pleasure and anxiety.

Sophie: **I need to talk to you. Where are you?**

That could mean anything. That she felt weird and wanted to get things back on an even keel. That she was upset about the kiss, after all. That she was still thinking about the kiss as much as he was. Okay, that last was probably wishful thinking, but he didn't care what she wanted to talk about. He'd drop everything for her.

He remembered Raleigh had said she and Kyla had been at Ardinmuir today for a pitch presentation.

Connor: **Are you still at the castle?**

Sophie: **Can you meet me at the shop?**

Because she wanted privacy for their conversation? Or because she'd gone back there to catch up on some kind of work? Maybe both.

Connor: **Of course. Give me thirty.**

She replied with a thumbs-up emoji.

He took the time to shut everything down, confirming his forge was properly cool and his tools stowed, then locked the door and headed for the village.

Glenlaig was big enough that he didn't know everyone, but small enough that damned near everyone seemed to know him and his family. The MacKeans were one of the oldest families in the area and had been the protectors of the region for centuries. That role had changed with the modern age, but the reputation had endured. As such, multiple people waved or nodded as he turned onto the high street. He passed the old stone church where the banns had been read about him and Afton. That felt like a lifetime ago. The crowd around the door of The Stag's Head told him the pub was already jumping. Depending on how things went with this conversation, he might stop in for a pint and a word with Ewan. Toward the end of the main row of shops, he took a right onto a side street and parked by the curb at the first open space. He found he wanted the short walk to settle himself before he saw her again.

Light spilled out of Village Blume, highlighting the snowy pavement. In the winter dark, it was harder to see the peeling paint and sagging eaves that were just a fraction of the signs John Milligan was a terrible landlord. Without the harsh light of day, he saw only the bright, cheerful oasis Sophie had created here. Racks crowding the front of the shop were overflowing with baskets and bowls and vases, all somehow arranged with an inviting sense of whimsy. He spotted the woman herself behind the counter, her inky black hair loose and spilling in waves over one shoulder as she studied something on her laptop. His fingers itched to thread in the silk of that hair. To lay his lips over hers again for more than a brief, performative kiss.

Sophie looked up, those striking grey eyes meeting his through the glass. For a moment, they stood there, and Connor thought he saw just as much yearning in her face as he felt. Then she was moving toward the door. When she opened it with her customary neutral expression, he told himself he'd imagined the whole thing.

"Thanks for coming." She stepped back, motioning him inside.

"Sure."

As he passed, Sophie dropped her gaze, which was the first sign things weren't okay. He followed her behind the counter, into the back room, where she did the bulk of the actual arrangements. Rather than sit, she immediately moved to one of the wide worktables and began restlessly organizing supplies that were already organized.

Sign number two.

Connor officially went on alert. "Are you all right?"

"We had a full pitch meeting today with Alyssa and Swayze."

Oh, bloody hell. "Did Swayze say something to Kyla about the engagement thing?"

Her hands stilled. "No, but it's only a matter of time. Alyssa signed the contract, and evidently Swayze will be hanging around until the wedding, overseeing everything from one of the estate cottages. She's planning to document the whole thing on social media, which could be huge for our business. But..."

"But my big fat mouth might put that in jeopardy because I couldn't be honest in the moment."

It was distress he saw in those pretty eyes when she met his again. "Maybe?"

"Shite." Connor tunneled a hand through his hair. "I'm sorry, Soph. That was never my intention. When I spouted off, I just thought to spare some hurt feelings."

"I don't care about that. You were trying to do a kindness. You couldn't have known it would backfire like this. But you and I need to be on the same page about how to handle her, because there's no way she'll be here for two months and *not* find out that what you told her was a lie. You'd know better than I how she might react to that. I mean, what do we need to do here? Is she the kind of woman who's going to get angry and talk her best friend out of using us? Do we need to tell her we broke up? Because even in that scenario, we'd still need some sort of story to tell people, and everyone's going to be completely and totally shocked, because we've never been involved. That's never how we've looked at each other."

Speak for yourself. But Sophie didn't know that, so Connor held his tongue.

"The truth is, I dinna ken how Swayze would react. We dinna ken each other that well, and our... involvement was two years ago. She disnae seem like the sort of woman who'd take my lie out on you, but I dinna like the idea of risking it. Even if Swayze doesn't retaliate, we dinna ken what kind of woman her friend is. She might pull the contract out of solidarity or something."

Sophie blew out a slow breath. "That's what I'm afraid of. So, what do we do?"

Connor considered the question. The answer was staring them in the face: Continue the fake engagement for the two-ish months Swayze was here. If that scenario also gave him a legitimate opportunity to get close to Sophie and prove to her she ought to give him a real chance, well, maybe he was an opportunistic asshole. But he was an opportunistic asshole who wanted to treat her like a queen. Surely, he could be forgiven for that?

"I think, rather than my talking to her or staging a breakup, it makes more sense to continue the ruse."

She blinked at him. "You... want me to continue to pretend to be engaged to you?"

"You and Kyla need this contract. You need the positive exposure that would come of staying on Swayze's good side and her using her platform to get the word out. I dinna think we can risk that she might use that platform for ill. So, continuing with the status quo, as far as she's concerned, seems like the smarter move."

"We can't just fake it for her, Connor. You know how village life works. If we do this, in order to actually sell it, we'd have to get the family on board with the fake engagement, because they're not going to believe that we're actually engaged. Then all of *them* are going to have to help us make the village think that this is real."

Act like Sophie's doting fiancé for two months in front of the world? Hell, yeah, he was on board with that plan. "I'm prepared to do that. Are you?"

She searched his face for a long moment. "We need the contract. So, yeah, I guess I am."

"Okay. When are we going to tell everybody?"

"Next family dinner, I suppose. It'll save us from having to call everyone together separately."

Connor thought about what he'd already promised Raleigh. That dinner was going to be a hell of a reveal. "Works for me."

"Okay, then. Fake engaged." She looked a little shell-shocked at the statement.

He crossed to where she stood and offered a hand. She glanced down at it for a long moment, frowning before curling her fingers around his and lifting his hand to stroke around the bandage.

"You hurt yourself."

Her touch felt about a hundred times better than the burn salve had.

"It's nothing." Connor didn't release his hold on her, didn't settle for a perfunctory shake. He couldn't. Not when the warmth of her skin against his reminded him of those all too brief moments with her in his arms. But he recognized that sealing the deal with a kiss wasn't the right move, so he pulled her into a hug instead.

"It's going to be okay. I promise."

As she slowly settled against him, she muttered, "I hope you're right."

The line of vehicles in the circular drive in front of the manor house at Lochmara told Sophie she was the last to arrive. She'd stayed late to put together a bright and happy arrangement for Bridget MacDonald to take to her sister, who'd just given birth to a brand new baby boy this afternoon. Bridget was over the moon and heading up to the hospital in Inverness to see the new addition.

Grabbing a bundle of flowers from the passenger seat, she walked around to the kitchen door. Before she could even knock, Connor was opening the door. Had he been watching for her?

"Let me help you with those." He moved in, neatly plucking the flowers from her arms and murmuring, "You okay?"

This was becoming a refrain from him lately. She wasn't sure how she felt about it. "Fine." At his arched brow, she amended, "A wee bit anxious." She had no idea what reactions they'd get to this insanity, but she knew they needed to get everyone on board sooner rather than later.

"It'll be fine. If everyone freaks out, throw me under the bus."

Even though this whole situation was patently his fault, she didn't like how easily he was willing to make himself a target. She'd agreed to the arrangement. That made her just as culpable. But he'd already turned to go back inside.

Trailing after him, Sophie spotted Charlotte at the hob, stirring something that smelled spicy and delicious. Malcolm stood behind her, one hand at her waist as he dropped a kiss to the juncture between her neck and shoulder. From where he stood chopping salad vegetables at the counter, Gavin made a comical gagging face, but it was clear he was really pleased to see the two of them together. Though nobody had seen that pairing coming, there was no denying Malcolm and Charlotte worked, so everyone had accepted it with little fanfare.

Sophie had no such expectation that she and Connor would

be as easily accepted. Not that their relationship was real. Which would, she knew, be the biggest sticking point when they made their announcement.

"I put the flowers on the dining room table."

She jerked her attention back to Connor. "Thanks."

He held her gaze a few beats too long, reassuring her in one of those silent couple communications. Which was entirely ridiculous, given they weren't a real couple. But that didn't change the fact that she could read him.

With a nod, she went to do her part by arranging the flowers.

It felt strange to share something with Connor that didn't involve Kyla. For all she'd known him his whole life, the past week had forced her to acknowledge that the two-year age gap between them was meaningless now. She hadn't been able to *unsee* him as an arguably very attractive man. One with quite the reputation among those of the female persuasion. A reputation that seemed well-deserved, based on that kiss. She hadn't managed to stop herself from wondering what it would be like to be the true focus of his attention and experience.

Which was absolutely idiotic. They wouldn't be taking this deception *that* far.

Although, some sort of public displays of affection would be necessary to make it believable. Couples touched. They held hands. They kissed. She definitely wouldn't mind kissing him again, without the haze of shock distracting her from the full effect. Just the idea of it had heat rising in her cheeks.

They should probably have a conversation to establish the ground rules around that sort of thing. Just so they were in agreement. Maybe they needed to practice...

"Did you see my email about the change from the caterer for this weekend's wedding?"

Sophie jerked so hard, she nearly knocked over the pitcher she was using for the flowers.

Kyla arched a brow. "You okay?"

She really wished everybody would stop asking her that. "Just daydreaming. Aye, I saw it and made the adjustments to the event timeline. Although we should probably do a dry run tomorrow—of moving all the tables and chairs out in the great hall between the ceremony and the reception—just to verify the timing."

"Good call." But instead of continuing to press on business, Kyla simply stood there, studying her.

Sophie fought the urge to fidget.

From the kitchen Charlotte shouted, "Come and get it, y'all!"

"We'd best hurry. I'm pretty sure Gavin has been eating to fill a hollow leg for at least the past two months."

"I'll be right along. Let me just get the last of these in water." Sophie gestured with a bearded iris.

Kyla looked like she wanted to say something, but got hailed by Raleigh from the other room.

Relieved for the reprieve, Sophie turned her attention fully to the flowers and worked to control her breathing. The anxiety had taken hold again. She needed to get this whole thing out in the open and over with, so she'd stop obsessing over what their reactions might be.

So, right after they all settled around the big table with bowls of rich beef stew and slices of warm, buttery cornbread, she blurted, "Connor and I have something to tell you."

Conversation screeched to a halt, and all eyes turned in her direction. Ewan still held the basket of cornbread aloft. Kyla slowly lowered the spoonful of stew that had been halfway to her mouth. The only sound to break the silence was Dugal, who playfully growled at a chew toy somewhere under the table.

Sophie felt vaguely ill. She laced her fingers together in her lap and launched in, explaining as simply as possible what had happened, without going into detail about what kind of involved Connor had been with Swayze that might scandalize the thirteen-year-old boy. "So, for the next two months, everyone has to think we're engaged."

The silence after this announcement was so profound, she

could hear Kyla's slow intake of breath. Stomach twisting, Sophie braced herself.

"Are you out of your mind?" She didn't shout, but Sophie flinched anyway.

Connor answered before she could. "No. We discussed the options. This is the best one."

"This isn't just some secret between the family. If you carry this out until the wedding, the entire village is going to find out." She turned her gaze on Sophie. "Are you really okay with that?"

Sophie shrugged. "It won't affect my dating life in the least. It's not like I'm seeing anybody for real." She'd never had suitors beating down her door. Would being linked to a man like Connor make her appear more desirable? Then again, did she want to waste her time on someone who didn't appreciate her for who she was to begin with?

"Will people actually believe it?" Raleigh asked.

Ciara propped her chin on one fist. "Sure they will. This is a classic best friend's sibling story."

"A what now?" Ewan asked.

"She's talking romance novels," Charlotte explained. "Best friend's sibling is a classic trope for a reason. They've known each other forever. They're comfortable together. And now that the marriage pact is no longer an issue, Connor's free to pursue whoever he wants. Why shouldn't that be Sophie? Anybody with an ounce of romanticism could believe that there were long-standing feelings that were never acknowledged because of duty. The only piece needed is the thing that makes them look at each other differently."

Like an unexpected kiss. Suddenly hot, Sophie shifted in her seat.

"I think I read that one," Ciara muttered. "Except it was set back in Regency era."

"Oh, honey, I've got a whole list, if that's your jam."

Sophie wasn't entirely sure how she felt about the application of romance novel logic to their situation. But before the conversation could devolve further, she spoke up. "We're not asking for your approval. That decision lies with me and Connor, and it's been made. We're asking for your help. Can we count on your support in keeping up appearances to avoid risking this contract?"

"Of course you can, lass." Angus cast a speaking glance to the rest of the assembly, which prompted a chorus of agreement with varying degrees of enthusiasm.

Sophie knew she'd be hearing more about this from Kyla, but she'd save it until they were alone.

"That's settled, then," Charlotte declared. "Let's get to this food while it's still hot."

Properly chastened, they dove into the meal. Conversation was a little halting at first but ultimately picked back up to normal. Connor caught her eye with another of those *You good?* looks. She didn't know what she was, but she appreciated his concern.

Angus had, per usual, provided dessert. Before everyone rose to clear the table, Connor cleared his throat. "I have another announcement."

Kyla sighed. "Now what?"

"Just... wait here a minute."

When he walked out, she turned to Sophie. "Do you know what this is about?"

"No idea. I'm only his fake fiancée, remember?"

Connor returned a few moments later, something in his hands. With great care, he leaned between Sophie and Munro and laid a sword on the table.

Sophie couldn't help but admire the gleam of the blade. "Are you entering the village Highland Games this year?" She glanced up in time to see his shoulders curl and noted that he wouldn't meet anyone's gaze.

"I made it."

"What?" Kyla asked.

Connor laid a hand on the hilt and looked at his sister, his voice a little stronger. "I made this claymore. I forged the blade, made the hilt."

Raleigh was the only one who didn't look surprised. "Finally."

Kyla stared at him. "You knew about this?"

"Yep. Been pushing him to tell you for months." At her mutinous look, he held up a hand. "It was his to tell. He's hella talented."

Charlotte bolted upright in her seat. "That wrought iron tree mug rack I wanted. You didn't find it. You made it!"

Connor made an awkward bob of his head. "Aye."

Sophie traced the MacKean crest etched into the hilt in intricate detail. "How long have you been doing this?"

"A few years now. I... um... have a forge out at one of the cottages on the estate."

He was an artist. A blacksmith. Suddenly those lean muscles took on a whole other meaning. Both were sides of him she hadn't expected.

Kyla rose and came around to examine the sword herself. "Connor, this is amazing. Have you done others?"

Another jerky nod. "An array of blades. Some architectural pieces. It's been a decent little sideline."

"I'd say it ought to be more than a sideline." Kyla studied him with a new intensity. "Why don't you make this a business?"

Connor was already shaking his head, both hands shoved into his pockets. "No, I canna do that. I've got too many other things to do with the estate. It's just a hobby."

Sophie heard what he was saying, but in the set of his shoulders and his refusal to look directly at anyone, she understood there was something else beneath it. As he dismissed the other questions asked, she filed it away to address later.

"I just thought you should know, as we were coming clean about secrets. Angus, can I help you plate up dessert?"

"Of course, lad."

They made it through the rest of the meal with no further

revelations. Connor fairly vibrated with restless energy, and Sophie knew he was ready to make his escape. So, once they'd cleared the table, she caught him in a corner of the kitchen.

"We have some details we probably need to discuss. Can I pop over to Ardinmuir after this?"

"Of course." He lifted his keys. "I'm leaving now."

"I'll be right behind you."

Seven

Connor's mind was full of a whole other set of worries on the drive back to Ardinmuir. A weight had lifted off his shoulders during dinner. The big revelation of his blacksmithing had gone smoother than expected. In the wake of the fake engagement to Sophie, his side hustle was no big deal. Given the objections, he'd expected Sophie to bend and ask the others if they had alternative suggestions for some other way to handle the situation. That she'd put her foot down and defended their decision had surprised him. She so seldom dug in on anything. But now he wondered if this whole charade would be too much for her.

Anxiety still seemed to crackle around her as she moved to start the tea. Maybe the reality of what they'd committed to doing was finally sinking in. Connor wanted to reassure her, but it was hard to find the right words when he was second guessing himself.

Whatever commentary Angus had on the situation, he was keeping it to himself. Connor knew that was entirely for Sophie's benefit. His great uncle wasn't prone to hiding his opinions. He put the leftovers Charlotte had sent home with them into the fridge. "I'm taking myself off to bed. Early day tomorrow." He gave Sophie a squeeze. "Good night, lass."

Eyes closed, she pressed her cheek to his. "Good night, Angus."

"Night, Uncle Angus."

With one last look that absolutely said, *Tread carefully, lad,* he left them alone.

Sophie filled the kettle and set it to boil. "If we're going to pull this off, we have some details to hash out."

So she wasn't planning to back out. Something inside Connor loosened. "Such as?"

"Well, obviously, we don't have to talk about how we met. But people will want to know how it is we actually got together. They'll want to know how long we've been together, and why we kept it quiet. We need to have our stories straight."

"Fair point." Connor kicked back against the island. He understood the point of this exercise, but he also wanted to give her as much of the truth as he could. "My whole life, my love life and my relationship status have been a topic for public consumption. My expected marriage to Afton was everybody's business. And I hated it. I hated the situation. I hated all the speculation. That's a big part of the reason, beyond simple respect for Afton, that I never dated close to home. But finally having the freedom to pursue a relationship with someone I actually choose, and being able to do that quietly, without anybody else nosing in and offering an opinion... That's a big deal to me. So I feel like that's a solid reason we'd have kept it quiet."

Sophie angled her head in concession of the point. "And how we got together?"

"That's no one's business. They might want some kind of a dramatic story for how and why things changed, but that doesn't mean there is one. As Charlotte said, we've known each other all our lives. For all they know, the feelings have been there all along, and we only just got the chance to pursue them."

Because he worried what might show in his face, when the kettle shrieked, he was the one who stepped forward and poured water into the waiting mugs.

"Fair enough. Simple is probably best in this situation, either way. Those are all secondary concerns."

Hearing something in the tone of her voice, Connor turned. "What's the primary?"

"Well, there's the matter of public displays of affection. I'm not..." She hesitated, seeming to search for the right words. "I'm not as easy with physical affection as you. The only reason I didn't blow it in front of Swayze and Alyssa in the first place was sheer shock. I worry we won't look comfortable together. Or that I won't, at least."

Connor weighed his words. "You're no' wrong. People will expect a certain degree of intimacy between us. But consent is a thing I take verra seriously. I crossed a line when I kissed you the other day. I willnae do it again without your permission." He'd hate it, because kissing her again had taken up probably ninety-five percent of his mental real estate since he'd stopped. But he didn't want to make her uncomfortable. "We can stick with hand-holding and hugs. That kind of thing."

"It's not that. It's just that it's been a really long time since I kissed anybody."

"It's been a long time for me, too."

One inky brow winged up. "Somehow, I expect our definitions of a long time aren't the same." She turned her back to remove the infusers from the mugs.

Connor couldn't be insulted by that. Not with the way he'd lived his life. "I havenae seen or been with anybody since the first banns were read announcing my wedding to Afton. So, I guess it's been about eight or nine months?"

That got her facing him again. "Really? Why?"

"Well, the banns were a sign of my impending marriage, so at that point, it was only respectful to cut that sort of thing off. And since Afton left, there's been a lot going on, and I havenae wanted to pursue anybody. The encounters I had served a purpose. Once I was freed from the marriage pact, that purpose was no longer relevant."

Her expression was full of compassion. "I don't think any of us really gave you full credit for how difficult a position you were put in. Certainly, Kyla didn't understand until she was in it herself. You were always just so easy and affable about it."

Connor shrugged. "It was the thing I was expected to do for my family. Now I get to think about a relationship purely for myself."

Sophie studied him. "Why couldn't you do that before? I mean, I've always understood that you expected to marry Afton, but I never understood why you didn't do exactly what Kyla originally planned. Marry, then divorce her. It seems simpler than trapping yourself in a marriage you didn't want."

It had been the obvious answer, and one he'd never fully considered. "I made a promise to my mother just before she died. She made me swear that I'd stick it out and do the work. I think, at that point, she just thought Afton and I needed to give each other a real chance. You ken how close she was to Afton's mum. Even without the pact, they loved the idea of us being together." He jerked a shoulder. "It was the one thing she asked of me, and then she was gone. So I hung onto that promise because it felt like the only thing I could still do to honor her."

Connor waited for Sophie to call him out on how it had been a foolish promise. That his mother's request had been selfish. Instead, he saw only empathy in her eyes.

"Promises are hard. Especially promises made under that sort of duress."

Yeah. She'd know all about that.

Wanting to change the subject, he accepted the mug she offered and leaned against the counter. "So let's circle back to the other thing. You've never seemed uncomfortable around me before."

She looked into her own mug. "It was different before."

"Are you worried it's gonna come across like you're kissing your brother?" That sure as hell wasn't how he felt about it. But if she wasn't actually attracted to him, he needed to mentally adjust his expectations for this whole endeavor.

A pretty flush worked its way up her throat and into her cheeks. "No."

"Okay, that's a start. So maybe we need to test things."

Her eyes lifted to his. "Test things? How?"

"You figure out where the line is between comfortable and uncomfortable and what we can do to put you more at ease. That way, you're in control, and you know what's coming. No more sneak attacks." She'd been given little enough control in her life in a lot of other areas. She deserved agency in this.

Sophie seemed to consider that for a long moment before nodding. "All right."

Setting the mug aside, she reached for his hand, lacing her long, slim fingers with his. Warmth spread from where they touched, palm to palm. He'd never in his life been aroused by simply holding hands, but Sophie was, it seemed, the exception to every rule. He held himself back from taking over, pulling her against him, but he couldn't quite resist brushing his thumb along the back of her hand.

"Feeling weird?"

"No."

"Good."

After another brief hesitation, she moved into him, sliding her arms around his waist. Connor set his mug on the counter and folded her in. They'd hugged before, many times over the years. But those had been casual, friendly squeezes. This was an embrace, one that allowed him to notice, for the first time, how perfectly she fit against him. Short enough that her head nestled against his shoulder, but tall enough he could turn his head to brush a kiss to her temple. Though he didn't. He simply held her, waiting as she slowly, gradually, relaxed against him with a sigh.

He wondered how long it had been since anyone had held her like this.

"Okay?" he murmured.

She tipped her head back to look at him. "Yes." Her gaze dropped to his mouth, indecision clear on her face.

God, he knew which one he wanted her to make. "Anything you want. You're running the show."

Her tongue darted out to wet her lips. Connor almost groaned at the sight of it. He saw the moment she decided and fought not to give in to his own elation. Sophie rose slowly to her toes and brushed her mouth to his.

It took everything he had not to haul her in and take over. He'd promised this was her show. So he held still, moving only his lips against hers with the same soft, questioning pressure. That slow exploration was maddening perfection. It wasn't as if he'd never been kissed by women. But he was usually the initiator. It was a whole different thing, being kissed by the woman he wanted.

As she went soft and pliant in his arms, he gave in and slid his fingers into her hair, asking for more and receiving it when her mouth opened under his on another sigh. She tasted of tea and spice and perfection. Connor wanted to drown in her. But he kept things easy, not fighting when she finally drew back.

Her eyes were huge, the grey of her irises the barest sliver of silver around her dilated pupils. A lovely flush warmed her honey-colored cheeks, and her mouth was pink and just a little swollen from his. She was utterly gorgeous, and it took Connor more than a few moments to find his voice.

"Okay?"

Looking more than a little dazed, she murmured, "Definitely not my brother."

Thank God. He swallowed. "Are you good? Or do you think we need to try that again?"

He definitely wanted to try that again.

"I think we're okay."

Connor searched her face when she dropped back to her feet and stepped back. She didn't seem to be making an escape.

To keep himself from reaching for her again, he picked up his tea. "What else do we need to cover?"

"I'm sure there will be other points that come up, but that's all I can think of at the moment." She drank down her abandoned tea. "I need to be getting home. We've got a long day tomorrow, with the bride and groom and wedding party arriving for this weekend's wedding."

He didn't want her to go, but he understood she needed to. "Okay. Text me when you get home?" Such a request wasn't the usual for him. "It's late, and we've kind of been through a lot tonight."

Her momentary beat of surprise turned to something he wanted to believe was pleasure. "I will. See you tomorrow, Connor."

He stayed where he was for a few long minutes after she'd left, because, for the first time in a long time, he was really looking forward to tomorrow.

———

The caterer's van was already in the castle drive when Sophie came flying up. So were a myriad of vehicles belonging to the wedding party and family who'd already arrived. They'd all be expecting to sit down and eat the rehearsal dinner at perfectly appointed tables with expertly crafted Scottish cuisine in ten minutes' time, so *of course* there'd been a delay with her delivery of the peonies for the centerpieces.

Thank God for Ciara. She'd been on hand to help Kyla greet and wrangle everyone, getting them settled into their respective cottages, before directing them to the great hall for the rehearsal. That had left Sophie free to finish the arrangements at the very last moment. Now, she just needed another set of hands to help transport the arrangements to the formal parlor, where the rehearsal dinner was to be held.

Connor must have been watching, because he stepped out of the castle before she'd even rolled to a stop.

Sophie threw the car into park and leapt out. "I need your hands!"

"I'm at your disposal, milady. Just one thing first."

She swung toward him, at the edge of panic. "What?"

His hands curled around her shoulders. "Breathe. There's time. One of the groomsmen has jetlag and overslept, so they're running through the processional one more time."

"Oh, thank God." She slumped against him. "My distributor was late, and just everything has gone awry today."

Connor folded her in, brushing his lips to her temple in a gesture that was oddly soothing. "Slow down. The emergency's over."

Sophie wished the whole day was over so she could stay right here, wrapped in his strong, capable arms. She hadn't known exactly how much she'd missed being held. Couldn't even remember how long it had been. But there were a-million-and-one details still to tend to, so she squeezed him once and stepped back to open the boot, where she'd stowed all the centerpieces. They were held in place by a grid of bungee cords she'd fashioned for transport.

Connor managed to juggle four. "Where do you need me to take them?"

She snagged the last two. "To the formal parlor."

They hurried through the labyrinthine halls of the castle. The tables were already draped and set with silverware and china. Cloth napkins had been folded in the shape of swans at each seat. Ciara's doing. Sophie immediately placed the first of the arrangements according to the plan she'd drawn up weeks ago. Connor dutifully followed her around so she could do the same at every table. He was so good about pitching in to help with these events, especially as they couldn't afford to pay him in anything other than beer.

"You're a lifesaver. You know that?"

He flashed a cocky grin. "What are fiancés for?"

Sophie's brain promptly offered a host of suggestions for more creative ways she could pay him back for his assistance. Starting with more of those toe-curling kisses. But there was no audience here. No one to perform for. So she shook her head and grinned back. "Cheeky. I'm gonna go find Kyla and let her know everything's on track here. Can you tell the catering team?"

"I'm on it."

The rehearsal was just wrapping as Sophie slipped into the great hall through one of the side doors. She caught Kyla's eye and signaled all was ready to go.

As the vicar concluded, Kyla stepped up to the dais. "You're finishing just in time. Ciara will take you to the formal parlor for the rehearsal dinner. The caterers are already on site, so you should be eating shortly."

"Right this way, everyone!"

While they all filed out of the hall, Sophie made a quick scan of the room. Everything was laid out for tomorrow's ceremony. The white aisle runner stretched the length of the room, flanked on either side by rows of regimented folding chairs. The tables for the reception were stowed nearby, just waiting to be rolled out the moment the ceremony was over.

"Caterers are activated. What's left for tonight?"

Sophie turned toward Connor, who'd slipped in behind her. "I need to finish the two massive arrangements flanking the altar. In the morning, all that's left will be attaching the floral decorations to the end of each row, and passing on the boutonnieres and bouquets to the family and friends who'll be handing them out to the wedding party. Those are already in the work fridge."

"Need another hand bringing in everything for the altarpieces?"

"I won't turn one down."

Kyla interrupted. "Actually, if I can steal you for a moment, Con, one of the cafe light strands has gone out. Weren't you the one who bought the extras?"

"Aye. They're in the... Actually, I cannae remember where I put them, but I'm positive I can lay hands on them."

"Go on. I'll help Sophie haul in the last of the flowers."

With a salute, he was off again.

"Flowers in the car?"

Sophie nodded and fell into motion. "Did the rehearsal go off okay?"

"No major disasters. I think we'll need to watch the groom's uncle. He keeps nipping from a flask in his pocket."

"Do you think he'll end up handsy or combative?"

"Never know. I'd rather be on guard and it turn into nothing, than not be aware and have Maureen and Tony's wedding ruined."

"Fair point."

When Kyla lapsed into silence, a fresh ball of dread formed in Sophie's stomach. She hadn't been evading her friend on purpose. The day really had gotten away from her with all the details of overseeing the wedding festivities. But she knew there were things Kyla hadn't been willing to say last night in front of the entire group.

Sure enough, as soon as they stepped outside, she started in. "This chance for our business is not worth mucking up your life."

"I'm not mucking up my life, Kyla. It's two months."

"You shouldn't have to pretend—" She cast a glance around to confirm they were alone. "—this."

"We need this exposure." More, she needed the success of this business to cover the higher business rent on her shop. But she knew exactly how Kyla would respond to finding out she'd already re-signed her lease, so she left that out. "Connor and I get on well. We've known each other forever. It's fine."

Kyla's face twisted. "But he's like a brother to you."

Heat gathered in Sophie's cheeks. "Not nearly so much as you think."

"What is that supposed to mean?"

"Just that he definitely does not kiss like my brother."

"He kissed you?"

"Oh, aye. That's how all of this came out when Alyssa and Swayze were here the first time." She explained the ambush.

"I canna believe he did that in front of clients." Kyla shoved a hand through her hair. "And it wasn't... weird?"

"It was a shock, certainly. But not gross or anything. I know it's an awkward situation for everyone, but it is what it is. This is what we're doing. He and I are fine with it, so you need to be, too." She ducked into the car and gathered up the first box of blooms.

"I'm just worried about you."

"Why?"

"Because it's hard to fake all of this without the heart getting involved. Trust me, I know. What happens if you develop real feelings for Connor?"

"So what if I do? What would be wrong with that? We're both single, consenting adults. And for the first time in his life, he's free to pursue someone for real."

Distress flickered over Kyla's features. "I mean, if that's how it happens, okay. But listen to what you're saying. You're talking about a—" She lowered her voice. "—*fake engagement* as if it's a real relationship. Dinna get me wrong. I love my brother. But he's a playboy with a short attention span. Long-term committed relationships are not exactly his wheelhouse, and you deserve better than that."

Sophie thought of his confession last night, that he hadn't been with anyone since the banns had been read months ago. "He only did that because he expected to be trapped in a marriage to someone he didn't actually want."

Belatedly, Sophie realized that made it sound like she thought he wanted her. But what if he did? There'd been no one to perform for in that kitchen last night. He'd kissed her back.

"I just don't want to see you get hurt. Either of you."

"Found it!"

They both turned to see Connor waving from the door, a strand of cafe lights in hand.

Sophie reached for the patience she habitually wore like a cloak. "I appreciate that. But I'm a big girl. I can handle this. Right now, the only thing you need to be concerned about is getting those lights up and making sure our guests stay moderately sober and on the proper wedding timeline."

Without waiting for a reply, Sophie headed back to the castle to finish her work for the night.

Eight

"Welcome to your home away from home." Connor opened the door to the cottage and stepped inside.

Swayze followed, smile blooming, her hazel eyes going wide with delight as she spun to take it in. "Oh, my God! This place is simply adorable."

Whipping out her cell phone, she tapped some buttons and started speaking into the camera. "Hey Sweethearts! This is Swayze coming to you live and in person at Ardinmuir Castle in Glenlaig, Scotland, where I have just booked the world's cutest cottage for the next couple of months. How cute is this place?"

Connor watched as she did a slow pan of the room, taking in the comfortable sofa and armchair clustered around the fireplace. Flowers bloomed in a vase on the little dining table and in bud vases on the mantle, beside squat pillar candles. Sophie's doing, of course. The kitchen was small but well appointed, with cookery implements clustered in a crock on the counter. Pots and pans hung from a wall rack he'd forged himself, and the open shelves held an assortment of simple cream-colored plates, bowls, and mugs. On the rustic little island that had been made from scraps of other cottages, a massive welcome basket waited for her perusal.

She pivoted in his direction. "And this is my buddy, Connor, one of the owners of the estate where I'm staying. Connor, say hi."

Knowing his part in this, he lifted a hand in a wave and put some extra brogue in his voice. "Hullo."

Turning the camera back to herself, she beamed. "I'm here for the next couple of months helping to plan my dearest darling bestie Alyssa's wedding, and y'all are gonna be brought along for the ride. Stay tuned, lovelies!"

With another megawatt smile, she blew a kiss to the camera and signed off.

From where he stood in the doorway, Angus angled his head. "You just... talk to whatever random strangers are out there on the internet?"

Swayze turned that grin on him. "A few million of them. Yeah."

Angus shook his head, obviously unable to conceive of such a thing. "Whatever makes you happy, lass. And I do hope you will be happy here. We've put together a welcome basket."

Shutting the door, he strode over to the basket and began to point out its contents. "Most of what's in here is local. Cheese and sausages from various crofts around the estate. Some beer brewed right in the village. And some fresh biscuits I baked myself this morning, if you've a sweet tooth."

"Oh, that's wonderful. And I remember how what y'all call biscuits and what we call biscuits aren't the same thing. Connor raved about your baking when we met, so I'm looking forward to getting a taste firsthand."

Connor pointed to the notebook they'd put together for every cottage. "There's a map of the village; a list of local restaurants, both in Glenlaig and the villages within about a half hour's drive; an assortment of brochures about activities in the area; and, of course, the Wi-Fi access information."

"This is amazing. Seriously. I can't thank you and your sister enough for letting me lease this place for the next couple of months."

"We're happy to have you." The long-term business was especially helpful, even if it came with some challenges. "I'll bring in your bags."

He hauled them in from the boot of her rental car, stacking them just inside the doorway of the lone bedroom.

"Thanks, Connor. Oh, and I really want to get video of you and Sophie together."

"Me and Sophie?"

"And Kyla, too, of course. To share the family aspect of the whole business. Viewers always love that sort of thing."

"Oh. Well, I'll talk to them about it." A big part of him hoped they'd say no, because the whole thing felt like just another opportunity for this farce to blow up in their faces.

"Fantastic. And I'd really love to have dinner with you and Sophie. She seems absolutely lovely. I know I'm going to be getting to know her better over the next couple of months as we work on the wedding, but I'd like to see the two of you together."

Why on earth would she want that? To verify the truth of their claim to be engaged? Or was he just that paranoid?

"Aye, well, I'm no' sure of her schedule. She's pretty busy between the event planning business and her shop, but I'll see what I can do." He had no idea how Sophie was going to react to the request. Needing to escape before Swayze found yet another way to put him on the spot, he took a step toward the door. "If there's nothing else you need, we've got a few things we need to get to. But welcome to Ardinmuir."

"See you soon!"

They left Swayze grinning from ear to ear and climbed into the 4x4 for the drive back to the castle.

"She's an enthusiastic wee thing," Angus observed.

"Aye. It's contagious. That's part of how she's gotten so big as an influencer. People like her."

"You don't?"

Connor glanced at his uncle, confused. "Of course, I do."

"But not enough to pick back up where you left off two years ago."

Shoulders twitching in discomfort, Connor kept his gaze on the road. "I wasnae looking for that when I ran into her in Edinburgh." Which was a bald-faced lie. He *had* been looking. He just hadn't been able to go through with it when faced with the actual opportunity.

Angus hummed a noncommittal note. "I just find it interesting that you entered this fake engagement with Sophie, when you havenae sought out anybody in the better part of a year."

He'd noticed? Uncomfortable with that, too, Connor shrugged. "There's been too much to do and a lot more important things to worry about." All true. Though the bigger truth was that he hadn't wanted anybody but Sophie since the door opened to the possibility of having a real relationship. Not that he'd admit that to his uncle.

Angus snorted. "Och, lad, do you really think I've never noticed how you look at her?"

A skitter of unease danced down his spine. "What do you mean?"

From the passenger seat, Angus just looked at him. "I ken you've been biding your time since you got free of the marriage pact, and you should ken, I support this a hundred percent. I just hope this particular tactic disnae blow up in your face."

"You and me both. Their business is counting on it."

"I think it's more than their business that depends upon this. Either way, there is something important that both of you have overlooked in carrying out this charade."

"What's that?"

Angus folded his arms. "The ring."

———

"Have you heard about Tom Chapman?"

Sophie had heard of little else since she opened the shop this morning. And by now, maintaining her professional demeanor was a struggle.

"A heart attack, they said," Betty McPhee continued. "I had it from Agatha Campbell at the butcher. Fell to his knees right there in the family lounge."

Sophie squeezed her eyes shut and prayed for patience as similar images of her own father's heart attack played on a reel in her mind. "Aye. Terribly sad for Neve and the family." She knew exactly what her former schoolmate was going through. Drawing deep on reserves of strength, she forced a half smile. "Did you want to send an arrangement to pay your respects?"

The question seemed to break Mrs. McPhee out of her gossip mode. "Aye. I would. What are my options?"

Sophie went over the options at each budget tier and wrote down the order, adding it to the stack of others she'd be slaving over when the base blooms arrived from her distributor. By the time the process was finished and Mrs. McPhee had left, she was exhausted and considering locking the door for a few minutes, just to give herself some time to breathe and process her own reaction to the news.

Her phone vibrated with a text. She pulled it from her pocket.

Connor: **Free for dinner?**

Dinner was hours away. Given how the day was shaping up, she'd do well to carve out time for another cuppa soup.

Sophie: **I've got a lot of work to do.**

Seconds after she sent the text, her phone rang. The corners of her mouth twitched as she answered. "Think you can be more persuasive in a phone call?"

"Of course I can. Come on, Soph. You've got to eat. I heard about Tom Chapman."

She groaned. "Not you, too."

"I ken that's going to bring some stuff up for you. Let me take you out tonight. Distract you."

That he knew her well enough to think of that gave Sophie pause. But of course he knew. He'd been there after her father had died and her life had been upended. He had, in fact, been just as much of a rock as Kyla. How had she forgotten that?

At her continued silence, he continued in a matter-of-fact tone. "It's midweek. There's no event this weekend, so you've got a little time before you'll be starting on the funeral arrangements."

"You know my work schedule?"

"Aye." She could hear the shrug in his tone. "I've been around. Besides, it's a logical deduction. The funeral willnae be until next week, when Neve and the rest of the family can get up here."

What else had this man picked up on, just from being around for so many years?

"Come on. I ken you dinna want Lorraine as company, so you've no excuse not to come out with me tonight. On a date. It's probably time for us to make our village debut, anyway."

A date.

He said it so casually. As if it were no big deal. And for him, it probably wasn't. For her, though... She couldn't remember the last time she'd been on a proper date. Not that this would be that. It was, at best, a meal between friends. With everyone talking about Tom's death, it was possible her going out with Connor would actually fly beneath everyone's radar for a bit. She was fine with easing into that. It would give her a little more time to wrap her brain around the idea that this wasn't actually real.

Those kisses were real enough.

Now was definitely not the time to think about that.

"Okay. Dinner."

"Excellent. I'll be by the shop to get you later. Unless I need to pick you up from somewhere else?"

"No, the shop is fine."

In the background, someone shouted, "Oy! MacKean! These beams willnae haul themselves."

"Dinna get yer knickers in a twist, Fergus. I'm having an important conversation with my lady."

His lady. Why did the idea of that make her go warm all over?

"Decide your place or hers later. Work now," Fergus insisted.

Well. That suggestion had a whole different sort of warmth coursing through her.

"No respect," Connor muttered. But there was no heat to it. "As you can hear, I've work to do. I'll see you tonight."

As the shop bell rang behind her, Sophie straightened at the counter. "Okay. I've a customer, anyway." They confirmed the time, and he rang off.

It seemed she was going on a date with Connor MacKean tonight, for better or worse. Despite all Kyla's warnings, the prospect of it made her just giddy enough to smile.

"That smile says you just talked to your man."

At the easy Southern drawl, Sophie turned to find Swayze on the other side of the counter. She forced down the little bump of trepidation. There was no hint of the malicious about the other woman. "Aye, that was Connor. I'm sorry... Did we have an appointment to go over wedding details?" There was none in her diary. She'd certainly have remembered it.

"Oh, no. I've just been exploring the village and wandered in to see what was what and say hello. The flowers you left at my cottage are just lovely."

"Thank you. Are you settling in okay?"

"Not too much settling to do. The cottage is just so cozy and perfect. I'm thrilled to be using it as my base of operations." She wandered the room, trailing a blue manicured finger over assorted displays scattered around the front of the shop. "You have a fantastic eye. The shop is just so inviting."

"I like to think so." She waffled for a few moments before giving in to manners. "Can I offer you a cuppa?"

Swayze's hazel eyes narrowed. "That depends. Do you happen to have any of Angus's biscuits to go with it?"

That provoked a full smile. "It happens, I do."

"Then I'll happily accept." She stepped up to the counter. "Could I come back?"

Sophie stiffened for a moment, not used to having strangers in her space. Then she relented. She could entertain this woman for a long enough to have a cuppa tea. "Of course."

Swayze followed her into the back room, looking things over while Sophie put on the kettle. The shop bell rang again.

"The box of teas is just there, if you'd like to choose one. I need to run up front for a moment."

It took longer than Sophie wanted to get through taking the next order—another arrangement for the Chapman funeral. She didn't like leaving Swayze alone back there.

The other woman was perched on a stool, a mug in her hands. "The kettle went off already. I took a chance and chose the chamomile for you. It seemed like you're having a bit of a hectic day."

Surprised at the thoughtfulness, Sophie took up her own mug. "I am. Thank you. There was a death in the village, so everyone's ordering flowers to pay their respects."

Sipping at her tea, Swayze nodded. "Back home, that'd mean a-hundred-and-one death casseroles. We Southerners express love and respect through food."

"Charlotte's talked about that some. It seems a lovely tradition." Sophie retrieved the box of ginger biscuits Angus had pressed on her after last weekend's wedding. "Here. Have some."

Cheerfully plucking two from the tin, Swayze bit in and moaned. "Oh, my Lord. I'm going to end up putting out a bunch of weight if I'm not careful. The things that man can do with butter, sugar, and flour are positively sinful."

Selecting her own biscuit, Sophie toasted. "You're not wrong. He's hoping it will eventually take him into the field as a contestant on *The Great British Bake Off*. He's waiting to hear about his audition."

"Really? That's awesome!" She continued to nibble. "I enjoyed meeting him. All of you, really. It's interesting to see Connor in his natural habitat."

"Oh?" To cover the return of the stiffness, Sophie focused on the biscuit.

"I don't actually know him all that well, I guess. I mean, how well can you know someone after a weekend two years ago?"

Well, enough in the biblical sense. The stab of jealousy was sharp. Sophie covered her wince with another sip of tea.

"But he talked a lot about this place. About all of y'all. It left me curious."

Where was she going with this? Keeping her tone and expression neutral, Sophie wrapped her hands around her mug. "One of Connor's gifts is making people comfortable. It's one of the things that made him a good guide."

"He is that." Her gaze was openly curious. "You've known him all your life, right?"

"Aye. I have. We've been friends for a long time."

"So what took y'all so long to get together?"

Was she looking for a chink in their story? A weakness in their supposed relationship?

Of course, they'd prepared for this question, deciding to give Swayze as much of the truth as possible because she'd hear about it through the village grapevine, eventually. "Well, the fact that he was supposed to have an arranged marriage had a lot to do with it."

The other woman blinked. "He was supposed to what now?"

"There was a marriage pact between the MacKeans and the Lennox families three-hundred years ago. It was meant to be a political alliance and stop a lot of feuding. Both their estates were to revert to the Crown if it wasn't carried out. Through a lot of terrible circumstances—accidents, fatal illnesses, multiple generations on both sides being the same gender—the pact couldn't be fulfilled until Connor and Afton Lennox were born. So this time last year, we were planning their wedding."

Swayze's eyes had gone round as saucers. "Except the wedding didn't happen?"

"No. Afton couldn't go through with it. She gambled her entire estate away in Vegas. The new owner was Raleigh Beaumont."

"Wait... When I saw him at New Year's, Connor said his sister had just gotten married. Did *she* have to do the whole marriage pact thing?"

"Aye. She did. It ended up working out, as she and Raleigh are perfect for each other. But that's certainly not what anybody would expect from an arranged marriage."

"This sounds like the plot of one of my sister's books."

"Your sister's a writer?"

"Oh, yeah. Paisley Parish. You might have heard of her. She writes romance."

Sophie set the mug down with a thump. "Your sister is Paisley Parish? I love her books!" Not that she had time to read them too often, but she enjoyed putting on the audio versions while she worked. Using headphones so as not to scandalize any customers who walked in.

"We're stupid proud of all she's accomplished. If you've got a particular favorite, I can get you an autographed copy."

"That would be amazing."

"I'll email her later tonight. Anyway, so Kyla married Raleigh, and you and Connor...?"

"Were finally free to pursue the feelings we'd always had but never acted on."

Swayze sighed. "That is so romantic. You two seem really great together."

"Thank you?"

On a laugh, Swayze put down her cup. "No, I mean it. And okay, let's acknowledge the elephant in the room. I know it's gotta be kind of weird having me here, when Connor and I have a history. I enjoyed my time with him. But I really am just here to help organize my bestie's wedding. I don't have any kind of designs on splitting you and Connor up or something. It's more than obvious in the way he looks at you that those feelings run super deep. I wish you both nothing but the best."

It was clear in every tone, every gesture, that she meant it.

"I can see why he likes you. Damn if I don't, too." The

moment the words were out of her mouth, Sophie wished them back.

But Swayze only laughed again. "Fair enough." She held out a hand. "I'd like to be friends with you, too."

Extending her hand, Sophie shook. "Friends."

She really hoped this didn't come back to bite her in the ass.

NINE

For once, Connor was grateful for the short winter days. It meant he'd been able to knock off work early without catching too much more flack from Fergus. He'd wanted time to shower and clean up for tonight's date with Sophie. More, he'd wanted the time to go over the options for an engagement ring. Not that there were many. But with a family legacy as long as the MacKeans, there were at least a few family pieces to choose from. Thank God for it. He certainly didn't have the funds to put into buying one for a fake engagement. And while he'd looked into the techniques for making one himself, such fine detail required skills and tools he didn't have. So, a family ring it was. For all that he knew this was merely a necessary part of their story, he took his time deciding which ring might suit those long slim fingers.

The winner was burning a hole in his pocket as he parked down the street from Village Blume. Uncharacteristic nerves tap-danced down his spine. Over the years, he'd been able to enjoy the company of a long and varied string of female companions because there'd been no risk with any of them. No expectation of more. Simply pleasure in the moment. This thing with Sophie wasn't that. Not that he'd be opposed to introducing her to a whole host of pleasures. But she came with stakes. He valued her friendship, even as he wanted so much more. Giving her this ring felt significant. He wanted her to like it. More, he wanted her to keep it.

Treading dangerous ground, lad. Getting way ahead of things. Start with the date.

She was on the phone when he stepped into the shop. Her eyes lit with relief at the sight of him. She mimed locking the door before turning her attention back to the call. "Give me one moment, and I'll get your total."

Connor turned the lock and flipped the sign to *Closed.* Without waiting for an invitation, he circled around behind the counter to see if there was anything in the back he could help with to speed things along. Spying the remnants of multiple cups of tea, he carried them to the sink in the kitchenette. He'd just stacked the clean mugs in the dish drainer when Sophie came to join him.

"Oh, you didn't have to do that."

"It was no trouble. I dinna have to ask if it was a busy day." With Tom's position in the village, she'd have been running around like a blue arse fly.

"Everyone wants to pay their respects. I'm sure there'll be more tomorrow. Give me just a few minutes, and I'll be ready to go."

He watched her go through the familiar close-up routine, pitching in where he could and otherwise staying out of her way.

"Okay. Now I'm ready." She shrugged into her coat, sliding both hands beneath her fall of hair to pull it free of the collar.

His pulse jumped. "There's just one more thing before we go."

"Oh?" Her lovely brows arched up in question.

Connor pulled the ring from his pocket. "This."

Color bloomed in her cheeks. "Connor..."

Was that pleasure or embarrassment?

"People will be looking for an engagement ring." When she only stared, he rushed on. "It's no' the one Afton wore."

Those grey eyes lifted to his. "But your mother's ring..."

That she recognized it immediately warmed something in him.

"It's what I'd choose to give my wife." And if she pushed him on this, he wasn't sure he'd be able to lie to her.

"Don't you want to save it for when you do this for real?"

Instead of answering directly, he told her another truth. "Mum would like you being the one to wear it. Even if only for a little while." The corner of his mouth twitched up. "She always had a soft spot for you."

Warmth softened the edge of the distress etching her features. "The feeling was mutual." With what seemed to be a bracing breath, she squared her shoulders. "Well, in that case, I'd be honored."

The hand she extended toward him trembled a bit. Connor gently grasped it and lifted his gaze to hers. The moment felt weighted, as if the world was holding its breath. Or maybe that was just him. Slowly, lest it be the wrong size, he slid the ring into place, feeling the faintest ridges of scars along her skin. Battle wounds from the literal thorns of her profession. A reminder that, for all her softness, she held so much strength.

He glanced down, rubbing his thumb over her knuckle, thinking how exactly right the rose gold band with the princess cut diamond looked there. As if it had been made for her. Unable to resist, he lifted their joined hands and brushed a kiss to her knuckles.

At her startled expression, he flashed a smile. "For luck."

Sophie's pupils were blown wide, and her breath hitched a little. Connor wanted to lean in and seal the whole thing with a kiss. But he hadn't asked the question, so he couldn't take this as an answer. He'd accept that she was moved by the gesture of the ring and go from there.

Shifting, he tucked her arm through his. "Shall we? I'm fair starvin'."

Squeezing his arm, she nodded.

"The pub okay with you? It's no' the most romantic, but it's close, and I have it on good authority tonight's special is venison ale pie."

Her mouth curved. "My favorite."

"I know." As soon as he'd heard the news about Tom that morning, he'd put in the request through Ciara.

Because they weren't too far from the pub, and the snow had stopped, for now, he left his 4x4 where it was. As they walked, he filled her in on the progress he and Fergus had made on the cottages, deliberately exaggerating here and there to get a laugh out of her. He'd seen the shadows in her eyes and knew she had to be thinking of her father after all the to-do over Tom's heart attack. His goal for the night was to erase them, if he could. That meant going full-on doting fiancé mode. Not that he'd ever really done that, but he'd seen a few of his mates do it, and he had a pretty good idea of everything it ought to entail.

Light spilled out the front windows of The Stag's Head, illuminating the snowy embankment on either side of the shoveled pavement. Scents of meat and grease and hops invited passersby to come in and warm up by the fire with a pint and a meal. Faint strains of The Who's greatest hits sounded beneath the din of conversation and laughter as they stepped inside. Assorted flat screen TVs mounted around the room showed differing coverage of the Six Nations Rugby Championship. Ewan moved behind the bar, a kitchen towel draped over one burly shoulder. Of course, he spotted them immediately and jerked a nod of acknowledgment.

Ciara appeared, order pad in hand, a pencil tucked behind one ear. "Braving the cold, aye? Are you here for a pint or a meal?"

"Both." Because he felt Sophie's hesitation in the tightening grip on his arm, he patted the hand tucked through the crook of his elbow.

The gesture drew Ciara's attention to the ring. Her mouth promptly fell open, her green eyes going wide. "You're going public, then?"

This hadn't precisely been part of the plan, but Connor saw where it could work to their advantage. "Aye. It seemed like time."

Toby Byrne, the village mechanic, sidled up, a pint glass in hand. "Going public with what?"

In answer, and because he didn't actually want to speak the lie, Connor lifted Sophie's left hand to display the ring. It seemed to flash in the lights of the pub.

"Holy shite! You're engaged? To each other?" At Toby's none-too-subtle exclamation, all conversation stopped and every head in the room swiveled in their direction.

The pulse of shock as they saw who he was standing with was palpable. Sophie took a half step back, and Connor promptly wished he'd chosen some other more subtle means of getting the word out. Wanting to put her at ease, he wrapped an arm around her shoulders, tugging her into his side and dropping his mouth close enough to murmur, "I've got you."

On the far side of the room, Laura Craig, one of the other long-time servers, broke her paralysis and began making her way toward them. "Well, I need to see the ring!"

As if she'd broken some spell holding the room still, everyone seemed to surge forward to see. Sophie tucked herself tighter against him, and he cursed himself. She hated being the center of attention. But he'd thought getting it out there quickly would be better than a long string of incessant inquiries. As they became the center of the crowd, he recognized his error. Questions peppered them from all sides.

"You and Sophie?"

"How long has this been going on?"

"You sly dog!"

"When did this happen?"

Wanting to shield her, Connor pulled Sophie more firmly into his arms. She came willingly, tucking her face against his shoulder. Looking over her head at the crowd, he summoned his most charming smile. "I ken it's a shock, but it's always been Sophie for me. I've just finally been free to pursue it." Because she trembled a little, he dropped a kiss to the top of her head. "Here now, love. They willnae bite."

"Certainly not." The crowd parted a bit as someone banged down a glass for emphasis. Connor spotted Flora McGowan. "I say this calls for a toast to their happiness. To Connor and Sophie!"

Glasses were raised around the pub. "To Connor and Sophie!"

There were stragglers among the toasters and a definite tone of bafflement from some, but the well wishes warmed him.

"Get over here, you lot," Ewan ordered. "You cannae toast without drinks yourselves."

Grateful for the interruption, Connor took advantage of the opening and ushered Sophie to the bar, where Ewan had their usual drinks waiting.

This time, when the next round of toasts rang out, they each had their own glasses to lift. Sophie met his gaze, tapped her glass to his and took a long drink.

Somebody shouted, "Kiss the bride! Kiss the bride!"

Connor glanced down at Sophie to find her gaze on his lips. That felt like permission enough. Setting his glass aside, he grinned. "I dinna mind if I do."

Pulling her in again was natural as breathing. This time, she wasn't flowing toward him to hide. Her mouth met his halfway, ready and eager. She tasted of hops from the beer and something darker, deeper, that was her alone. No matter how awkward she was afraid of being, this was easy. This was real. Desire kindled between them, and Connor slipped deeper, burying his hands in her hair as their audience fell away.

Only the enthusiastic whistles and catcalls brought him back. Sophie's fingers flexed against his waist in protest as he pulled back. Her lips were rosy and kiss-swollen, and damn if he didn't want to spend the next year or ten memorizing every millimeter and learning what else made her eyes go dark with arousal.

"In honor of my cousin and his new fiancée, a round of drinks on the house!"

Ewan's proclamation and the resultant cheer of the crowd brought Connor fully back to himself. Now was not the time. But he thought they'd done a right solid job of believably debuting themselves as a couple.

Scooping up his beer again, he pressed another kiss to Sophie's temple. "Best pace yourself. I suspect there will be a lot of toasts tonight."

———

By the time Sophie managed to extract Connor from his adoring crowd—she was under no delusion that the villagers were sticking around for her—he was definitely no longer fully sober. Everyone had wanted to toast to their engagement, and Connor hadn't paced himself quite so well as she had. As they waved their last goodbyes, she slid an arm around his waist for the walk back to her house—both because it felt nice to be that close to him, and because she wanted to assess exactly how intoxicated he was before she let him drive back to Ardinmuir. He draped his arm around her shoulders and pressed a smacking kiss to her cheek. His level of open physical affection dialed up proportionate to his alcohol consumption. She filed that tidbit of information away as they began to walk.

While his boldfaced announcement wasn't at all how she'd have preferred to handle things, the night hadn't gone poorly. Despite how awkward she'd felt at the shock and all the questions, the overwhelming attitude of everyone had been well wishes, which was far more than she'd been expecting. Reluctant as she'd been, she had to admit she'd retained some warm fuzzies from the experience. Whether that would remain as the gossip spread like wildfire through the village remained to be seen. For now, she'd take the win.

She wished the reactions of their friends and family had been as positive. Then again, all of *them* knew that this was a setup. Deep down, Sophie knew that was the part that worried everyone. If she and Connor had really fallen in love and decided to be together, she felt certain they'd have everybody's support. Once they got over the abject shock.

Thoughts of that family dinner reminded her of something else she'd been meaning to ask Connor. "Tell me something."

"Hmmm?"

"The blacksmithing. Why don't you do it for a business, really? Because, obviously, you've been juggling this alongside your other duties as estate manager for a long time. You're incredibly talented, and it seems like you really love it."

He sucked in a long breath. "The truth?"

Sophie glanced up. "Is it that bad?"

"Bad...? No. It's no' that. The truth is, I dinna ken the first thing about running a business. Not the technical sides of it. Spreadsheets, profit-and-loss statements, all that shite. That's Kyla's love language. But they're beyond me. My brain just disnae work that way."

"That's it? That's all that's stopping you?"

His body went stiff. "It's no' a small thing."

Realizing she'd inadvertently insulted him, she squeezed. "No. That's not what I meant. It's just, those are all things you could get help with. *Those* are the parts of a business that can be farmed out. Spreadsheets are also *my* love language. I can help you with all of it. Make a website so you can take regular commissions, help you with accounting and whatnot. I've run a small business for years now, even before the event planning. I understand how it all works, so it would be no trouble for me to help you set it up and keep it running."

"I canna ask you to do that. You've already got so much on your plate."

"You're not asking. I'm offering. We're in this together, aren't we?"

He stopped walking, right in the middle of the pavement, and drew her in, searching her face. Sophie was exquisitely aware of his arms around her and the rise and fall of his chest against hers. Would he kiss her again? God, she hoped so.

"You'd really do all that for me?" Even in the dim glow of the streetlamps, she could see the uncertainty in his beautiful blue eyes.

"Of course. If it helps you make a real go of something you truly love, why wouldn't I? You helped me so much as I was getting my shop up and running."

That uncertainty turned to something else as he stared down at her. Sophie's pulse beat slow and thick. Snow had begun to fall again, and he reached out to brush some flakes from her cheek with his thumb.

"If you truly dinna mind, then I'd be grateful."

She tipped her face into his hand, loving the warmth as it curved against her cheek. "Then it's settled."

They smiled at each other, and time took on that treacly sensation. At least until a passing car cheerfully beeped its horn.

"I should get you home."

So he was back to the gentleman. Sad the moment was broken, Sophie stepped back and began to walk again. "Not far now." And, in fact, it took only a few more minutes to reach her front walk.

Not ready to say goodbye, and still hoping for a goodnight kiss, she towed him up the walk. "You should come inside for a cuppa. You need a little longer to sober up before you get behind the wheel."

"Fair enough. We'll see if Dame Coriander deigns to honor me with her presence."

Sophie was grinning for once as she stepped inside the house.

From the lounge, Lorraine called out, "Sophie? Is that you?"

Of course, she hadn't gone to bed. "Yes."

"It was terribly inconsiderate of you not to let me know you'd be out late. I need you to do several things for me tonight. I've got my ladies of the village luncheon tomorrow, and I need you to wash my—" As she began to reel off her list of demands—definitely not requests—Sophie's cheeks heated.

It had been years since she'd allowed anyone into the house while Lorraine was here. Not since she'd acquired the shop and claimed that as her space. She was too embarrassed by how her stepmother treated her. It was mortifying to be addressed as if she were a servant in her own home.

Needing a little distance to regain her composure, Sophie turned to start on the first thing that registered.

Connor stepped forward and grabbed her hand firmly, clearly growling, "No."

"What do you mean, no? Who is that? Who else is there?" Footsteps sounded from the other room, but Sophie couldn't look away from Connor's face.

She'd seen frustration and irritation from him and Kyla both over her situation before, but not like this. Color rode high in his cheeks, and a muscle ticked in his strong, stubble-covered jaw. His shoulders rose and fell with short, quick breaths, and a vein throbbed in his temple. The eyes he turned on Lorraine as she stepped into the room were glacial.

Sophie squeezed his hand. "Connor, don't." She didn't know what she was telling him not to do. She knew only she wanted to derail this impending sense of doom.

He stepped in front of her, zeroing in on her stepmother. "She's no' your servant. No' your employee. She works two jobs and is, so far as I can tell, the one who puts the food on the table in this household. You can wash your own damned clothes."

Lorraine's head pulled back into her neck, reminding Sophie of nothing so much as a turkey. If she hadn't been so very aware of her stepmother's precarious moods, she might have found it funny. But there was nothing amusing about the haughty expression on her face.

"I allow her to live here rent-free. It's only right she help out."

That had been her argument from the beginning, and Sophie had never wanted to risk fighting her about it. Not when this was her home, and she had no backup plan. "Connor, stop. It's fine. I can just—"

"It's *no'* fine. And it's no' right! You do everything around here, and she does *nothing* but work you to the bone. I willnae have it."

Wait. What?

His impassioned declaration had completely derailed Sophie's frantic calculations for how she could salvage this situation.

Connor paid no attention to her as he took another step closer to Lorraine. "You are a spoiled, selfish waste of space, and your days of using Sophie as live-in free labor are over."

Oh, shite.

Before she could step forward to stop him, he kept going. Because of course he did. The dam had broken, and apparently, everything he'd ever thought about Lorraine was spilling out. "If Robert had lived long enough to see the abominable way you treat his daughter, he'd never have stayed married to the likes of you, you racist, bigoted cow."

Nausea roiled through Sophie at his words. His opinions on their living arrangement she might have been able to work around once he'd gone home. But this? For all Lorraine's many faults, Sophie knew she'd loved her father in whatever way she was capable. There was no lower blow he could make.

Lorraine's face went chalk white for a few humming seconds before color raced into it again. "Who are you to make decisions for Sophie or to stick your nose into any of this?"

With an unmistakable air of menace, Connor took one more step toward her, lowering his head so he was at eye level with the smaller woman. "The man she's going to marry." He issued the proclamation with a growl that was nothing short of magnificent, for all that it was a lie. A terrible lie that was going to ruin everything.

Lorraine's head snapped back in shock, and Sophie simply closed her eyes. She knew this news would have reached her by tomorrow. But hearing it through the grapevine wouldn't have done nearly so much damage. She had no idea what the ramifications for Connor's statements would be.

Determined to play peacemaker and mitigate the damage he'd caused, Sophie opened her mouth—to say what, she had no idea.

But before she could speak, Lorraine's eyes narrowed. "Fine. Get out."

Horrified, and thinking of the long ago promise she'd made her father, Sophie stepped forward. "Mum—"

Her stepmother's cold glare swung in her direction. "No. As has been rightly pointed out, I'm not your mum. He cares so much about your living conditions, go live with him. Get out."

Sophie absorbed the order. When she didn't move fast enough, Lorraine began to shriek. "Get. Out!"

The woman meant it. Truly.

Connor's glower cracked, as it seemed to finally register that he'd crossed some kind of line. But it was too little, too late.

Devastation swamped Sophie. Not because she had any affection for this woman. But she was being kicked out of her father's house. Forced out of her home. The last connection she had to his memory, other than Cori. Heart breaking, she turned away from the pair of them, still locked in some kind of standoff, and moved to the stairs.

Connor followed her up.

She considered telling him not to, but she'd need his help to pack her things. He'd gotten her into this mess. He'd have to do some work before she figured her own way out of it.

She opened the door to her room, at a glance taking in the window seat where she'd spent so many rainy afternoons reading, and the desk where she still spent hours every night working. Cori leapt up onto the bed and yowled in a tone that clearly said, *What the fuck?*

What the fuck, indeed?

Moving inside, she stroked a trembling hand over Cori's head and knelt to haul bags out from beneath the bed. There was no way she could get everything tonight. Maybe if she gave Lorraine time to calm down, she could come back later.

In the doorway, Connor hesitated. "Sophie, I..."

She couldn't look at him right now. Couldn't fully think yet about the consequences of what he'd done. "Don't, Connor. Just... don't."

Ten

All Connor's life, Sophie had been one of the few people he could be silent with. If she had nothing worth saying, she usually didn't speak. That had always been okay with him.

But now... now her silence was terrifying.

Other than the occasional clarifying instruction, she hadn't said a word as she efficiently packed her things and rounded up all the accoutrements for the cat. She'd pulled in on herself with the same restrained sort of grief he'd seen when she'd lost her father. He didn't understand it. She was finally moving out of her step-monster's house. Maybe this wasn't the way she intended to do it, but surely it was freeing on some level.

He'd retrieved his 4x4, and they'd filled the back with as much as she'd been able to hurriedly pack. It was more than she'd intended to take, but he'd pushed her to gather up anything she deemed important, because he feared that Lorraine, vindictive bitch that she was, might retaliate by destroying Sophie's things. When he'd brought up the possibility, she'd lost another shade of color in her usually honey-warm cheeks.

He felt like the worst of the worst.

But she'd packed.

Cori was the only one to break the silence as Sophie placed her carrier into the little Fiat. The elderly feline objected to everything about the arrangement. Maybe she thought they were headed to the vet. Either way, her piteous yowling was clearly audible, even through the closed car door. That surely wouldn't improve matters during the drive out to Ardinmuir. And crap. What kind of house-proofing did they need to do to the castle to accommodate a cat? Connor added that to his mental list.

Lorraine was watching them from the window of the lounge. It was too dark to see more than her silhouette, but he could feel her disdain as she kept an eye on the proceedings.

Sophie took one last look at the house, her face inscrutable, before sliding into the driver's seat of her car without comment.

Okay then.

He got into his own vehicle and pulled onto the road, continually checking the rearview mirror to see that Sophie followed. The moment his Bluetooth connected, he dialed Angus.

"I already heard about the announcement at the pub tonight. Ewan said the drinks flowed freely. Are you needing a ride home, lad?" Connor could just see the amused smile on his uncle's face.

"No. But I do need your help."

Picking up on the seriousness of his tone, Angus lost the teasing edge to his voice. "What's wrong?"

"I fucked up." The knowledge of that had done more to sober him than any amount of coffee. He'd behaved badly, letting his righteous anger get the better of him. If he'd believed for a second that an apology to Lorraine would have made a difference in this situation, he'd have choked one out, no matter how insincere. But he'd pretty thoroughly cut that option off, hadn't he?

In broad strokes, he explained what had happened, leaving off the part where he'd gone off the rails and acted like Sophie's real fiancé. "Lorraine kicked her out."

Angus loosed a spate of curses that were a step beyond what Connor had already lobbed in the stepmonster's direction. The instant vitriol was at least a little vindicating. "That woman... Well, what's done is done. I'll go make up a room for our Sophie."

"Thanks. We're about twenty minutes out."

"I'll be ready."

As soon as he rang off, he dialed his sister. No doubt she'd come down on him like a ton of bricks—deservedly so. But she needed to be apprised of what happened, so she could be there for Sophie. He doubted Sophie wanted anything to do with him just now.

"Hey Con. You just caught me before bed."

He winced. "Sorry. I didnae realize how late it was."

"It's fine. It something wrong?"

"You could say that. I... kind of told off Lorraine Cameron."

The sound of a mattress shifting told him Kyla was sitting up in bed. "You did what?"

"I took Sophie out to the pub for dinner tonight. There were a lot of toasts to our engagement, and I wasnae quite fit to drive by the time I walked her home, so I went in for a cuppa to sober up, and Lorraine started in on her, like she does. And I just... lost it."

"Oh, Connor. You didn't."

"I did. It was bad."

"Is Sophie okay? What am I saying? You're calling me, so I'm guessing she's not."

"Lorraine kicked her out."

"Fuck."

"Aye. That's about the right of it. We've packed up most of her things and the cat, and we're on the way to Ardinmuir. Angus is readying a room."

When Kyla said nothing, Connor's shoulders hunched at the implied recrimination.

"I ken I should've kept my mouth shut. Sophie's been verra vocal for years that she didnae want us to butt in." Why the hell hadn't he been able to remember that in the moment?

"Maybe so, but I'm glad you did it, anyway. God knows, I've

wanted to often enough. Living that house has been killing something in her. She'll not thank you for the boot now, but I think, once she's had some time away, she'll see that it's for the best."

He hadn't expected the support and appreciated it. "I sure as hell hope so."

"What's next?"

"I dinna ken. She hasnae actually spoken to me since it happened, other than to say what should go where. She'll stay at Ardinmuir for tonight, then we'll figure the rest out tomorrow."

"I've told her this before, but I'll tell you the same: If she wants to stay at Lochmara instead, we've plenty of room and would welcome her."

Connor hoped like hell Sophie didn't choose that option. "Thanks. I'll remind her." He turned onto the castle drive. "We're here. I need to go."

"All right. If I need to talk her off the ledge, call me. I'll stay up a while longer."

"Let's hope that's no' necessary. Night."

Angus had all the exterior lights on, such that the castle looked like a jewel against the snowy night. Perhaps he'd thought it would make the place feel more inviting. And maybe it would have under other circumstances.

He parked around the side, by the kitchen door. One of the other entrances might make more sense, once he knew which room she'd be moving into, but they'd start here. Sophie parked beside him and got out, not looking his way before circling around to retrieve Cori, who'd stopped yowling and begun hissing instead.

What was she thinking? What was she feeling?

Connor couldn't bring himself to ask. Not yet. He was too afraid of the answers.

Angus threw open the kitchen door, all smiles. "Hello, Sophie, love. I've your room made up for you."

"Thank you for your hospitality." The words came out stilted and entirely un-Sophie-like.

"Nonsense. You're family. It's not hospitality. Here. Hand over the she-beast and get the necessities. You'll not want to lug everything up tonight. It's getting late."

She reluctantly transferred the carrier to him. Instantly, he began crooning to Cori, who talked back in an alarmingly human tone, as if to say, "You wouldn't *believe* what my human got up to tonight."

"Is that right now? Why don't you tell me all about it while I get you a wee bit of cream for your trauma?"

Cori declared she liked that idea.

They both stared after him as he went into the house. With a shake of her head, Sophie moved around to the boot of her car.

"What all do you need for tonight?"

She grabbed a small suitcase and laptop bag. "Just this. You can get Cori's things, just there."

He hefted the box and followed her inside.

Angus was still talking to the cat, a part-empty pint of cream and a bowl in one hand. "Right this way."

He'd put Sophie in the garden room, so named for the patterned wallpaper that dated to a previous century. The understated feminine grace seemed to fit her. Lamps were already on, and the bed had been turned down as if just waiting for her. "There are fresh towels in the bath, and plenty of room for herself to roam without getting into trouble, once you think she's settled enough to let out."

"Thank you."

Setting the carrier down on the bathroom counter, he poured a little of the cream into the dish. "I'll just let you give her that when you think she's ready. If you need anything, don't hesitate to let me know."

Sophie unbent from her stoicism enough to give him a squeeze and a kiss on the cheek. "Goodnight, Angus."

Then they were alone. She lowered the laptop to the ottoman by the armchair in the corner and laid the suitcase on the tapestry bench at the end of the four-poster bed and unzipped it. For every moment that passed when she didn't look at him, Connor felt his anxiety ratchet up.

"Please say something. Is this really that bad? You're finally getting away from that harpy."

She turned to face him, and the ravaged look in her eyes was a knife to the gut. "It's not about her, Connor. You just got me kicked out of my home. My father's house. The last connection I have to him, other than my extremely geriatric cat. You just destroyed that."

Oh fuck.

In the wake of Robert's death, the house had passed to his wife instead of his daughter. They'd all just mentally started thinking of it as Lorraine's house. It was certainly how she'd behaved, how she'd made everyone feel. But it had been Sophie's home long before Lorraine had come along. She'd lived there almost all her life, with *both* of her parents. Connor hadn't given a single thought to the memories it still held. And, damn it, he should have. He, of all people, understood the memories tied to a place. It was why he'd been busting his arse alongside Kyla for years to keep Ardinmuir in the family.

Sick at the idea that he'd taken that foundation from Sophie, he took a step toward her. "You have to know, that was no' my intention."

She closed her eyes and sighed. "I know. None of that ever crossed your mind. Not yours and not Kyla's. And I never told either of you. I guess I should have."

"Christ, dinna take that on yourself, too. This was all on me. I just... I couldnae take seeing what she does to you anymore. I needed to get you out of there. Kyla and I have been telling you for years that you're welcome to stay here as long as you want. You're family. If you dinna want to stay here in the castle, then one of the cottages on the grounds."

She shook her head. "No. Those are meant to be estate income, and right now, I can't afford to pay rent. That's the whole reason I haven't moved out before. I thought I was going to be able to do it this year, but business rent has gone up substantially, so that's set me back."

Connor bit back the string of curses he wanted to spew about John Milligan. The bastard. That wouldn't help matters just now. Instead, he reiterated what Kyla had said. "Lochmara is also an option. They've plenty of room."

"I'm not going to impose upon your pregnant, newlywed sister. Even if she is my best friend. No. For now, I'll stay here. I don't really have much other choice."

Connor hated himself for inadvertently backing her into a corner when all he'd ever wanted was to give her options. As he took in her resolute posture and grim expression, he vowed to do everything in his power to make her comfortable here so that she didn't regret it.

Her shoulders straightened. "I need to know something, though."

"Anything."

"Why did you do this?"

She didn't get it. Even with his outlandish declaration, she still hadn't put it together. Maybe that was for the best.

Swallowing hard, Connor struggled to find a way to explain that wouldn't push harder than he already had. "I've watched you be used and abused and endure unspeakable, ridiculous demands from this woman because of a promise you made to your dad. And the truth is that he wasn't around long enough to know the true character of the woman he married. If he had, I firmly believe he never would have made that ask of you. He never intended for you to be a slave in your own house. And I guess I had just enough alcohol tonight to obliterate the self-control that's stopped me from saying it a thousand times before."

Shock overlaid some of the pain in her face. It was clear she'd never considered the situation from that angle. But he still couldn't read more than that in her expression.

At last, she slowly nodded, some of the anger fading. "I appreciate your willingness and desire to defend me."

He always wanted to be the one to defend her. To protect her. She deserved so much goodness in her life.

But he didn't say any of that. Instead, he asked the more important question. "Are we gonna be okay?"

With a world-weary sigh, she finally closed the distance between them, wrapping him in a hug. "Yes."

Connor hugged her back, wanting to communicate through touch how very sorry he was, and how much he valued this connection. They stood that way for a long time, until she'd relaxed enough against him that he registered how very tired she must be.

Pressing a kiss to her brow, he stroked a hand down her spine. "Let's get you settled in."

———

"You sneaky minx! Snagging Connor MacKean right under our noses without so much as a hint." The broad, delighted smile from Brenna Napier took any sting out of the words. "Let's see the ring, then."

As she held up her left hand, Sophie had yet another moment to be grateful she'd thought to put it on this morning. She almost hadn't. But she'd found it oddly comforting to feel the subtle weight of the band on her finger. A reminder of the early part of last night. The good part.

"Never thought I'd see the day the likes of that one settled down."

Feeling her cheerful smile freeze, Sophie retracted her hand. "Was there something else I could help you with? It's time for me to close up for the day." For once, she was determined to get out of here on time.

It was more than obvious that the woman had only stopped by for gossip confirmation, but Sophie was pleased enough when she bought one of the loose bouquets to take home and brighten up her kitchen. The moment she was out the door, Sophie threw the lock and exhaled a slow breath.

The day had been full, with another flood of orders coming in for the Chapman family, along with a considerable string of the curious who'd heard the news of the engagement and wanted to come see for themselves. Most people had been gratifyingly cheerful about it, which allayed some of her original fears about whether they'd be believed. It seemed Ciara and Charlotte's romance novel logic held up.

It took only fifteen minutes to go through the routine to close up. She'd made it a dozen steps toward home before she remembered it wasn't home anymore and she'd have to drive out to Ardinmuir. She was meant to meet Kyla out there anyway, to go over details for the retirement party coming up and review some options to present to Alyssa. With an about-face, she trudged through the snow to her car.

Though it would have been the more direct route, Sophie deliberately avoided driving by her house. No sense in doing anything to stoke the grief. But as she took the winding road from Glenlaig out to the estate, she couldn't deny she also felt relief that she wouldn't have to face down a laundry list of bullshit from her stepmother after a long day.

She'd calmed down enough to acknowledge—to herself, at least—that was the part Connor had reacted to. That was the part he'd wanted to save her from. For all his frequent lack of seriousness, he was a good-hearted man. She knew he hadn't meant to cut her off from that connection to her father. If it had happened on another day, when she wasn't so mired in memory and so ultra-sensitive to the topic, maybe she would have handled it better. But she was only human, and she had a right to her grief.

Kyla's car wasn't in the drive when Sophie got back to the castle. She didn't spot Connor's 4x4 either. He was probably at his forge. As she parked by the kitchen door, she wondered where it actually was. Did anybody but Raleigh know? She'd need to have him take her out there for pictures. Better, he should bring

Kyla and her camera. They could use those for his website, when she got to it. But that was putting the cart before the horse. She needed to have a long talk with him about the specifics of his business before she could build him spreadsheets and a business plan. And that was all going to take more bandwidth than she had right now.

Figuring she had a little while before Kyla showed, she elected to go change clothes and bring in more of the stuff from her car. Her mind was spinning over logistics when she opened the door to her room and stopped dead. One end of the big space was full of neatly stacked boxes that hadn't been there this morning. Someone—Connor, no doubt—had brought in all the things they'd packed last night. But they hadn't had more than a couple of boxes when they'd gathered her things. Moving to the nearest one, she pulled it open to find some of the stuff she hadn't deemed first priority for getting out of the house. Checking another, she found some of the family pieces she'd believed would be safe in the attic, including her mother's jewelry and some of her embroidered silks.

Overwhelmed, she wandered to the bathroom to let Cori out. The castle was far too large and unfamiliar to simply give her free rein. Sophie planned to confine her to these two rooms for now, until they'd done some cat-proofing. She didn't want her baby getting injured or trapped, and she certainly didn't want any spite pooping or vomiting on any of the antiques that filled the place.

As soon as she opened the door, Cori slipped out, weaving around her ankles and arching against her legs, even as she made her displeasure at the arrangements known at top volume. Or maybe that was the lack of more cream. Sophie scooped her up and went to sit on the bed, staring at all her possessions. Cori circled twice and eased her bony frame onto Sophie's lap, kneading at her thigh. Automatically, Sophie began to stroke her head.

"He went to all this trouble." They hadn't packed any of this last night. Which meant he must have made a trip back to the house today to retrieve the rest of it. More than one trip, given the size of the stacks. This was basically everything she owned. Had he had help for this? Or had he done it entirely on his own?

"Maybe he's right. Maybe this is for the best."

The door swung open and another huge box came through. Sophie recognized Connor's legs below it, though he didn't spot her until he'd turned to set his load down.

"You're home." He hesitated. "I thought you might have to work late, with all the orders for the Chapmans. I was hoping to have all this finished before you got back."

"It's been a long couple of days. I actually closed on time." Settling Cori on the bed, she crossed to the box he'd brought in. *Kitchen* was scrawled on the side in her own handwriting. With trembling fingers, she opened the top and peered inside, seeing exactly what she'd known would be there: all the traditional cookware and utensils of her mother's homeland that Lorraine hadn't allowed her to use in the house, because she couldn't bear the smell of the rich spices that had marked Sophie's childhood. She'd packed them herself years ago so her stepmother wouldn't throw them out.

Connor rested his hand on the edge of the box. "I remember when she forced you to put these away. I was going to just leave them in the kitchen so you could use them here, but I thought it best to make sure you still planned to stay."

Sophie couldn't stop the tears from welling. "Connor—"

His eyes were so earnest and full of apology when she turned toward him. "Oh God, I'm sorry. Did I fuck up again and overstep? I just... I worried what Lorraine might do in retribution. I thought she might block you from the rest of your things or try to hold them hostage, so I bullied my way in today and got everything. All the boxes you held onto in the attic. The family pieces I knew you wouldnae want to lose. Everything she made you lock away."

The tears spilled over. He may have accidentally cut her off from her father, but with this, he'd given her back her mother, and that was a gift she hadn't expected. She threw her arms around him, squeezing tight. "Thank you."

After a nanosecond's hesitation, he wrapped around her, one big hand cradling her head against his chest. "I want you to be happy here. And I dinna ever want you to feel like you have to put any part of yourself away to make someone else comfortable."

Moved beyond words, Sophie pulled back and lifted a hand to cup his jaw.

She'd underestimated this man in a big way. All day her mind had circled back to the fact that when push came to shove and alcohol had undermined his restraint, his instinct had been to act as if their engagement was truly real. To defend her in a way no one ever had. She'd always known that he and Kyla hated the way she was treated. It wasn't new. They'd all talked about it before. But having someone step into the breach to truly defend her, to shield her, was a powerful and attractive thing.

But this went beyond the bounds of their fake engagement, and it felt like so much more than friendship. It showed he not only cared; he understood her in a way she'd never guessed. And *that* was more attractive than the muscles or the blond-haired, blue-eyed good looks, or any alleged prowess between the sheets. That was the stuff real relationships were made of.

Stroking a thumb along his cheek, she murmured his name. Connor's arms tightened, his broad palms somehow cradling her as if she were precious. His head dipped toward hers.

Footsteps and voices sounded from down the hall, breaking the spell.

"—where to put the table."

And suddenly Kyla and Raleigh were crowding in the doorway. Each of them carried more of her mother's family pieces she'd squirreled away.

Kyla's face melted into surprise at the sight of them. And no wonder. Sophie still cupped his cheek, and Connor was still smoldering down at her.

"I—oh. Um... I'll just leave this here, and—"

Refusing to be awkward about any of it, Sophie took her time stepping back. "No, it's fine." She glanced back at Connor. "I see you had help."

"I had help." There was still heat simmering in his eyes, along with something else.

Sophie put a mental pin in that and crossed to her friends, hugging them both. "Thank you. Truly. This means so much to me."

"You're absolutely welcome," Raleigh said. "I'm actually gonna go get another load from the truck."

"I'll help," Connor announced, and followed his brother-in-law out of the room, quietly shutting the door behind them.

The moment their footsteps faded, Kyla took her by the shoulders, eyes searching her face as she brushed at the lingering tears. "Are you okay?"

With a quick jerk of her head, Sophie wiped at the tears herself.

"Is this because of Connor? Because of what he did?"

"Yes. And no." He'd cut her off at the knees in the worst and best way possible, and she was still reeling.

"I know he went about it wrong, and I know this is not what you wanted. But he meant well."

"I know that."

"He cares about you." Kyla shot a worried glance at the door, where he'd disappeared. "More than maybe I realized."

"I'm starting to get that."

"What are you going to do about it?"

There were so many questions within that one. *What are you going to do about Connor? Do you care for him, too? Is this fake engagement turning into something real? Do you want it to? Will the two of you be okay on the other side of all this?*

Sophie didn't have an answer for any of it.

"I don't know. But I'm here now, so there's no better time to figure it out."

ELEVEN

Spreadsheets were the devil's tools. Connor was convinced of it.

He wasn't a Luddite. He could use social media and all the bells and whistles on his phone. Multiple gaming systems were hooked up to the TV in his personal lounge. But the intricacies of doing more than the most basic maths in a spreadsheet simply eluded him. Why did everything have to be so bloody complicated, anyway?

At least Charlotte was handling the lion's share of the bookkeeping related to the cottage rentals on both estates. That was a huge weight off Connor's shoulders. He simply had to keep up with the day-to-day running of things, which he stayed on top of using old school spreadsheets his mum had created before he'd even hit puberty. They worked. Mostly.

Except when they didn't.

He'd fouled something up with one of the formulas and hadn't been able to track it back.

"Bloody fucking hell." Disgusted, he shoved back from the desk and scrubbed both hands over his face.

He shouldn't be trying to do all this when his brain was elsewhere.

Not just anywhere.

On Sophie.

If he'd expected to see more of her now that they lived under the same roof, he'd been sorely disappointed. She'd put in late hours to prepare for last weekend's event, in addition to going in early to finish all the arrangements for Tom Chapman's family on top of her usual business. He didn't think she was avoiding him, but what did he know? That night in her room, it had felt as if disaster had been averted. It had felt like a hell of a lot more than that before his sister and Raleigh had interrupted.

There'd been no time to address any of it since then, and he'd been trying to figure out how to bring it up.

Hey, so, I felt like we were having a real Moment before. Do you think you might want to date me for real? Because I'm right crazy about you.

Yeah, no. He couldn't just blurt that out. What if she said no? Worse, what if she felt some kind of pressure to do it anyway, simply because of the fake engagement situation? He didn't want to coerce her into anything.

Do you like me? Check "aye" or "no."

Direct and to the point, but still with strong potential for rejection. He needed to feel out where she stood after the chaos he'd inadvertently introduced to her life. Which would require actually seeing her for longer than five seconds in the hall.

"Is this a bad time?"

He dropped his hands to find the object of his thoughts hovering in the doorway, as if conjured by his longing. Everything in him lifted. "You are a sight for sore eyes." He waved a hand at the computer that sat upon the battered desk. "Please look at this and tell me what I've fucked up."

She slipped into the room to peer over his shoulder at the screen. "The books for the estate?"

"Aye."

Reaching for the mouse, she glanced back at him. "May I?"

"Please." He happily ceded his seat to her and peered over her shoulder, watching as she clicked around.

"This is a really old version of Excel."

"We've been taking an 'if it isnae broken, dinna fix it' attitude. Except I think I broke it."

"Looks like you just accidentally overwrote one of the formulas." She did some more clicking and tapped a few keys, and the caution sign disappeared. "There. No harm, no foul. I can fix it so that field can't be accidentally changed, if you like."

"Just like that? Christ, I've been beating my head against this for forty-five minutes." This. This was why he had no hope of running his own business.

Her lips curved. "This is why you need me."

This and so many other reasons.

"Which reminds me," she continued. "You and I need to have a sit down to go over the details of your blacksmithing business. I'll need more information in order to pull together the spreadsheets that will work for you, so I need to ask you a bunch of questions about things like your process, your supplies, your cost basis, how you arrive at what you're going to charge and so on and so forth." She looked up at him through those impossibly long lashes. "And I was really hoping to wrangle a tour of your forge."

As if he'd deny her anything when she looked at him like that. "You want to see the inner sanctum?"

Her smile was easy, affectionate. "I understand it's a bit like your Fortress of Solitude, but I think it'll give me a better grasp of the business and what else I might need to ask. And, I confess, I'm just plain interested."

Nervous pleasure fizzed in his blood. He'd never taken anyone out to the forge on purpose, but he found he wanted to share this with her. "Sure. I'll take you after dinner."

"Great. That brings me to the other reason I came to find you. I went to Inverness today to do some shopping."

He'd wondered what she'd gotten up to on her day off. "Oh? Did you need help carrying in all your purchases?"

"Not quite." She bit her lip, which made him want to soothe it with a kiss. "I might have gone a little overboard, but I've been poring over my mum's recipes since you got all the kitchen stuff out of storage. I want to host family dinner and cook for everybody, but I'm not really ready to just put myself out there without doing some trial cooking first, because it's been a *really* long time since I've used any of Mum's recipes. I was hoping you'd be my guinea pig."

His belly grumbled in anticipation. "Well, it seems my stomach has spoken, but I'll second that I will always eat. I loved your mum's food. Do you want any help in the kitchen?"

Her smile spread slow and a little shy. "Yeah."

Happy to abandon the books for now, he straightened and offered his arm. "Milady." Ridiculous pleasure coursed through him when she slid her hand into the crook of his elbow. That was his only excuse for what he blurted out next. "I've missed you this week."

Connor waited for the inevitable excuses, the recitation of all the things she had going on that would prove she wasn't avoiding him. She was just busy.

"I've missed you, too. Things should slow down a little, now that Tom's funeral is past. C'mon. You can catch me up on everything you've been up to while we cook."

Pleased with the idea of it, he escorted her to the kitchen, where he stopped dead in the doorway. "Holy shite. You weren't kidding."

Dozens of bottles, boxes, and bags of ingredients were set on the big wooden island at the center of the kitchen. Most of them were spices and herbs, but there was a bag of onions, several heads of garlic, potatoes, some kind of flour, ghee, a massive bag of basmati rice, and an array of other vegetables peeking out of a canvas shopping bag.

Color leapt into Sophie's cheeks. "I know. But I couldn't decide what to make, and it's hard to get away to the city, so I bought the ingredients for basically anything." She hesitated, looking uncertain. "Is it too aromatic? Lorraine wouldn't even allow Indian spices in the house. She said the smell made her ill."

Though Connor wanted to growl, he kept his tone matter-of-fact. "Lorraine is horrible, and she's been missing out on something wonderful. I never ate a bad meal in your house growing up."

"Neither did I. But I'm never quite sure how much of that is true and how much is nostalgia for my mum's cooking."

"Both can definitely be true. So, what actually *is* on the menu?" Taking her hands, he looked into her eyes with the most soulful, begging expression he could muster. "Please say samosas."

"Well, since you asked so nicely. Go wash your hands."

He did as told, rolling up his sleeves and cracking his knuckles. "Put me to work."

"There's a packet of boneless chicken thighs in the fridge. I need you to cut them up into chunks."

"I dinna remember there being chicken in samosas."

"There's not, but there is in biryani. It'll need to marinate while we work on other things." Sophie dug out several bowls, setting one aside for him.

Connor pulled out the chicken. "I remember your mum's biryani. She brought it to a New Year's Eve party here when I was maybe... six? It was the first time I ever saw her. She was dressed in this magnificent sari—dark red and gold with these little sort of feather accents on the fabric."

"Like peacock feathers?"

"Aye, that's the one. I took one look at her and thought she was a queen. She was the most beautiful woman I'd ever seen." At least until Sophie had hit about sixteen. "I think I fell half in love with her on the spot. Then I tasted her food and fell the rest of the way."

Smiling, Sophie measured spices into a bowl. "She was stunning. My father used to call her his Indian rose. I still have that sari packed up, along with some others. I kept it thinking I might wear it one day, but I'm taller and wider in the shoulders than she was."

"Could you repurpose it? Turn it into something else you'd be able to use? Decorative cushions or something? Or would that be disrespectful?"

"No, I think Mum would have liked the idea of my finding another way to use her saris. I've thought about it from time to time. There's ample fabric to do something with it. But I just... never have."

"Because of Lorraine." The knife thunked against the cutting board as he drove it through the chicken.

"Partly. I got trained not to talk about her. At first, my father framed it as a matter of respect. Lorraine was his wife, and she was uncomfortable with reminders of who came before. He was convinced she'd get easier with it over time. But she never has. I think a big part of that was because he still loved my mother, wholly and completely, and Lorraine knew it, deep down. He was with her because he couldn't stand to be alone. It was hard to watch."

"And then he died and left her alone with you."

"The perpetual reminder of the woman who took up his whole heart." There was no bitterness in her tone, only resignation. "It's made me think a lot about relationships and what I want in one long-term. What I want in a partner."

Connor's heart kicked into high gear as he scraped the chicken into the bowl and washed his hands again. Was this just casual conversation, or was she leading up to something? "That seems natural enough."

"I suppose. I've second-guessed a lot whether what I remember of my parents before Mum died was real, or whether I've polished it up in my own memories into something better than it was."

"Why does it matter whether it was the absolute truth? That disnae change that you deserve everything you want. Is that perception of what they had why you havenae really dated much?" Or maybe she had, and he somehow just hadn't known.

"Some," she conceded. "All of my focus has been on getting

out of my stepmother's house, making my business a success on my own. No one seemed worth the extra effort. They all seemed like more work." She stirred the spices in the bowl and carefully leaned over to sniff, a delighted smile spreading over her face as she did. "Here. Smell. Careful not to breathe in too much."

Connor bent toward the bowl she held up for him. Scents of cinnamon, cumin, cardamom, pepper, and he didn't know what else tickled his nose. The combination was earthy and rich, with hints of something sweet that made his mouth water. "It smells like her. Exotic."

"It's garam masala. The recipe that's been passed down in my family for generations." Closing her eyes, Sophie inhaled again. A peace seemed to settle over her, and something in her face relaxed. "It's home." Those eyes opened again and fixed on his, clear grey pools. "Thank you for giving that back to me."

Connor swallowed, his throat going thick. "You're welcome."

As the moment spun out, they leaned toward each other, drawn together by some invisible force neither could control.

The back door banged open. "Something smells absolutely amazing."

With a rueful smile, Sophie eased back, and Connor held in a curse. He was getting really damned tired of being interrupted.

"I'm cooking tonight," she announced.

"Indian food?" Munro asked hopefully. "I love Indian food."

"Good. I hope you brought your appetite, because I'm making enough for a small army."

Angus moved over to buss her cheek. "Put us to work, lass. The least we can do for you feeding us."

"Peel up four of those potatoes and put them on to boil while I start on the samosa dough. It'll need to rest for about half an hour before we can roll it out to form the pockets."

As she gave out more orders, Connor told himself he just had to bide his time. They'd be alone at the forge tonight, and then he'd have an opportunity to make his next move.

———

Good food filled more than the belly. The fragrant chicken biryani, buttery garlic naan, and crisp samosas had fed something in Sophie's soul she hadn't realized was starving. Cutting off that side of her heritage had been a survival mechanism around Lorraine. But bringing out those recipes, filling the kitchen with spices and aromatics, laughter and good conversation, had brought her such joy. As had the stories they'd all shared about her mother. Naya had been dearly loved. It was good to remember that. And as those memories had been unearthed like her recipes, the world seemed all the brighter for them.

Or maybe it was because of the man unlocking the door to a cottage deep in Ardinmuir's forests. Connor had inhaled seconds of everything and already put in requests for other favorites he remembered from childhood. All before insisting he and his uncle and Munro do the dishes.

Now they were stepping into his private sanctum.

As he flipped on the overhead light, she could see that he'd done some work on the place. There were none of the roof or window issues they'd seen with many other cottages on the estate. But everything here was set up for function over form. Worktables ran the length of two adjacent walls. Tools hung from hooks and pegs above one of them. A big machine that might have been some sort of sander sat on the other. Opposite them were industrial shelves full of neatly organized bins of materials. She spotted the anvil in the center of the stone floor, and past it, some sort of long square tube, open at either end, with three pipes sticking out of the top. Some kind of hose attached to them and snaked down behind the wooden table the thing sat on. Weapons in various stages of completion hung on a rack that took up most of one narrow wall, and she spotted what appeared to be gates leaning against another.

"It's not what I expected."

His grin flashed. "Were you imagining some big galumphing thing with bellows?"

"I mean... yes? Literally, my only exposure to blacksmithing is in historical romances and television shows." And if that had led her to imagining him working shirtless, muscles gleaming in firelight, well, he didn't need to know it.

"That one's heated with propane. The coal forge is out back."

He led her through another door and into a sort of covered courtyard. Here a square tray of some sort was mounted on legs. There was a huge metal hood on the back and something with a handle mounted below.

"The coal goes in there. Instead of bellows, I've a hand crank blower that feeds air to the fire from the bottom. And the hood there helps direct the fumes and heat. I use this for bigger projects."

He gave her the full tour, pointing out tools and materials. He tried to skip right over the bulletin board, but Sophie zeroed in on the sketches tacked there. "Are these your designs?"

He shifted on his feet, rubbing at the back of his neck. "Aye. Just ideas I've had."

Some sketches were clearly of blades. Others were smaller components. Designs he intended for hilts or as accents to the blades themselves. She traced a finger over a drawing of an axe with an exquisite knotwork design. "Connor, there's true artistry here. In the drawing and the bringing them to life."

He made a dismissive noise, and she backed off for the moment, knowing he was embarrassed by the praise. "Tell me how it works. Are you making what you want to make and then posting it somewhere online for sale? Or is it commission only?"

"I've done a little of both. Most of my business has been through word of mouth. I entered a few contests and placed well. That was how I got the word out in the first place. But that wasnae where any of it started. I wanted to see if I could manage some of the repairs around the castle, because obviously we have a lot of custom ironwork. It was only after that I veered off into bladesmithing. That's where my passion lies. Because that's where I can really create things of beauty."

The sigh of steel filled the room as he pulled a blade from a sheath and held it out for her to inspect. "This one is a work in progress. A rapier."

"It's beautiful." The hilt was a complex twist of metal encasing the grip.

"Aye, beautiful, but no' balanced. There's too much heaviness in the hilt." He demonstrated with what should have been a fluid swishing sort of motion, but the tip of the blade dove toward the floor. "Until I figure out how to bring that down, it willnae be a functional blade. It's a learning piece."

"What percentage of your work falls into that category versus something you can actually sell?"

He replaced the sword. "I dinna ken. A lot of what I've done has been for Ardinmuir itself, so I've not been paid. I havenae thought much about the rest. I suppose the ratio would change with a more formalized business plan."

She knew it wouldn't have even occurred to him to expense the estate, so she didn't ask. "We can talk about the options there later. What are your expenses?"

"I can give you a list. But I think the best way to get a feel for this kind of work is hands on."

Sophie's pulse jumped. He wasn't talking about the kind of hands on she was thinking of. Was he? "You mean actually make something?"

"Aye." He moved to the workbench and retrieved a leather apron, leather gloves, and safety goggles. "Here. Put these on."

While she did, he grabbed up some other tools and a small metal rod from a bin. She had to wrap the ties of the apron around her waist twice, and the gloves came up to her elbow. With the goggles perched on her brow, she felt a little like a mad scientist. Nothing sexy about that.

Connor moved to the forge and adjusted something. Sophie heard the telltale hiss of gas. He fiddled with a valve on what she realized now was a burner and lit it. A roar instantly filled the room.

"What you're looking for here is a blue flame."

She eyed the forge. "Is that really safe on a wooden table?"

"Aye, it's well-insulated. We're just going to use the first burner for this project for now."

"What *is* this project?"

His lips curved. "You'll see. Now, this is your steel. Hold it with the tongs like this." He closed her hand around the tool. "You want to grip it firmly. The last thing you need is to drop burning hot stock."

"Like this?"

He adjusted her hold, then turned her toward the forge. She could feel the heat coming off it like some kind of living thing.

"Extend the bar in like this." He guided her hand closer, so the steel was beneath the flame. "We're waiting for it to get to a bright orange."

Sophie was achingly aware of his chest pressed to her back, his arm extended along hers. Helping hold the thing up? He didn't touch her anywhere else, and his gaze was firmly fixed on the forge as they slowly twisted the steel beneath the flame. Maybe she'd been wrong about the purpose of this hands-on demonstration. Maybe it was just a demonstration, as she'd originally assumed. More was the pity. The warmth of him behind her was almost more distracting than the heat pumping off the forge.

"Okay, now we're pulling it out and taking it to the anvil."

Moving as if she were carrying a live grenade, Sophie eased the rod out of the fire and pivoted to the anvil. Behind her again, Connor positioned the steel where he wanted it and handed her a hammer.

"This is a flat-faced hammer. We're going to use this to taper the hot end about an inch and a half. You'll strike it with angled blows, turning it 90 degrees after each blow." Closing his hand around hers, he brought the hammer down.

Sophie felt the vibration all the way to her shoulder. "Oh!"

He helped her rotate it and repeated the motion until she understood what he wanted. Then she took over. Each blow sang up her arm. There was a startling physicality to it that went beyond what she'd imagined. As the rod turned to a proper square, Connor had her switch to rotating the steel 180 degrees each time, effectively creating a front and back that she pounded on to make the steel thinner and thinner.

"We need to get it to about a sixteenth of an inch thick."

"I have no idea how thick that even is by eyeballing it."

"Here, I'll help."

This time, when he wrapped his arms around her, Sophie knew she hadn't been entirely wrong about this demonstration. He snugged up closer, tucking his head over her shoulder and wrapping his bigger hand over hers on the shaft of the hammer. There was something oddly intimate about moving together to make something, and it definitely distracted her from what they were doing. Connor, thankfully, was paying more attention. When they'd flattened the end to his specifications, they returned the steel to the forge to repeat the process on the other end.

As they waited, he reeled off more of the details about the materials and expenses she'd asked about. She did her best to commit it to memory, but it was hard to focus on anything but the closeness of him and the desire for more. Once the second end had been flattened, Sophie found her breath coming short, and she was grateful when he took the tongs.

"I'm just gonna do this bit."

A handful of hard, precise strikes straightened the slight warp of the steel, and then he plunged the piece into a bucket of liquid. Steam billowed, and a ball of flame erupted.

Sophie leapt back with a squeak of alarm.

"That's called the quench. We dip it into oil to cool it quickly."

"What kind of oil?"

"You can use a lot of different kinds. This is rapeseed oil. Cheap and with a verra high smoke point."

Once the piece was cool, he brought it over to one of the worktables. "Okay, now you're going to measure and mark the center just there. Aye, that's right. And now an inch from the center on either side. Now we take it back to the forge to heat the whole length."

He lit a second burner for the purpose. "Hold this here and keep it moving until we have that nice, high orange color again. I'm going to set up the vise."

She followed his instructions, carrying the heated steel to the waiting vise, where he clamped it in up to the marks she'd made. He moved behind her again, guiding her hands through the use of the twisting wrench for one full revolution. Then it was back to the forge again.

The work was repetitive. Sophie imagined some people would find it boring. But Connor seemed almost meditative as he moved from one step to the next. Perhaps if it had been someone else doing the teaching, she'd have found it relaxing, too. As it was, the only thing stopping her from turning in his arms to take the mouth she hadn't been able to stop thinking about, was the threat of third-degree burns for one or both of them if they got fully distracted.

"Okay, now place it flat against the anvil with about a half inch hanging off the edge. Aye, just like that. You're going to strike hard, with the idea of bending into a sort of L-shape."

She did as he instructed, twisting and pounding to make a tiny scroll at the end. Still with no idea what they were making, she returned the steel to the forge and repeated the process on the other end, so it made a sort of squat horseshoe shape. Except it was much too small to be one of those.

Connor went hands-on again as they worked together to smooth out and taper the sides up to the twist they'd made. Then it was back to the forge again. He retrieved a wire brush and took the tongs from her at last.

"I'll just finish this last bit. It can be tricky to scrape off the slag."

"Slag?"

"It's the scale that forms from repeatedly heating steel."

She watched him run the brush over the thing with quick, practiced movements. Then he began dousing it in the oil again, over and over. Steam billowed up from the bucket.

At last he pulled it free, turning it this way and that, before nodding in satisfaction. "Congratulations. You just made your first bracelet."

"Oh, *that's* what we were making!" She could see it now. Her wrist would just fit in the gap between the ends of the C.

"The other easy alternative was a coat hook, but I thought you might like to have something to take back with you."

Emboldened by awareness of the dance they'd been doing, she tugged off the gloves and arched a brow in challenge. "Or something to keep on me to make me think of you?"

A trace of uncharacteristic uncertainty lit those blue eyes, and his mouth quirked as he set the bracelet aside to cool. "That depends."

She stripped off the apron. "On?"

"On whether thinking of me makes you smile or if it just reminds you of what you've lost."

He'd taken her upset to heart and done everything he could to rectify the situation, but he was still beating himself up for telling off Lorraine and getting her kicked out.

Sweet, thoughtful man.

Wanting to reassure and needing to touch him, Sophie crossed the two steps to him and pressed a palm to his chest. His thundering heart belied his otherwise calm demeanor and gave her more confidence. "I was hard on you last week. I'm sorry for it. You were right. I needed out of that house, and at the rate I was going on my own... Well, the dynamite method was far more effective."

He brought a hand up to cover hers. "I'm still sorry for all the collateral damage from my thoughtlessness."

"Thoughtlessness? Connor, you've thought of me more in the past two weeks than I think anyone ever has."

His mobile face twitched as he seemed to struggle over what to say. "You... matter, Sophie."

At his confession, warmth bloomed in her chest. She hadn't kissed him since that night at the pub when their engagement had been announced, and suddenly she was tired of waiting for an excuse or another opportunity. She *wanted* to feel his lips on hers. Wanted to feed this simmering need that had been bubbling inside her.

Cupping his cheek, she tipped her face up and whispered a confession of her own. "So do you. So much more than I realized."

Heat sparked in his eyes, as hot as the forge's flame as he muttered, "Oh, thank God," and yanked her to him.

His lips were a fever against hers. There was none of the patient, gentlemanly restraint he'd shown her before. This was want, pure and simple. And it electrified her. She rose to him, wrapping her arms around his neck and answering his demand for more by opening her mouth beneath his. The taste of him flooded into her, rich and potent.

With a growl, his arms tightened, and he lifted her. Sophie wrapped her legs around his waist and felt the unquestionable evidence of his arousal. A fresh wave of heat rolled through her as he strode to one of the worktables, perching her on the edge so he could settle more firmly between her thighs. The feel of him pressed against her center wrenched out a whimper. Her head fell back on a moan, and he took full advantage, trailing open-mouthed kisses along the column of her throat that set her on fire.

She wanted that mouth and those hands everywhere. As if reading her mind, his fingers dipped beneath her jumper to skim up her sides and around to claim her breasts. God, she needed to feel those hands on her skin, rolling her nipples, and she wanted to get her own on the length of him straining for release behind his fly.

Shocked by the direction of her thoughts, she gasped his name.

He lifted his head, looking hungry and lust drunk, but he stopped moving. "What? Too much?"

"Yes. No. Maybe? I need to catch my breath." That wasn't at all what she *wanted*, but there was still a shred of sanity that he hadn't obliterated with arousal, and it was screaming at her to actually consider the ramifications of what they were doing.

Connor pulled his hands from her sweater, planting them on the table as he eased his hips back a fraction. "Okay. You're still driving this train, aye?"

Unable to muster any words other than *Come back* or *Take me*, she just nodded.

They stayed that way, painfully close, but not quite touching, until their breathing slowed and the rest of her sanity returned. This was a huge step and deserved proper consideration, because she wasn't one of his out-of-town flings. If they crossed this bridge and it didn't work out, they'd still be in each other's lives. She was still his sister's best friend and business partner.

She skimmed a thumb along his cheek, loving the rasp of his golden stubble. "It's late. We both have work tomorrow. We should probably get back."

His eyes searched hers for a long moment before nodding and pressing a kiss to her temple. "Okay."

When he started to pull away, she pulled him back again, suddenly needing some reassurance and clarity of her own. "This isn't just... It's not fake anymore, aye?"

He brushed a soft kiss over her mouth. "It's never been fake for me."

"Oh." It was all she could manage as the shock of that reverberated through her like the impact of a hammer on steel.

Connor lifted her down from the table. "Come on then. You've a long day tomorrow."

As he moved around the room, shutting off the forge and

putting things to rights, she pressed a hand to her heart. He'd given her a *lot* to think about.

"Connor?"

"Aye?"

"Thanks for the lesson."

His grin flashed brighter than a solar flare. "Anytime."

TWELVE

Connor made sure Sophie got to host her big family dinner. And he was absolutely on hand to be her sous chef, fetching, chopping, stirring as instructed. If it gave him the opportunity to be close to her, stealing a touch here and there, well, tonight he was a happy opportunist. He'd take what he could get. Their family and friends had arrived, the bulk of them flowing in and out of the kitchen, setting the table and otherwise prepping the dining room for the fragrant feast he'd been drooling over for more than an hour. Sophie herself looked like an exotic ballerina, dancing from dish to dish. His bracelet adorned her slender wrist, and joy added a lightness to her steps. He couldn't help but smile, knowing he'd given her that.

Her clear grey eyes met his as she loaded fresh naan into a basket. "You're looking very self-satisfied."

"I'm about to be eating a pure dead brilliant meal made by one of my favorite people, and it's going to start with dessert. What do I have to complain about?"

Her brows knit. "Dessert? What are you—"

Because the kitchen was clear for the moment, he darted in and stole a kiss. Just a peck, rather than the lingering taste he wanted, but it left her with a dazed expression that was almost as satisfying.

Someone cleared their throat, and Connor realized the room hadn't been as empty as he'd thought. Sophie blushed and began ladling butter chicken into one of the hammered copper serving bowls.

Well, they'd address that as they needed to.

"Come on and grab a dish!"

At Sophie's call, everyone flooded in and began transferring the food to the dining room. When they settled at the table, instead of taking her usual seat down by Kyla, Sophie sat beside him. A unit. No muss, no fuss. Stupidly pleased by that, Connor grinned at her and hooked his pinky finger with hers beneath the table.

Ciara cleared her throat. "So I'm just gonna bring up the elephant in the room. Are you two...?" She waved a hand between them, encompassing a whole range of possibilities for what she was suggesting, all of which meant some variation of him and Sophie being actually together.

Which they were. In some form or fashion. Despite the shift in their relationship, they hadn't defined it or discussed what to tell anyone else. He didn't want to hide their relationship, and certainly his behavior toward her hadn't been that of an indifferent fake fiancé. But he was committed to letting Sophie set the pace, so he stayed quiet and let her field the question.

Unperturbed, Sophie unfolded her cloth napkin with a snap and laid it in her lap. "Yes."

There was a beat of silence and surprise as everyone waited for her to elaborate. Instead, she reached for the bowl of dahl, leaving them all to draw their own conclusions.

From the opposite end of the table, Charlotte pumped her fist. "Called it."

"Damn it," Ciara muttered. "I had two more weeks in the pool."

Sophie lost some of that ineffable calm, her gaze snapping up as something more than embarrassment heated her cheeks. "You're betting on us?"

"I mean, not like, huge betting. But my cousin's a charming guy. Any woman would eventually succumb to his attentions. We just had differing opinions on how long you'd last."

Uncomfortable with the reminder of his past conquests, Connor grabbed up the hammered-copper bowl full of rice. "It's no' like that."

Ewan shot his sister a bland look. "Smooth, you wee numpty."

Now Ciara's face went ruddy. "I didnae mean... Sorry."

Sophie passed the dahl to Munro. "We don't have to make a big thing of it. There's just... less to lie about now."

From the head of the table, Kyla looked like she wanted to make something of it. She met Connor's gaze, her own full of concern, but she held her tongue.

Angus spooned butter chicken onto his plate and cleared his throat. "Well, not to take all the spotlight, but it seems the perfect time to announce that I had a phone interview for *The Great British Bake-Off*."

That effectively took the heat off of them. God bless his uncle.

Cheers and exclamations rounded the table, followed by a volley of questions.

"If I go on to the next round of selection, I'll be called in to do an in-person audition to prove it's me doing the baking."

Conversation flew fast and furious as they all offered opinions on what he should bake if he got a callback. By the time talk shifted to business, the disquiet he'd sensed in Sophie had settled.

Connor didn't like seeing her upset. Didn't want to think that being involved with him would bring her more grief or stress. For now, she seemed happy and on the same page as he. That was more than he could've hoped for. Despite where things had been headed that night in his forge, he wouldn't push her to go any faster or farther than she wanted. The stakes were too high, and he wouldn't risk fucking things up with her.

"—bridesmaid dresses are on order," Kyla said. "Since we've got a couple of weeks until the next event, we've got time to really buckle down with Swayze on the rest of the details for Alyssa and Ryan's wedding."

Swayze. Right. The person he inadvertently had to thank for his current relationship. He hadn't seen her much, but he knew from the social media posts she'd been making that she'd been exploring the village and other surrounding areas in between work on the wedding. Sophie hadn't brought her up, and he hadn't seen a reason to.

"Did you see the latest in the email thread?" Sophie asked. "Alyssa and Ryan have decided to add a unity candle to the ceremony."

"That's straightforward enough."

"It is, but they want to do something special to really make it stand out. I was hoping you could help with that."

Connor realized she was looking at him. "Me? How?"

"Well, I told Alyssa you might be able to design and make the stand to hold the candles."

"A candlestand? I've not made one of those before."

"There's usually a center mount for a large pillar candle and then flanking cups for two smaller tapers, or sometimes more, depending on how many families are being represented. Certainly we can purchase something that would suit, but if you're game, she'd really like to commission the piece from you. Pending approval of design, of course."

The request both excited and mildly terrified him. He'd tackled custom pieces before. The whimsical iron tree for mugs that Charlotte had wanted had been a fun and unique challenge. But she hadn't known he was making it. He'd taken a few commissions before, but those were for blades and other architectural pieces he already knew how to make. This was something else.

Still, it meant something to have her believe enough in his

capability that she'd ask. "It's a little out of my wheelhouse. Can I think about it?"

"Of course."

Conversation shifted yet again after that, but Connor missed most of it. He was turning over design ideas in his brain, his fingers itching for a pen and paper to sketch things out. Did the flanking candles have to be tapers? If each one sat on a sort of plate, with a spike to hold it in place...

When the meal ended, with everyone full and happy, dishes were cleared to the kitchen.

"Sophie is officially off dish duty," Charlotte announced. "You cooked. We'll all wash up."

"I won't argue." She reached out to grab his hand. "Connor, come on. There's something I wanted to show you."

He'd have sworn he heard Ciara mutter, "Is that what they're calling it now?" but when he looked back, she was already filling the sink with soapy water.

When they were down the hall and out of earshot, he shook his head. "I'm sorry if that made you uncomfortable."

"They'll get used to us." The easy confidence in her statement had his chest swelling. Because that suggested she expected them to last long enough to be a thing to get used to.

Sophie led him to the room across the hall from her bedroom. She'd co-opted the space and turned it into an office. As he stepped inside, he could see that she'd not only scrubbed and dusted every inch, she'd actually unpacked a few boxes, adding framed photographs and knickknacks in a way that said she was settling in. Given her initial reluctance to living here at Ardinmuir, the shift pleased him.

She dragged a chair around behind the desk. "Sit."

He dropped into it and waited as she opened her computer.

"I finished your spreadsheet. We'll probably need to make a few tweaks as you go, but this is the start. This page is where you'll enter your expenses. There's this drop-down menu here to categorize each one. I can go back and add anything I've left out. This tab is where you'll list your income, which I've broken down between commissions and direct sales, in-person or via the web. That, too, can be tailored as we go."

She took him through it, showing him all the features and how the formulas linked across sheets to update and auto-calculate... everything.

"And I've protected all the formulas so they can't be accidentally changed."

Connor stared at the screen. "You did all this in less than a week?"

"I did most of it in a couple of hours."

He turned his stare on her. "A couple of hours?"

She shrugged. "You get the benefit of my years of familiarity with the program."

"You are a wonder, Sophie Cameron." He leaned in, intending to give her a smacking kiss, but she stayed him with a finger to his lips.

"I'm not finished."

"There's more?"

"This is just the guts of the business side. The stuff you'll need for taxes and such. You still need to market yourself. That means you need a proper web presence. Once you settle on a name for the business, we can nab the domain and social media real estate, but for now, I've mocked up a basic site." A few more clicks, and she opened a slick website. "It's just got a simple shop that will show a gallery of available products. You can either do that all custom stock that isn't posted until it's made or have photos showing examples of what you can make that they can order in advance."

Big. Everything about this felt big. "I'm no' sure I'm ready to put myself on a deadline. No' when I'm still juggling all the responsibilities of the estate."

"You don't have to start huge. Lean into that artistic bent. Make what you want to make and post that."

"Even if there are only a half dozen things on there at a time?"

"Even if. That suggests scarcity and makes what you do have all the more valuable. You could keep another gallery simply showing what you have made. And if you want, a contact form for people to use if they're interested in commissioning a specific piece. That way you're not locked into anything, and you can negotiate custom pieces on an individual basis, depending on the current costs of materials and whatever else you have on your schedule. Then there's the newsletter—" Her gaze swung back to him, and she flashed a rueful smile. "I'm overwhelming you."

"A little, aye. This is amazing. You did all this for me?"

Her smile was soft. "Of course I did. This is the base. We can dial it in however you need. And just to really make your head explode, technically, you need a social media presence. I can direct you on the basics there, and you have some experience already from your tour business. But honestly, you're friends with Swayze, so she'd probably be a better person to consult about that."

The idea of getting Swayze involved, with the possibility she'd somehow make his stuff go viral, made Connor downright queasy. "I'll take that under advisement. All of this as it is feels like... a lot. I'm afraid it'll get too big for me." It was easier, somehow, to make that admission to Sophie. Because he knew she wouldn't judge him.

"Then you start small. You don't have to do all the things at once. But start with this commission for the wedding."

It was easier to grasp on to the notion of a physical product. A thing he could create with his own two hands, even if he wasn't entirely sure how to do it yet. "Okay."

"There's just one more thing."

"*More?*"

She opened another file. "I took the old books for the estate and updated them to the newest version of the software. All the sheets have been protected, so you literally can't mess the formulas up."

He thought of how much time he'd wasted fighting with the damned things and gripped her hands. "You are a goddess."

She was laughing as he took her mouth in a long, grateful kiss.

Connor still tasted her smile when he eased back. "Thank you."

Her eyes shone. "We make a really good team."

"Aye. That we do."

———

One unexpected side effect of having moved to Ardinmuir was that Sophie found herself with occasional actual free time. Having been used to working herself to the bone at her two jobs and dealing with the vagaries of her stepmother's demands, she didn't really know what to do with herself. Being still, doing nothing productive, left her feeling twitchy. And guilty. She wasn't paying rent. Wasn't being allowed to contribute to the utilities. The only thing Connor and Angus hadn't argued with her over were the groceries she'd brought in, and even that was largely because all the cooking she'd been doing made her happy.

She didn't feel as if she were earning her keep.

Not that Connor or Angus or Kyla had expressed such a sentiment. She knew none of them operated that way. But she had years of programming from her stepmother on that front, and she couldn't quite get past that whispering voice in her conscience that said she was taking advantage. The spreadsheets and website for Connor were something, but those felt more personal. A way to give something back to him after he'd given her so much.

She hadn't been back to the house. Hadn't tried contacting Lorraine at all. It had been easier to do than she ever would have imagined, and the guilt and sense of obligation hadn't been strong enough to force her back into a situation where she would inevitably be mistreated. Her father would have been appalled at the behavior of his wife. Connor had been right about that.

He was off meeting with a local contractor this afternoon, to determine whether all the cottages still to be renovated would need masonry work that had to wait until warmer weather, so she found herself wandering into the kitchen, where she knew Angus was working on a new bake.

"Is there anything I can do to help?"

Too late, she spotted Munro's hand low on Angus's back and sensed the crackling tension in the air.

Angus picked up a bowl and began whipping something with manic energy. "I've got everything in hand just now, but bring back your appetite in a couple of hours."

"Understood. I'm just gonna..." She pointed back toward the hall and withdrew, not wanting to interrupt whatever was happening.

The two had been friends most of their lives, and for a stretch, they'd been more. Neither Connor nor Kyla knew what they'd fallen out over, but since Munro had come back into Angus's life after his heart attack last year, they all been hoping for a reconciliation. Looked like they were on track to get their wish after all.

Too keyed up to simply sit and read or watch TV, Sophie wandered the castle, searching for something to do. As children, she and Kyla had explored the whole thing, with rare exceptions of rooms shut off due to safety concerns. Over the years, their territory had shrunk to Kyla's room and the sections in the newer part of the castle that had been added on. They hadn't been banned from anything, per se. They'd just stuck to habitual territory. Sophie left that territory now, curious what might have changed in the years since she'd explored.

When she found herself outside the master suite in the castle proper, she hesitated. It had been nearly ten years since she'd been up here. Not since she'd helped Kyla clean out and pack up her parents' things a year after their deaths in a plane crash. Back then, the whole room had been covered in dust. They'd cleaned the whole suite then, Kyla not wanting the place to become a shrine. But no one had moved into the rooms. A fact that was more than evident by the stale air that assaulted Sophie's nose as she pushed open the door.

Dust was a pale gray shroud over everything. It muted the deep jewel tones of the rugs and hid the warm luster of the antique wood pieces that had been in the MacKean family for generations. A cloud erupted when she shook the velvet curtains hanging from the four-poster bed, making her sneeze. It was entirely possible that no one had been in here for years. Sophie understood how memories lingered in a place. Being in here was probably difficult for Kyla and Connor both. But she hated to see the signs of neglect. These pieces had lasted for centuries because they'd been cared for. Giving the whole suite a bit of a spiff up would work off her restless energy, even if no one ever knew, and she'd feel like she'd done something to care for this place.

Decided, she went in search of cleaning supplies. It took about twenty minutes to track down the vacuum and lug that and the assortment of rags and oils and cleaners she gathered in a bucket up to the suite. Then she got to work, starting from the top by beating the dust out of those velvet curtains, following up with the upholstery attachment on the vacuum until the rich green was no longer muddied. She stripped the bed, swapping the linens for some she found in a cedar-lined chest and piling the dusty ones in a corner to wash. Every surface was wiped down, the glass cleaned, the wood dusted. She emptied the canister of the vacuum twice as she sucked up every speck of dust from the floor. Then she started in with the lemon oil, cleaning and conditioning the heavy, gorgeous wood pieces that anchored the space. There was something meditative about this kind of deep cleaning, watching years of grime disappear and the beauty of the room beneath begin to shine through. That tangible, visible mark of progress was incredibly satisfying.

The light outside the mullioned windows faded, but Sophie barely noticed as she moved on to the master bath. The counters here were clear of the array of bottles and pots of beauty products that had once filled them. As Sophie wiped down the marble top, she remembered the makeovers Kyla's mum had given them when they were little girls, sitting them just here in front of the mirror so they could watch as she arranged their hair and swiped on mascara and blush. It was a good memory. A happy one she hadn't thought of in years. She was smiling as she knelt to start on the baseboards with a bucket of hot, soapy water and a scrub brush.

"What the bloody hell are you doing?"

Sophie registered the sharp whip of Connor's voice and dropped the brush as she twisted toward the doorway.

He stalked toward her, his face a thundercloud as he reached down to clasp her arm, pulling her to her feet. "What. Are. You. Doing?"

She'd made a mistake. Kyla hadn't wanted to make a shrine of these rooms, but maybe Connor had. And she'd just stepped all over that.

"I'm sorry. I... I just wanted to—"

"This is no' why I brought you here," he snarled.

Fury pumped off him in waves, and Sophie could only stare, wide-eyed. "I—what?"

"You're not a servant. Not an employee. You dinna have to earn your place here."

"I know that. I just—"

"Do you?" he demanded. "Look me in the eye and tell me you weren't trying to find some way to pay me back."

He had her there, and she flushed, uncomfortable with the truth of it, and with the fact that he knew her well enough to understand a big part of her motivations.

When she said nothing, he scowled. "You're a part of the family. This is your home. And I dinna *ever* want to see you on your knees ever again."

Baffled and a bit embarrassed at his vehemence, she searched his face. "Why does this matter so much to you?"

"Because you matter to me," he roared. "You've always mattered to me!"

He'd said much the same that night at his forge. But this felt like something more. Something deeper. Older.

His breath came in ragged bursts, as if he'd been running. Releasing his hold on her, he paced a few steps away, tunneling both hands through his hair. "If not for the damned marriage pact, I would've pursued this years ago. Gotten you out of that house before she had time to twist you up inside, do anything to make you think you're less. Because you're not." He turned back to face her, blue eyes blazing. "You're everything."

His words hit her directly in the sternum, and all her breath wheezed out. No one had ever said such things to her. Hearing it from him, seeing how much he meant it, if his level of agitation was anything to go by... He'd wanted to rescue her. For *years*. And he'd been hamstrung by circumstances.

"I should've done it sooner, but I couldnae figure out how. No' when I was suddenly free and had to contend with the reputation I'd built for myself. Why would you ever believe I'd be serious? And why would you even look at me? I was just your best friend's little brother. So instead I landed you in this insane fake engagement because I didnae know how to just tell you I want a real, lasting relationship. Not because of Swayze or the wedding or any other lunatic reason. But because I'm finally able to choose for myself." He heaved a breath, as if giving voice to all this was an unburdening. "I choose you, Sophie. I'll always choose you. If you'll have me."

Of all the women he could've wanted, all the women he could've had—and she knew the list was long—he wanted her. He'd *chosen* her.

No one had ever done that. Not like this.

And as she stared at this man she'd known practically all her life, she understood that there was so much more to him than the playboy and the clown she'd seen most often. Even more than the loyal friend. Those were simply masks he'd worn to hide his true self from the world.

The true self he was showing to her.

The true self she was pretty sure she was falling in love with.

Sophie closed the distance between them to take his mouth. He wrapped around her, at once both fierce and gentle. Emotions rioted in her chest, and she poured all of them out, wanting to tell him everything she felt without words. Desperation. Gratitude. Need. So much need it made her knees weak. She tasted an answering recklessness in him and knew there was no going back to before.

She didn't want to go back.

"Take me to bed, Connor."

He fumbled, his hands stilling in her hair. "That's not… I wasn't pushing…"

Rising to her toes, she nipped at his jaw. "You chose me. Am I not allowed to choose you right back?"

Cautious joy lit his face. "Are you sure?"

"Positive." To settle the matter, she took his hand and led him toward the door. "Your room or mine?" Neither was close, but they'd manage.

Connor tugged her to a stop, shutting the door to the suite and throwing the lock. "Here's closer."

"So it is." And with a sense of giddy anticipation, she let him lead her to the freshly made bed.

Thirteen

A sense of unreality settled over Connor as he backed Sophie toward the big, four-poster bed. She'd made it up fresh in her feverish early spring cleaning of the room, leaving it folded down, as if waiting just for this. He doubted she'd had that in mind, but he was thankful, nonetheless. There were a lot of halls and a floor-and-a-half between here and his room. Even more to hers. He didn't want to wait that long. Didn't want to give her a chance to change her mind. If she did, he'd certainly respect her wishes, but he was positive he'd cry.

He hadn't really believed he'd ever be here with her. Hadn't really thought she'd want him as he wanted her. And he sure as hell hadn't expected this to be the outcome when he lost his shit over finding her literally scrubbing a floor on her knees. He intended to make the most of it, taking his time and using everything he'd ever learned about pleasing a woman to worship her like the queen she deserved to be.

Only the palest sliver of grey showed in her dilated eyes. She was all long, lovely limbs and arousal. Connor wrapped an arm around her waist, drawing her close for a deep, drugging kiss. She was pliant in his embrace, following his lead when he circled her into a slow dance to the rhythm of his thrumming heart. With his free hand, he slowly worked at the buttons of her shirt, flicking each one open as he drank her in. The shirt slid down her arms and fluttered to the floor. He pulled back, wanting to see her. Her breasts were offered up like a gift in pale pink satin with a lacy edge. Somehow, that very feminine choice for his ever-practical Sophie was even sexier.

Connor drew her in again, skimming his hands along the soft, supple skin of her torso, exploring. She shivered beneath his touch, those long lashes dropping to cover her exquisite eyes.

"If anything's off limits or too much, just tell me to stop, and I will," he murmured.

"Don't stop."

Encouraged by that breathy note to her voice, he continued his seduction, slowly unwrapping her like the very best present. Every inch of new skin he exposed was a treasure he paused to explore with his hands, then his mouth. Every valley, every dip and curve, each spot of softness and strength, was a wonderland. When he released the catch of her bra and drew it off, she trembled but didn't stop him, only watched as he wrapped his tongue around one dark, budded nipple.

Her breath burst out, and her fingers threaded in his hair, holding him to her. He sucked and laved, cupping the other breast in his palm and stroking until he felt her knees go weak. Following the momentum, he lowered her to the bed, stretching out over her. With a little moan, she brought her mouth back to his, her hands getting busy on his shirt with rather less dexterity.

"I want to feel you," she complained.

Connor promptly tugged his shirt straight off over his head and tossed it to the floor.

Her fingers, those lovely, long fingers that were dotted with scars from her work, traced over his chest, lingering at the assorted tattoos. Her hands were heaven, but he dragged himself away. There was far more pleasure to give her before he gave in and sought his own.

He lowered his mouth again and took a lingering journey

down her body, worshiping her breasts, exploring that little soft-ness around her belly and lower, until he hooked his fingers in the waistband of the matching underwear and drew them down her legs, leaving her bare.

He half expected her to curl up in embarrassment or reluc-tance. Instead, she stayed splayed there on the rumpled comforter, a goddess to be admired.

"God, you're beautiful."

She sat up and reached for him, but he nudged her back. "I've been dreaming about this for years." Lightly, he curled his hands around her thighs. "Will you let me taste you, Sophie?"

Her throat worked, and he spotted the hummingbird beat of her pulse, but she nodded. Gently, he spread her open, watching her face as he skimmed one knuckle through the wetness at her core. Her head dropped back on a whimper, her hands fisting in the bedding.

"Too much?"

"N... No."

"Let me know if that changes."

Settling her legs over his shoulders, he lowered his mouth, exploring her with his tongue, his fingers, learning what made her sigh, what made her shudder, and ultimately what made her scream moments before she erupted around him, her hands diving into his hair, her legs locking around his shoulders.

Connor had never felt more like a god.

He brought her down slowly, easing her through the after-shocks of the orgasm, until those slumberous eyes opened and found his. When she beckoned, he crawled back up her body, stroking her quivering muscles along the way.

Sophie studied him for a long moment when he stretched out beside her. Lifting a hand that appeared too heavy for her arm, she caressed his cheek. "Did I pull your hair?"

She had, and he considered it a mark of a job very well done. But it seemed bad form to mention it. Instead, he pressed a kiss to her collarbone and continued to nuzzle the velvety skin there. "You didn't hurt me."

On a sigh, she relaxed back against the bed. "I just have to say that whatever practice you've had was absolutely worth it."

Delighted with the praise, Connor rolled on top of her, braced on his forearms. "Oh, love, we're just getting started."

He felt her hands at his belt as he took her mouth again. She'd evidently recovered some dexterity because a few moments later, the zipper was down and she'd wrapped those long, strong fingers around his length.

He hissed, arching into her grip. "Christ, I dinna want to spend myself in your hand."

"Then hurry up and get inside me."

This wasn't his plan. He intended to draw things out, give her another orgasm or two.

"Connor, please."

As she drew her thumb through the moisture beading at his crown, Connor decided he could be flexible. Give her those extra orgasms after.

Rolling away, he quickly shucked his jeans, grabbing the wallet and fishing out a condom before shoving it all to the floor. Coming to his knees above her, he ripped the foil packet and watched her as he sheathed himself. She was spread out on the white linen sheets, flushed with desire and mussed from his hands, waiting with hungry eyes.

With a sense of wonder, he settled into the cradle of her hips. He was no stranger to sex and intimacy, but this was so much more than he'd felt before. This trust from this woman absolutely leveled him.

"Sophie." Her name was more breath than sound as he found her entrance.

With a smile, she framed his face in that way she had and kissed him once, softly, before wrapping her legs around his waist to urge him inside. His whole world narrowed down to her as he slid slow and deep. She arched against him, tightening her legs, drawing him deeper with a satisfied groan. Her body fisted his, an exquisite torture. He held there, basking in her tight, wet heat, until she relaxed a little, her body adjusting to his girth.

This was perfection. She was perfection. And she'd given him a chance. He didn't plan to waste it.

"Connor?"

"Aye?"

"I need you to move."

"As you wish."

He caught the flash of amusement that he'd quoted her favorite movie. Then everything else was lost beneath the tide of desire as he began with short, shallow thrusts and picking up momentum until her hips were rising and falling with his and he felt her body already beginning to coil. He drew on all his skills and prowess in an effort to stretch things out and make it last, but she was climbing too high, too fast, and it was too much to finally be here with her. They plunged and gasped together, each stroke a desperate lunge toward madness.

And when she quaked beneath him, he felt the world fall away as he spilled inside her.

———

Sophie woke with a gasp, heart hammering, certain she was late.

But it was still dark in Connor's room when she roused to consciousness all snugged up next to him, her head tucked against his shoulder, one leg thrown over his. The man was a furnace—something she wouldn't complain about, given the frigid winter air of his bedroom in the castle proper. They'd migrated here late in the night, after making a kitchen raid for sustenance. She'd intended to move back to her own bed before morning, as she had early client meetings, but evidently Connor had reduced her to a sexual coma sometime well after midnight.

She wouldn't complain about *that,* either. Every inch of her body felt delightfully used in the best possible way, and she suspected it would show the moment she got out of bed. Did she have time for a soak in the tub to ease some of those pleasurable aches? A quick check of the bedside clock said maybe a quick one if she could escape in a hurry. Much as she wished she could linger and bask in the closeness, memorizing the scent of Connor's sleep-warmed skin, he needed whatever rest he could get, and she had work to get to.

Brushing a soft kiss against his pec, she began inching away with infinite care, biting her lip as the mattress creaked. Though he made a soft groaning noise and rolled toward the warm spot she vacated, he didn't actually stir. So far, so good. In the glow of the LED clock, she padded around the room, gathering up her clothes. Her shirt was MIA, and she wasn't about to bother with the bra for this dash down the stairs, so she scooped up Connor's flannel button-down and slipped it on with her loose cotton pants. She could find the shoes later. Clutching the rest of her bundle to her chest, she tiptoed across the room, her toes sinking into the lush pile of the rug. At the door, she glanced over her shoulder, seeing the faint outline of him in the big wooden bed.

Connor MacKean. Her best friend's brother. Her lifelong friend. Now, her lover. And definitely something more. They'd have to talk about that at some point. But she was satisfied knowing they were together and exclusive. That was as far as they'd gotten last night. It was enough. They didn't have to have all the answers now.

The door gave the faintest of squeaks when she tugged it open, but there was no sudden movement from the bed, so she backed out into the hall and hardly dared breathe as she pulled it shut behind her. The squeak of a floorboard from down the hall had her whirling to see Munro coming around the corner, his salt-and-pepper hair tousled, a similar bundle of clothes clutched in his hands. He stopped, a guilty flush creeping up his olive complexion.

Angus's room was on the opposite side of the tower. More to

the point, Munro didn't live here. Apparently, their reconciliation was complete?

Wanting to put him at ease, Sophie flashed a sheepish smile and jerked her head toward the stairs.

"See you at breakfast," she mouthed.

Munro's shoulders dropped, and a rueful smile bloomed.

Neither of them was under any delusion about what this meant. She refused to think of it as a walk of shame, and she hoped he wouldn't either. There was absolutely nothing wrong with being intimate with someone you cared about.

Back in her room, she paid the adoration toll to Cori, who had definite opinions about the fact that she'd spent the night anywhere but available as a feline mattress. Sophie scooped her up and carried her into the bathroom so she could start the water. Cori immediately twisted and began climbing up to her shoulder.

"This is not for you, she-beast. Mama needs a soak after last night."

"Mrrrowwww."

"Yes, I am aware you disapprove, and I shouldn't have left you alone all night since you're still getting comfortable here, but your mum has needs."

Two scoops of peppermint and rosemary bath salts for muscle aches.

"Mrroww?"

On a sigh, she cuddled the cat against her chest. "It was amazing. He's amazing. I never imagined him like this before—well, the whole fake engagement. But being with him for real? Getting to see what's underneath this mask he presents to the world? It's such a privilege. And he wants *me*."

Cori made a noise that had to be the feline equivalent of "Duh," an impression further backed up by her unmistakable smirk.

Laughing, Sophie nuzzled her soft fur. "He makes me feel cherished and adored. And he's quite possibly ruined me for other men. That reputation of his is well-earned. And that, my dearest Coriander, is why Mama needs a soak this morning."

Setting the pacified cat on the floor, Sophie stripped down and slid into the steaming water.

Nearly an hour later she headed downstairs, hair dry, face freshly made up, and dressed for business, with a scarf tied around her throat to hide the beard burn and love bite she'd found when she got out of the bath. Angus and Munro were already in the kitchen, both dressed and looking dapper, as usual, as they worked their way through most of a full Scottish breakfast, with only one of the artery clogging meats, in deference to Angus's more heart-healthy diet.

Her step hitched as Connor turned from the kettle. For a long moment, she wondered how she was supposed to act. Her brain was replaying every moment of last night on a high-definition reel, which made fresh heat pool low in her belly. The burn of it crawled up her throat and into her cheeks.

"I started your tea." Connor lifted a mug, and suddenly everything was okay again.

Sure, she knew what he looked like naked now—amazing— but he was still the thoughtful guy who'd been trying to take care of her in big ways and small for far longer than she'd realized.

Crossing over to him, she took the tea and slid an arm around his waist. His eyes searched her face, and she recognized his silent question of whether she was okay. She gave a little nod and tipped her face up for a kiss. In deference to their audience, he kept his brief and sweet. She couldn't stop the sigh or the foolish grin as he kept his hand hooked possessively on her hip.

From the table, Angus beamed over his coffee. That did nothing to banish the blush, so Sophie changed the subject instead. "Kyla should be here any minute. We've got client meetings this morning."

As if invoked by the utterance of her name, the back door opened and Kyla strode in, a travel mug in hand. "I know they say the decaf tea tastes the same, but they're lying. As soon as this baby arrives, I want the world's biggest London Fog latte."

Connor tugged Sophie out of the line of fire as Kyla marched straight to the kettle and filled it to make more tea.

"Are you allowed to have more?" he asked.

"I can have one real cup a day. As I'm definitely not getting that at home, due to my cowboy's new anti-caffeine stance, I haven't had any since he found my contraband stash last week."

"Your secret's safe with us, love," Angus assured her. At least Sophie was pretty sure he was talking to Kyla.

So they all kept out of her way as she made her first proper cuppa in a week. As soon as she had the mug clutched between her palms, she inhaled as if it were the purest ambrosia and took a sip.

"Thank God." Everything in her posture relaxed. As her eyes fluttered open, they fixed on Sophie, still standing next to Connor, with his hand on her hip. "You look fantastic today, Soph."

I will not blush. I will not blush. I will not blush.

In time-honored tradition, she lifted her own mug to hide her face. "I had a great night's sleep." It wasn't a lie. The sleep she'd had between the stupendous sex had been good. The sleep of the utterly sated and exhausted. Quality over quantity.

"Well, you're gonna need it. We've got a lot to do today. Our client should be here in about half an hour. I'd like to go over some details before they get here. Are you good with that?"

"Of course." Sophie grabbed a couple of tattie scones from the plate of extras Angus had left. "These'll do me."

With one last squeeze of her hip, Connor dropped his hand. "We're waiting on supplies to come in for the next phase of cottage renovations, so I'm at the forge today. Catch up later?"

"Dinner for sure. I'll be headed into town to the shop as soon as the meeting is over." She had dozens of Valentine's orders to finish and have delivered.

Look at us being all domestic.

"It's my turn to cook."

Sophie grinned. "Does that mean takeout from the pub?"

"Hey, my repertoire is wider than that. Just because I've deferred to Angus's expertise doesn't mean I haven't picked anything up over the years. I feel like my skills are being questioned."

"Then, by all means, cook whatever you like to impress me. I shall be grateful for whatever you make."

He saluted them both with his cup of coffee. With one last brush to his hand, Sophie trailed Kyla out of the kitchen, carrying her breakfast with her. Her business partner was already talking about details for the meeting as they navigated through the halls. Sophie was only partly paying attention. Her head was in the clouds.

As they stepped into the parlor and began setting up for the meeting, Kyla turned to face her. "I really hope you know what you're doing with him."

Blinking, Sophie dragged her attention back to the present. "What are you talking about?"

Kyla strode over and began to fuss with the scarf. "You'll have to do better than this to hide that nookie badge on your throat."

The blush came back at radioactive levels. Obviously, she wasn't fooling anybody.

Swallowing hard, she laid a self-conscious hand over the mark on her throat. "I don't know how to talk to you about this."

Kyla untied the scarf and began refolding it. "You don't have to talk to me about it. Just tell me one thing."

"What's that?"

She looped the silk around Sophie's neck and met her gaze. "Are you happy?"

"Yeah. I really am."

Nodding, she retied the scarf. "Whatever happens, that's the important thing right now." With a few more tugs to adjust, she stepped back. "Now. No one else need know about your escapades."

Sophie couldn't hold back the grin. "Nobody would imagine I'd had any."

Kyla's own smile was twisted with a bit of a grimace. "Given you had them with my brother, I need a while longer to mentally readjust to the idea. But good for you."

That was as close to a blessing as she was likely to get. Sophie decided it was good enough for now.

"Let's get to work."

Fourteen

Connor held up the newly finished piece of iron frame, examining it for warp or other problematic imperfections. Deeming it satisfactory, he added it to the collection of others he'd be hauling to the greenhouse when weather permitted. There were enough of them here he'd be able to complete most of the repairs on the north wall. He'd already tackled the trusses of the ceiling, so once he finished this, it would be down to installing the replacement glass. Depending on his workload, he might be able to finish the project entirely by summer's end. Less if he could bring in enough money to hire some professional help.

He'd been dreaming of presenting the finished greenhouse to Sophie for ages, but after last night, his brain took a decidedly sexy turn when imagining her reaction and how she might prefer to express her gratitude. Maybe he could string up some of the millions of fairy lights they had around for events. Make the whole place look like some enchanted midnight garden, complete with a picnic and champagne. She'd love all of that. And if it led to making love under the stars... well, he couldn't imagine a better setting. Not that he needed setting. Hell, he'd been semi-hard every time he'd walked into his forge since he'd kissed her up on that worktable. But he wanted to give her romance. He didn't think anyone ever had. Probably a lot of people would assume she didn't want or need it, given she was such a practical soul. To his mind, that just meant she deserved it all the more, because she wouldn't expect it.

Connor enjoyed surprising her. Reveled in finding those little things that made her life easier or brightened her day, and seeing the expression of baffled gratitude in those gorgeous grey eyes because it never occurred to her that anyone would think of her first. After so many years of feeling he had nothing to offer, being able to show her he knew her—he *saw* her—was oddly empowering. And yeah, okay, maybe a part of him felt like he needed to keep doing it to make sure she didn't regret taking a chance on him.

She hadn't made an issue of his reputation as a playboy. No question, she'd enjoyed the expertise that had come from it. But Connor couldn't quite shake his own discomfort with the life he'd led.

He'd had his reasons, of course. That Afton hadn't wanted him had always stung on some level. Never mind that they'd had no chemistry, and he hadn't had feelings beyond friendship for her. They'd been a duty to each other, to their families. Little more. But not being chosen by the person he was meant to marry had wounded something in him. All those casual one-night and weekend flings he'd had fed the part of him that needed to feel wanted. But that had never been the real him. Not all of him. It had been surface. Simple. Physical.

Nothing with Sophie was simple or surface. They had history. Friendship. Ties that were deep and messy. She was seeing the real him, which was equal parts exhilarating and terrifying.

And she'd chosen him, anyway.

That was his own personal miracle. The fact that she believed in him, believed he could actually turn his passion into a business, was just icing on the whole glorious cake.

Which meant he had to buckle down and get to work on the

designs for this commission instead of daydreaming. He'd done some internet searches to get a better idea of what sort of ready-made options were out there, but he hadn't gone further. The problem was, he knew next to nothing about the bride and groom. Not their tastes or styles or family histories. Nothing that could inform the basis for his designs. The obvious answer was to ask Swayze, who he'd been avoiding.

Better to bite the bullet.

Connor pulled out his phone and sent a text. **You busy?**

Her reply came back almost immediately.

Swayze: **Not with anything important. What's up?**

Connor: **Was hoping to do a consult with you about this unity candlestand. Can you come out to my forge?**

Swayze: **Absolutely! I've been wanting a tour. Send me directions.**

So he did.

Half an hour later, she stood on the stoop, bright and bubbly as usual. "Hi!"

"Thank for coming."

Her inquisitive gaze scanned the space. "I'm so glad you asked me out here. I've been hella curious since Sophie said you could make something custom. I had no idea you were into any of this."

Because she'd asked, he gave her the 50p tour and showed off some of his projects. There was less shyness in showing her than there had been revealing his inner sanctum to Sophie. But that night had been about more than simple business.

Swayze pointed to the pile of iron frame pieces. "What's all that?"

"Part of a restoration project at the castle." No reason to mention specifics. The last thing he needed was Swayze wandering around to find the greenhouse and posting a video that somehow made it back to Sophie.

"You're just full of surprises. Seriously, all this is amazing. You totally need to have your own social media channel. A hot Scot working as a blacksmith? People are gonna eat that up. I mean, they already did with your tour videos just to hear you talk. But this? This is next-level. You totally need some Instagram lives and TikToks and all the things."

Connor rubbed at the heat on the back of his neck. "Sophie said the same. I just havenae gotten around to it." He was still coming to terms with the glory of the spreadsheet and fleshing out the website Sophie had built him.

"Well, there's no time like the present. C'mon. Let's set up your accounts."

"Right now?"

"Yes, right now. Why not? What is your business name?"

"Ardinmuir Ironworks." It was what he'd finally settled on after a lot of thought.

"Awesome. Pull out your phone."

In her perpetually cheerful way, she bullied him through setting up the accounts and even filmed an introduction to cross-post on both platforms. It wasn't much, but it was, as she'd said, a beginning. Everyone had to start somewhere.

"Now, how would you feel about making an instructional video with me? Like, is this something I can be taught how to do? I mean, obviously, I'm not going to become a blacksmith, but can you walk me through something simple? Because then I can introduce my followers to this side of you, and you'll have a solid launch, right off the bat."

"I'm not sure about that. Even simple projects are a fairly long process. You wouldn't want a video that long." On top of which, he wasn't sure he was ready for the potential impact of being launched to all her followers. Right now, the level of growth felt manageable. If something went viral, who knew what might happen?

"Oh, it wouldn't be a live. I'd take multiple videos of each step and splice them together, so it's short and to the point. And in between, while we're waiting on stuff to cool or heat or whatever,

I can tell you a little bit more about Alyssa and Ryan to give you some ideas about who they are as people and as a couple to hopefully inform your design."

Connor considered. How much actual business would he get from exposure to Swayze's audience? A huge portion of them would likely just follow him as a thirst trap. The volume of women who'd followed his other videos purely because of his accent and his looks had been incredibly gratifying. But that wasn't his motivation here. Surely, out of all that, the number of legitimate clients who might come out of it ought to be manageable. Exposure couldn't be a bad thing, right?

"Okay."

She clapped. "Wonderful! I'll get my tripod and ring light out of the car."

While she hauled in and set up equipment, he gathered his own materials and tools for a quick project. He'd show her how to make a coat hook. Making a bracelet felt too much like a kind of betrayal of Sophie. Because that had been important. Having her here in his space had meant something. Swayze being here was just business.

"Hey Sweethearts! Swayze here with Connor MacKean of Ardinmuir Ironworks in Glenlaig, Scotland. He's being kind enough today to give me a one-on-one tutorial here at his forge. What are we making? You'll have to stick around to find out."

Connor gave the obligatory safety warnings, and then he took her through the process, step-by-step. Despite the fact that the project began exactly as the bracelet had, it felt so different from what he'd done with Sophie. There was none of the underlying tension, no subtle flirtation. Even when he had to adjust her grip or wrap his arms around her to correct her technique, he felt not a flicker of the attraction that had drawn him to Swayze's bed two years ago. And that was… interesting.

"It's a coat hook! I made a coat hook, y'all!" Swayze beamed into the camera before flashing that megawatt smile at him.

Connor grinned back, pulled in by her enthusiasm. "Just a little souvenir of your time in Scotland."

"There you have it, Sweethearts. Don't forget to comment and like this video. And follow Ardinmuir Ironworks for more videos from one of our favorite hot Scots."

She shut off the camera and caught the bottle of water he tossed her.

Connor tipped back his own and took a long pull. "So that's it then?"

"Yep. I'll do the editing and splicing and upload later."

"Do you think you can hold off for a week or so? I'm trying to finish getting my website updated." And this would light a fire under his arse to actually complete the project.

"Sure, just let me know. Do you think you got what you needed for the design?"

"Aye, I think so. I've got something more to go on now. Thanks for your help."

"It's no problem. At this point, there hasn't been as much to film with the wedding planning as I'd hoped. But there will be a lot more of that going on closer to the wedding, when there'll be all the behind-the-scenes stuff with the flowers and the caterers and decorations and such. But it's hardly a hardship to be on the ground here, with plenty of time to explore the region with this as my base. I think it just makes Alyssa feel better that someone from her team is here to step in if the need arises. Not that anything has arisen, because your sister and Sophie are amazing at what they do."

Connor felt a glow of pride at the praise. "Aye, they are. Your friend is in good hands."

Swayze picked up the now cool coat hook and held it up. "Thank you for the demonstration! I really enjoyed this." She hesitated, gaze dipping to the ground before lifting to meet his again. "I confess I sort of felt like you've been avoiding me."

Guilt pricked his conscience, but before he could think of anything to say, she rolled on.

"Which is totally not fair of me because I get that it has to be weird for you to be around me when your fiancée is here. You and Sophie are great together, and I just want you to know that I fully respect your relationship. You and I were over a long time ago. But while I'm here, I'd really like to be friends. Because I really just like you as a person."

He soaked that in, not sure what to say. This woman had been the inadvertent catalyst that set him on the path to finally have a real shot at his dream girl. It seemed the least he could do to be her friend.

"Aye. I can do that."

Swayze lifted her water bottle in a toast. "To friendship."

"*Slàinte.*"

She leaned back against one of the worktables and fixed him with an impish grin. "So, do you have big plans with Sophie tonight for Valentine's Day?"

Something hitched in his chest. "Today's Valentine's Day?"

Swayze went brows up. "It is."

"Shite." It hadn't even been on his radar because... well, dates tended to slip out of his brain seconds after they popped into it. And Valentine's Day had never mattered to him because he'd never been with anyone special for the occasion. But Sophie was different.

He tossed his empty bottle into the bin. "I hate to teach and run, but I've got a lot of work to do."

"No problem. And good luck."

At this last minute, he was going to need it.

———

Kyla slumped her way out of the shop's bathroom, face still looking a little green. "Oh God. If all women experience morning sickness, how does anyone ever have more than one bairn?"

With a sympathetic wince, Sophie offered a mug of freshly

brewed peppermint tea. "I'm reasonably sure a great many of them aren't planned. Here. Sit down with a fresh cuppa. It should settle your stomach."

"There's also that thing where you forget after the bairn arrives, what with all the cuteness and sleep deprivation. Having another seems like a good idea because you've basically been subject to torture tactics and are no longer thinking soundly," Ciara added.

Sophie shot their young assistant a glare. "Well, that's a cheery thought. Planning to have a brood, are you?"

"Not for at least another decade. And I'd be entirely okay with doing multiples. Getting the whole sorry mess over with at once. But only after I've found the right guy, who understands that he *will* be changing nappies and helping with middle-of-the-night feedings."

Kyla wilted into a chair and clutched the tea as if it were a healing elixir. "Multiples she says. I promise you'll be grateful those don't run in your family. It's hard enough incubating one. I had no idea I'd be this *tired*."

Sophie moved back to the table to continue assembling centerpieces for the weekend's wedding. "It'll pass. And thankfully, you *did* find the right guy who's hardly letting you lift a finger."

"And I love Raleigh for it. Bless the man. Still, I feel terrible about how much I've let slide onto the two of you for this weekend's vow renewal and anniversary party."

"It's fine. We're managing," Sophie assured her. "Ciara's getting a handle on everything, and I can bring in Mrs. McNeary if I need help with the flowers. Her arthritis is much better since she sold the shop to me, and she loves to keep her hand in from time to time."

"It may come to that if this wee monster disnae settle down." Kyla rubbed a hand over her faint baby bump. "Now, where were we?"

"Going over this weekend's checklist," Ciara announced.

But before they could resume the discussion, the bell over the shop door jangled. Pasting on her customer smile, Sophie stepped out front.

"Welcome to Village Blume. How can I—Oh, Swayze. Hello."

The other woman beamed. "Hey, girl! I was in the village, and I just wanted to pop in to let you know Alyssa has approved the design for the unity candlestand. She's totally in love with Connor's concept."

An instant surge of pride swelled in Sophie's chest. "I knew she would." He'd been so nervous to send the design off to the bride, but she'd known instantly that it was perfect.

"He's so freaking talented! I already passed the news on to him directly so he can get started, but I wanted to take a chance and come by to see if the rest of the team was here."

"They are, as it happens. We're right in the middle of a summit meeting about this weekend's event."

"Then I won't take up too much of your time. Could I come back for a few minutes? Sort of see behind the scenes?"

It was hard to resist the other woman's avid curiosity and enthusiasm. "I don't expect it'll be too interesting, but you're welcome to join us."

Swayze followed her into the back of the shop. "Hey, y'all!"

"What can we do for you?" Kyla asked.

"Well, I'm sure you heard me telling Sophie that Alyssa approved Connor's concept for the unity candlestand. I was just hoping to be a bit of a fly on the wall to see more of what y'all do. I haven't posted nearly as much video as I expected."

A fact for which Sophie had been grateful. Having a camera around made her totally self-conscious. She returned to her work-table and began weaving greenery into the centerpiece. "I'm sorry there hasn't been more opportunity for you to film things. The fact of the matter is that planning a wedding is mostly a lot of boring meetings and paperwork and phone calls. Things that are vital, but not too interesting to watch."

Swayze waved a hand. "Oh, it's fine. I've really been enjoying my time here in Scotland. I was only here for two weeks last time I came to visit, so getting this longer stay to see the things I couldn't fit in before has been fabulous. And, in fact, to fill my time, I've got a date with Angus later."

That sparked Sophie's curiosity. "With Angus? For what?"

"I told him I'd help him set up his own YouTube channel for his bakes. Or maybe TikTok. We're still discussing. So even if his *Great British Bake Off* aspirations don't end up taking off, he can still share his love of baking with the world."

"Oh, he'll love that," Kyla murmured. "Thank you."

"It's no hardship to spend time with him. He's adorable, and his skill in a kitchen is unparalleled. I'm happy to trade my social media expertise for cake. So, you'll be seeing me around the castle a bit more for a while."

Sophie wasn't entirely sure how she felt about that, but as no one seemed to expect a response, she stayed quiet, continuing the work.

"Can I get you a cuppa?" Ciara offered.

"I'd love one."

As they went through the expected social ritual, Sophie listened to the conversation with only half an ear. Swayze asked a lot of questions of Kyla, who showed off the spreadsheets and timeline documents they'd constructed around the weekend's event. Noises of admiration were made over their organizational prowess. Sophie finished the centerpiece and moved on to start the next one.

"So, Sophie, when are you and Connor tying the knot?"

The shears in Sophie's hand snapped shut with a click, cutting the stem on the hydrangea far too short. But she was too shocked by Swayze's question to react. Brain scrambling, she gave the only answer she could. "Oh, we haven't set a date."

"I guess it's pretty hard to do when you're planning everybody else's wedding. Hard to squeeze your own into the schedule."

It was a reasonable assumption, so Sophie didn't contradict her. Her brain was too busy spinning over the question. Despite the fake engagement they were maintaining, the idea of it hadn't crossed her mind before. Not really. She'd simply been living in the now. And why not? The now was so very good. She and Connor were unquestionably together. Over the past month since she'd moved into the castle, they'd fallen into an easy and comfortable routine she never would've imagined possible. Things were great between them. They fit. But actual marriage? Was that something he was thinking about?

Behind her, the conversation continued without her input.

"I can confirm," Kyla said. "Raleigh and I eloped."

"But didn't you two have that whole marriage pact thing to fulfill? So you had to get married in a hurry?"

"There was also that," she conceded.

"Wasn't that scary? Marrying someone you didn't even know? I mean... I've read tons of romance novels around that trope, but I can't imagine actually *doing* it."

"Oh, it was utterly terrifying. But the Universe apparently knew what it was doing, throwing us together. What started out as a business arrangement turned into something more. Now, I can't imagine my life without him."

Swayze loosed a gusty sigh. "I love love."

"It seems that runs in your family," Ciara observed. "I adore your sister's books."

"She writes damned good ones." Pride and warmth filled Swayze's tone. "Which brings me to the other reason I stopped by. I have that autographed copy I promised, Sophie."

She dug around in her purse. "I wasn't sure which your favorite was, so I figured I'd err on the side of reality with a best friend's brother romance, given your relationship with Connor."

Flustered, Sophie accepted the copy of *Say You Won't Let Go*. "Oh, this is so kind of you. Thank you."

"Of course! Ciara, if you've got a favorite, too, let me know. I'll be here long enough for Paisley to send more."

"Truly? Oh, you're a gem, you are."

"Just text me which one you'd like. You, too, Kyla." She set her mug on the counter. "Well, I'm off. I've taken up enough of y'all's time, and I don't want to be late to meet Angus. See y'all later!"

They all called out farewells after her retreating figure.

Nobody moved until the bell jangled, signaling her exit.

Ciara stacked the used mugs in the sink. "She's like a tornado. But it's hard not to like her."

Sophie set the sheers aside and turned to face her friends. "She is very likable. She's a truly nice woman. I'd just feel more comfortable if she wasn't also one of Connor's exes."

In the beat of silence, Kyla studied her face. "Well, he's got quite a few of those. Does that bother you?"

"Mostly, no. I mean, he never hid it. And we certainly weren't together when any of that was going on. I'm not remotely concerned that he'd be unfaithful. It's just awkward being in a room with someone else who's seen him naked."

Looking a little green again, Kyla held up a hand. "I'm happy if you and Connor are happy. I've always thought of you as a sister, so if you ultimately become an actual sister, I will be delighted. But I don't think I can hear about your love life. That's just a little too weird."

Sophie laughed. "That's completely fine with me. I'm not up for discussing."

Ciara rolled her lips out in a pretty pout. "Well, color me disappointed. I, for one, have always wondered if the rumors are true."

"Gross. He's your cousin!" Kyla protested.

"It's no' in an I-want-to-experience-it kind of way. Just out of sheer academic curiosity."

"Well, I have no intention of kissing and telling." She caught Ciara's eye and winked. "But, aye, they definitely are." She thought of the erotic surprise he'd come up with for Valentine's Day. "If anything, they might undersell him."

Kyla stuck both fingers in her ears. "La la la! I canna hear you!"

Snickering, Sophie held up a hand for peace. "I'm finished. And we've work to do. No more talk about anyone's love life."

"Are we sure we've gotten it out of our systems?"

"As the two of you are the only ones *with* love lives to discuss at the moment, I'd say yes," Ciara announced. "So, who's making the final call to the caterers?"

They got through the work, confirming and finalizing last-minute details with phone calls and emails. Then they scattered to the winds and the rest of their assignments, leaving Sophie to wrap up the last of the floral arrangements that could be pre-made. Ciara would be back later to help her haul them all to the castle for storage in the spare fridge.

All in all, it was a good, productive day, boosted by her weekly interaction with the ever-adorable William Fraser, so Sophie was in an excellent mood when the shop bell announced the arrival of a customer just before closing. She stepped out front and spotted the older woman standing in the entryway, one hand clutching the strap of her purse.

"Welcome to Village Blume. How can I help you?"

She looked vaguely familiar, but Sophie couldn't place her.

The woman stepped further into the store and raked a judging gaze over her. "Shameful."

Taken aback, Sophie could only blink. "I beg your pardon?"

"She housed you. Fed and clothed you. And you just up and walk away from your poor stepmother. Living it up with that MacKean boy. *Engaged.* As if a ring will stop that one from wandering."

Temper spiked at the insult to Connor.

So, this was one of Lorraine's friends. Sophie shouldn't have been surprised. But when this much time had passed since she'd been kicked out, perhaps the bigger shock was that it hadn't happened before. She dug through her brain, trying to come up with the woman's name, as she squared her shoulders.

"Lorraine asked me to leave. That was her choice, not mine."

"And you havenae even checked on her once."

Ariah Richardson. Sophie recognized the unwavering judgment in her tone. Recognizing it didn't diminish the sting of guilt that arose from her accusation. It was true enough. She'd been so consumed with Connor, and so much happier out of that house, she'd given her stepmother very little thought. "She didn't leave me with the impression she wanted to continue contact."

"She was hurt. And you couldnae even apologize."

No doubt Lorraine was passing that version of events around to anyone who would listen. There was no sense in pointing out that she wasn't the one who owed anyone an apology.

Putting on her best professional face, Sophie moved toward the woman. "It's closing time. I'm afraid if you aren't here as a customer, I must ask you to leave, Mrs. Richardson."

With a disgusted sniff, Ariah turned toward the door. "I've said what I needed to say. Gave you something to think about. Mark my words. You'll be sorry you left a good woman to fend for herself while you shacked up with that... playboy."

Sophie followed her to the door, immediately throwing the lock as soon as she was outside on the pavement. Her hands were shaking.

How dare this woman come into her place of business to try to guilt her over living her life? Regardless of the fact that she wouldn't have heard the true story of what had transpired that last night at the house, who the hell did something like this?

The bitter and the angry, who resent that the world doesn't work the way they want.

Perhaps Connor had forced the issue, but Sophie had made the choice for herself to cut off contact with her stepmother completely. As she watched her accuser disappear into the night, she wondered if she'd been too harsh. Too hurt.

She *had* promised her father she'd look after Lorraine. Maybe it was time to try to mend fences. It didn't mean she had to go back, but she maybe she could be the bigger person, make the overture.

It would have to wait. This weekend's event came first.

Pushing the whole thing out of her mind, she went to text Ciara that it was time to transport flowers.

Fifteen

The bride and groom had cut the cake, and the reception was rocking and rolling after a flawless—so far as all the guests knew—vow renewal. Connor grabbed Sophie's hand. "C'mon. We're taking ten to disappear to the kitchen. You havenae eaten a bite in hours."

"Just let me check in with Ciara." As she stepped away and spoke into her headset, the phone in his pocket vibrated with a text.

Expecting something from his sister, he was surprised to see Hamish's name pop up on the screen. The sight of it caused an instant spasm of guilt. Since New Year's, his friend had withdrawn, busy with work and divorce proceedings, and Connor had been so wrapped up with Sophie, he hadn't checked in as often as he should.

Hamish: **I thought I'd pop by, but it looks like there's a big to do going on.**

He was here? At Ardinmuir.

Connor: **Vow renewal and fortieth anniversary party still happening. Are you still on the grounds?**

Hamish: **Down toward the end of the drive. There are cars everywhere.**

Connor: **Come up to the kitchen. I'll meet you there.**

Hamish sent back a thumbs up.

Sophie took off her earpiece and looped her arm through Connor's. "I'm clear for at least fifteen minutes and intend to make the most of them."

"I'll see you're fed. Hamish is here."

"Oh! Did we know he was coming up this weekend?"

"No."

They hurried out of the great hall, toward the kitchen, where they found an exhausted Hamish just stepping through the back door.

Connor instantly felt even more guilt. "I'm sorry you had to walk in."

"No. That's what I get for showing up more or less unannounced on a weekend. I guess this is the new norm around here?"

"It's getting to be." Sophie stepped forward to wrap him in a hug. "It's good to see you."

He gave her a squeeze. "And you. So the event planning business is going well, I take it?"

"It's taking off. With luck, by midsummer, we should be able to hire more staff so this one isn't having to work for favors." With a cheeky grin, Sophie popped up to brush a kiss against Connor's mouth.

Hamish went brows up at the sight, which Sophie missed because she'd already turned to the fridge to dig out one of the sandwiches Angus had left for them. Hamish waved a silent finger between the two of them, clearly asking, *So you and she...?*

And the guilt just spread on thicker because Connor hadn't told his best friend about any of it. How could he share his joy when Hamish's marriage was falling apart? So he simply nodded.

Sophie swung around with a full plate and caught the end of the silent exchange. Her own brows rose in understanding. "Right. It seems you two have a lot to talk about. I'm going to leave himself to explain." She paused to squeeze Connor's arm in wordless support. "Hamish, I hope you'll have time to stop by tomorrow when things are a little less chaotic."

Connor saw his gaze fall to that hand, to the diamond glittering there

"I've got some time, aye."

"Good. I'll see you later."

She started to walk out, but Connor caught her hand.

"Do you need me for anything?"

"Not for a while yet. The party will be going on for at least another couple of hours. Likely longer. If it ends as late as we expect, most of the tear-down will wait until tomorrow."

"Okay. If that changes, text me."

"Will do." She brushed her lips to his again, lingering just a moment, he knew, to settle his nerves. Then she strode out with her food, leaving an awkward silence in her wake.

A full ten seconds passed before Hamish spoke. "Was that...?"

"My mother's ring? Aye."

He sucked in a measured breath. "I feel like I've missed a lot."

"Aye, well, I figured you had enough on your plate just now. How is... everything?"

Hamish fixed him with the hard lawyer stare. "You're just gonna drop that bomb about you and Sophie being a... something and think I'm going to let it go?"

Twist, twist went the guilt knife.

"We'll get to that," Connor promised. "I want to hear about you."

The exhaustion dropped back onto him. "That conversation would go smoother with whisky."

"Got you covered."

They relocated to the library, where there had always been a decanter of whisky. As Connor poured them each a glass, he admitted, "It always feels strange, drinking in here. Even after all these years, I keep expecting my dad to come in and box my ears for getting into his stash."

"Not surprising. He chewed us both but good after we wiped out his Macallan."

"You only turn eighteen once. It seemed worth the sacrifice."

"Not so sure it was worth the sick." Hamish sank heavily into one of the leather chairs. "Without belaboring the details, the divorce is in process. No contest. She's not trying to hide the affair. It should go fairly quickly, as Dayna isn't even fighting for primary custody of Freya."

Disgusted, Connor prowled closer. "That's awful. But easier, maybe? It's what you wanted, aye? To bring Freya back to Glenlaig?"

"Of course, I want her with me, but I had thought we'd at least give her the choice. Instead, Dayna was talking up the idea of Freya living with me here and being closer to her grandparents, and how they'll have great girl time during their weekend visits."

Because he had no idea how to respond to that, Connor sat. "How did Freya take that?"

"It's hard to say. She's more like me than her mother, and she loves it here, so right now, all she can see are the positives. But the realities of a split custody arrangement, where she only sees Dayna on weekends and holidays, is something else entirely." He scrubbed a hand over his face. "How long is it going to take her to feel like her mother doesn't want her?"

Connor had no idea how to respond to that. "You ken we all do, aye? You're family, blood or no."

The corner of Hamish's mouth tipped into a pale imitation of his usual smile. "It's the biggest reason I want to come home."

"So that's the plan for sure, then? Moving back here?"

"Aye. I'll be on the hunt for a house. That's part of why I'm here. Taking some time to update my parents and also get the lay of the land, so to speak. They'll offer for us to stay with them, and of course, I know we're welcome here. But we'll need our own place. I think we'll both need that fresh start. The plan is to move as soon as the divorce is finalized and the school term ends. I dinna want to cause any more upset than necessary."

"What about your work?"

"I'll be transitioning. Ultimately opening my own office here, but still doing remote work for the firm in Edinburgh until I can hand my responsibilities off to someone else."

Lots of changes on every front. "Do you ken whether she's continuing to see David?"

Hamish winced. "I haven't asked. I moved into the guest room right after I confronted her, so for all intents and purposes, we're separated while still living under the same roof. It'll all be over soon."

But not soon enough. Connor could see the strain in his friend's posture and couldn't imagine the toll it was taking for him to hold everything together to make things as okay for his daughter as they could be.

He raised his glass. "To your impending freedom."

"I'll definitely drink to that." And he did, draining half the whisky in one gulp.

Connor took a more leisurely sip and asked the thing that had been circling around in the back of his brain. "Have you tried to contact Afton?"

Hamish hesitated before lifting his gaze. "No. Has she contacted any of you?"

"As far as I ken, no."

With a nod, Hamish tipped back his glass again. "I have to think she's not coming back. What does she have to come back to?"

Clearly, you. But Connor didn't give voice to the thought. Hamish needed time to work through the fallout from his divorce before he could even think about pursuing something with someone else, whether that was Afton or not.

Time to change the subject.

"Look, Hamish, I want to apologize for not being there for you like I should the past couple of months."

"You've clearly had a lot going on here. So, you and Sophie?"

"That calls for more whisky." Connor refilled their tumblers and explained how their fake engagement had come about, and how things had progressed from there.

"I always knew you'd had a bit of a thing for her, but I assumed it was just a case of fancying your sister's very attractive best friend. Because she was always around. I never suspected this."

Connor shrugged. "What was the point? I was supposed to marry someone else. I didnae see any reason to get her emotionally involved when we couldn't be together. Or myself, for that matter."

"But you're emotionally involved now?"

"I'm in love with her." It was the first time he'd spoken the truth aloud. The first time he'd fully admitted it to himself. "I have been for a long time."

Hamish merely accepted that in his quiet way. "Have you told her?"

"I've circled around it. I havenae actually said the words. I dinna want to spook her off. Because while this has been long-standing for me, it's still pretty new for her. So we're just enjoying things, and trying to take our time."

"Seems sensible. I rushed things with Dayna, so there was no time to notice the warning signs. Better to take things slow and make sure you're feeling what you think you're feeling before crossing any lines that can't be uncrossed."

Connor fought not to bristle. He understood Hamish issuing such a warning. But he knew what he felt. "I ken we got into this under false pretenses, but nothing has ever felt more real or perfect in my life."

Hamish went brows up again and studied the golden liquid at the bottom of his glass. "I don't think I ever really felt that way about Dayna. Not deep down. If you're sure, that kind of feeling is worth hanging onto, brother." Draining the last of the whisky, he set his glass aside with a thunk. "I'm gonna get out of your way because I know you've got work to do, and I owe my parents a visit and an update as well."

Connor rose and pulled his friend in for a tight, back-thumping hug. It was as much intended comfort as a promise that he'd be a better friend. "See you tomorrow?"

"Absolutely."

After seeing Hamish out, Connor went in search of Sophie. The thump of music told him the reception was still going strong. He stepped into the great hall, scanning the periphery of the crowd for her familiar face. She'd keep herself off to the side, watching out for any potential problems so she could head them off. Spotting her on the far side of the room, he retreated, winding his way through back halls to a door on the opposite side. It opened into an alcove largely hidden by a heavy drape. They stored tables and chairs back here when events weren't in progress. Slipping free of cover, he stepped up behind Sophie and slid his arms around her waist.

It gratified him that she didn't jump, only leaned back into him. She'd learned his touch.

"Everything okay with Hamish?"

"As okay as it can be, for now. He'll be moving home with Freya in the summer, after the divorce is final. Everything going okay here?"

"The DJ is planning to pack it in at the end of the hour. So far, everyone's behaving themselves. No creepers, and I don't think we'll be finding anyone making inappropriate use of dark corners."

"In that case..." Tightening his hands around her waist, he pulled her backward into the alcove.

Sophie laughed, but followed. "What are you doing? I'm working."

"You've just pointed out everything is well in hand, and I want to dance with you."

As if he'd planned it, the music rolled into something slow and sweet. With a little spin, he settled Sophie into his arms and began to sway. After a few moments' hesitation, she relaxed into him, resting her head against his shoulder, exactly where it was meant to be.

Hamish was right. This kind of feeling didn't come along every day. Connor was prepared to do anything he had to in order to keep it. And as he circled her in the shadows, basking in the stolen moment of perfection, he wondered if Sophie felt the same.

———

On her next day off, Sophie stood at the end of the walk, in front of her father's house.

Lorraine's house.

This was probably a terrible idea. She could just imagine the fit Connor would throw if he knew she was here offering an olive branch. But she hadn't been able to stamp out the flicker of guilt ignited by Ariah Richardson's accusations. For the sake of her own conscience, she needed to at least try to make amends.

Nerves dampened her palms. A strange sense of unreality draped over her. So much had changed in the past month. She'd changed.

The key weighed heavy in her hand. Should she use it? It was her key to her house. Given to her by her parents. But she didn't live here anymore. Just walking in felt... wrong somehow. But neither could she summon the will to go knock on the door.

What if Lorraine wasn't home? What if—

The door swung open, and the woman herself stared out, one hand clutching at a four-footed cane. Her whole posture seemed stooped, as if she'd shrunk in on herself over the past weeks. The usually neatly coiffed ash blonde hair was disheveled, as if she hadn't washed or brushed it in days. For once, she looked truly ill.

That flicker of guilt flared high and propelled Sophie closer. "Are you all right?"

Something flashed over Lorraine's face before she sniffed. "Dinna act like you care."

A dozen placating excuses clogged in Sophie's throat, but she swallowed them back down. For better or worse, she'd stayed away. What other conclusion was there for her stepmother to draw?

Tightening her grip on the basket in her hand, she took another step forward. "May I come in?"

"Why?"

Drawing on all the poise she'd learned at her mother's knee, Sophie sighed. "I was hoping we could talk."

Lorraine hesitated, her gaze dropping to the basket, where she could no doubt see the familiar packages of some of her favorite treats. Sophie hadn't been above making this olive branch a little bit of a bribe just to get in the door.

At last, her stepmother yielded, shuffling back so Sophie could pass.

Something in her chest eased at passing this first test. At least until she got inside.

The smell hit her first. Stale air and a musk of rot from trash that had been left to molder. A quick glance around showed a thick layer of dust and dirt. The floors beneath her feet crunched with grit from the salted winter sidewalks. She resisted the urge to remove her shoes as usual because it appeared that absolutely nothing had been cleaned or disposed of since she'd walked out weeks before.

"You'll have to excuse the house. I haven't had any help, and I just haven't been able to take care of things."

That flame of guilt shot up as if doused in petrol, as Lorraine had probably intended.

But what if she truly was incapable? Surely she wouldn't be living like this if she had the option?

Trying not to breathe through her nose, Sophie slipped into her familiar role here. "Why don't I make us a nice cuppa tea?"

A tension eased in Lorraine's shoulders. "That would be nice. In the lounge. There's nowhere to sit in the kitchen."

Sophie saw why as soon as she stepped into the room. It was filthy, with empty takeaway containers scattered everywhere.

Dishes were mounded in the sink, with baked and burnt on crud that had clearly begun to decay. Every surface—from the counter, to the table, to the chairs—was covered. Repulsed and driven by habit, Sophie began to clear things away, starting by emptying the overflowing trash bin. By the time she'd made the offered tea, she'd taken out two more bags of rubbish and started the dishwasher running. These were all the things she'd done every day to maintain the household.

Carrying the tea into the lounge, she found this room not much better. Lorraine seemed to have made a nest on the sofa. Another overflowing bin sat to one side. Sophie didn't comment, though she itched to tidy up in here, too. Instead, she handed over one of the cups and perched on the edge of an armchair with her own.

"Look, there were some harsh things said when I was last here. Connor has very—" Sophie struggled to come up with a way to frame what she wanted to say without indicating he was wrong. "—strong opinions and wants to protect me. He said some things that I know were extremely hurtful to you, and you reacted. Understandably. But I wasn't the one who said those things."

"You left." The words snapped out, the bite of a wounded animal.

Taking a firmer grip on her patience, Sophie didn't allow her voice to rise. "You kicked me out."

"And you didn't come back." Legitimate surprise seemed to underscore the words. As if she'd never imagined such an outcome, and the reality of it hurt her.

"You kicked me out," Sophie repeated. "And I believe you did it because you were hurting. Because he lashed out at you, and you lashed back. But we've both had some time apart to calm down. And I hoped that you'd be amenable to resuming our relationship."

A flash of satisfaction leaked through the wounded routine. "You want to come home."

Sophie glanced around, beyond the mess, and realized that

this house wasn't home anymore. Everything that made it her home was gone. And that made this next part a little easier.

"No. It was time for me to go. I'm grown, and I have my own life. But you and I are the only connection to Dad that either of us has left, and I hoped we could work our way toward finding a new kind of relationship." She didn't know what that would look like, only that her conscience needed her to do *something*.

"I'd appreciate it if you could come by a few times a week to help out. Do the washing up and the cleaning and the dishes."

Was she serious?

The hold on her patience was waning. "No. That's not what this is about. If you need help around the house, I'm happy to help you interview people to find someone trustworthy that you can pay for the service. That won't be me."

Lorraine sniffed. "So you're too good to help family now?"

She wasn't getting what she wanted, and the mask was slipping. Sophie could see it in the ugly set of her mouth, and realized she'd been played. Coming here was a terrible idea. A knee-jerk response to quell the shame she wouldn't even feel if not for the manipulation of this woman and her cronies.

"No. I just recognize my own value. And I find it interesting that you only pull out the family card when you want something." She shook her head. "You know what? Connor was right. You have never looked at me as a daughter. You've never looked at me even as an equal human being. You only look and see what you can get out of me because you think that I'm lesser, and I therefore exist to serve you. Well, guess what? I don't. I have two successful businesses, and I don't have time to be your maid, especially when I've never received a pound of payment or a thank you —ever—for anything I have ever done for you."

"You ungrateful brat. After everything I did for you, you'll speak to me in such a manner?"

Sophie absorbed the blow, soaking in the ugliness of the words and allowing them to chill her from the inside out. "I'm sorry that you were hurt. I'm sorry that Dad died before he could find out what kind of person you really are. But I'm done. I won't do this anymore." She shoved to her feet.

"Leave the key." The order snapped out with finality.

This was it. The true end to her connection to this house, this woman.

With a level stare, Sophie pulled the key off her ring and laid it on the messy coffee table. There was relief in the gesture. Her father was gone. His memory was no longer here.

Lorraine's color was up, and she was sputtering, furious she wasn't getting her way. "You think you're all high and mighty, now that you're living up at the castle with that manwhore. He'll never be faithful to you. Men like that never are."

What do you know of faithfulness?

"You're a miserable woman, Lorraine. I do hope you'll take this as an opportunity to reflect on your choices. Perhaps it'll lead you to make better ones in the future."

Ignoring the shouts, Sophie walked out of the room and out of the house for the very last time.

Sixteen

Hamish rocked back on his heels in the crushed gravel driveway outside Ardinmuir. "I think it has to be the farmhouse."

Connor went brows up. "Are you sure you want to offer on it? You've got time to see if other properties come on the market. No reason to rush into anything." The half-dozen houses they'd toured since the weekend hadn't exactly screamed, *Buy me*.

"You heard what Vera said," Hamish argued. "The turnover in the area is fairly low. The number of properties that have come available in the past year is less than twenty, and most of those aren't detached. It'll be disruptive enough moving up here. I don't want to let a place, only to have to uproot Freya again in a year or two on the off chance that something better comes along."

His logic made sense, but Connor still couldn't quite see his friend moving from his posh New Town neighborhood in Edinburgh to a sprawling farmhouse that had been added onto over the past couple hundred years. "It's a long way from your townhouse."

"That is the biggest appeal. It's a place Dayna would never even have set foot in."

That Connor understood. Still, he had to make one more

effort at steering his friend in a more sensible direction. "With all the changes coming, do you really want to take on a project? Because that's what that house will be."

Folding his arms, Hamish slumped back against the hood of his car. "I want a new start for both of us. And I want to give Freya the kind of childhood we had. The kind of freedom she could never have in the city. The farmhouse has plenty of room for us to spread out. And there's a garden and room for a dog. You know she's wanted a dog since she was wee."

Connor wondered which of them he was trying to convince, but he knew when to fold. "Well, if your mind is made up, then you ken I'll be here to support you, whatever happens. I've certainly got experience making repairs on cantankerous old houses."

"I appreciate that, brother."

The sound of a car pulled their attention to the drive. Sophie's little Fiat zoomed around the still dormant hedges at the front of the castle and circled around to park near the kitchen.

Connor knew the moment she slid out of the car that something was wrong. He had a lifetime of watching this woman. Years of recognizing her small, subtle tells. As she strode in their direction, he watched her slip on the mask, stuffing down whatever she felt in the name of being unruffled and pleasant.

He hated that mask.

"Are you okay?"

"I'm fine." She flashed a smile that wasn't her real smile and came straight to him, wrapping an arm around his waist and snuggling in.

Connor tucked her closer and registered the tension in her body.

"How did the house hunting go?"

"I think I've settled on one. Connor thinks I'm mad, but I'm banking on Freya thinking the whole thing is a big adventure."

"Not mad, precisely," he qualified. "Just... overly optimistic."

"No house is perfect. And it's the imperfections of this one that draw me to it."

"That sounds like a story," Sophie murmured. "Will you be staying for dinner?"

"No. I've got to get back to Edinburgh. But thank you for the invitation. It's been good to see you both." Hamish stepped forward to hug each of them. When he pulled back from Connor, he shot a meaningful glance toward Sophie.

See to your woman.

She wasn't fooling either of them with this false bravado. Maybe she'd gotten out of the habit over the past month. Or maybe he just knew her that much better now.

With one last round of goodbyes, Hamish was gone.

Once his car was out of sight, Connor pulled Sophie in. "I'll ask you again. Are you okay?"

Was that grief in her eyes?

"I will be." She twined her arms around his shoulders. "Will you come upstairs with me?"

She so seldom asked for anything that he ignored the disquiet and followed her inside.

She led him to her room, perhaps because it was closer. They'd bounced back and forth between each other's beds since they'd become lovers. He wanted her in his for good, but he'd let her set the pace on that. If she needed to feel she had a separate space where she was more in control, he wouldn't deny her. In truth, he didn't know how to deny her anything.

The moment she had him across the threshold, she pressed him back against the door, using the momentum of his body to close it. Her mouth was already on his when he heard the lock turn. There was a fevered desperation in her kiss that told him she was more upset than he'd realized.

Framing her face, he gentled. "Sophie, love, what's wrong?"

"Nothing. I just need... I need..."

He watched her search for the words, emotion twisting in her face. "What do you need?"

"You. Just you." Then her mouth found his again, her tongue stroking against his, stoking the desire that was never quite banked around her. Whatever was bothering her would still be there on the other side, and maybe she'd find it easier to talk about once he'd banished the shadows with pleasure.

Picking up on the frantic edge to her kiss, he responded in kind, his hands tugging at clothes, seeking flesh. They stripped each other in a rush, falling onto the bed in a tangle of limbs. She shoved him back, her high, firm breasts swaying as she straddled him. Those striking eyes seemed to glow as she rolled on the condom, then sank down to claim him in one hard, fast slide.

Her head fell back on a cry that was part pleasure, part pain. Before he could find breath to check on her again, she was riding him. There was no mistaking the feverish desperation in her movements, as if she were trying to outrun her demons. With every roll of her hips, she whipped the frenzy between them higher. Recognizing that she'd need more to get over the cusp, he rolled, reversing their positions and pressing her leg back so he could drive deeper, harder, angling his hips to get just a little more friction where she needed it most.

She splintered beneath him, around him, yanking him into his own brutal release.

For long minutes after, there was no sound but the harsh rasp of their breathing.

Connor felt hollowed out and had no idea what to say.

A yowl of protest sounded from somewhere beneath the bed as the beleaguered Dame Coriander voiced her displeasure.

Sophie started to giggle. Then the giggles turned into full-blown whoops of laughter that left her gasping. Connor snorted and carefully rolled to the side to dispense with the condom. He spotted an irritable twitch of furry tail disappearing into the bathroom.

"I think we may have scarred her for life."

"She's still getting used to sharing me."

Connor eyed the partly open door. "If I go in there to clean up, am I risking my bollocks?"

"Maybe just grab a towel from the basket of laundry by the chair for now."

"Wise words."

When they settled back in the bed a few minutes later, he felt the difference in her as she snuggled against him. He stroked a hand along her spine and looked into those lovely eyes. The shadows were gone.

"No' that I dinna appreciate an enthusiastic afternoon romp, but that wasnae what that was about. Are you better now?"

"I am."

"Do you want to talk about it?"

"No." She pressed a kiss to his chest, just over his heart. "I just want to be here with you."

It wasn't the heart to heart he'd expected. He'd thought she'd confide in him once they'd driven away whatever darkness was dogging her. But maybe he didn't need her to tell him. This was something to do with Lorraine. He understood that well enough. Maybe Sophie had seen her in town. Or maybe she'd come by the shop. The village was small. They couldn't avoid each other forever. If Sophie didn't want to dwell on the encounter, who was he to argue? She'd come home to him for comfort, hadn't she? That was what mattered.

———

"Thank y'all so much for letting me pitch in with this!" From across the kitchen table, Swayze beamed. "It's fun to see behind the scenes how y'all run things. I do promise not to post a single thing without your approval, though."

Sophie couldn't help but respond with a smile of her own. "It's us who owe you the thanks. I'm not sure if we'd have managed to pull this off on such a short timeline without your very enthusiastic extra set of hands. Who decides to have a formal engagement party with less than a week's notice?"

"Someone with enough friends that three-quarters of the cottages are rented across both estates for the night," Connor added.

"Somebody who lives in the moment," Ciara suggested. "Or who disnae believe in wasting time."

"Well, either way, we're thankful for the business and everyone's help." Kyla looked down at the clipboard that held the final checklist and reached for some of the assembled meat, cheese, and crackers on the charcuterie tray in the center of the table as she began to go over the remaining details. "Connor, you're on duty with the van to shuttle guests from cottages to the party and back again later tonight, so no one's driving under the influence."

He dangled the keys. "Aye. We're set on that front. The van holds ten, so it'll likely take a few trips to gather up everyone who chooses that option."

"I'll be sending texts in waves to let them know when you're on your way, so they'll be ready." Ciara passed him a sheet of paper. "Here's the list of cottages, grouped by location, and number guests on pick up."

Kyla continued. "Sophie, you and Swayze will greet the guests on their arrival, check them against the list, and direct them on to the great hall for the party. That'll be a two-woman job to keep people from getting lost or being generally nosy and wandering the castle."

Swayze looked both intrigued and vaguely horrified. "Do people do that?"

"Not many. But people are curious about a place like this. And especially once the alcohol starts flowing, they'll often forget it's actually a private residence. We try to post staff on all the exits to the great hall, to make sure we don't end up with strangers snogging or worse in a closet or something."

"And we keep Connor and a few other of our men on the premises in case any guests decide to make inappropriate advances to us or other guests," Sophie added. "Tonight, that's Ciara's brother Ewan, who's also playing bartender, and Raleigh, once he wraps up some business at Lochmara."

"Huh. I had no idea how much of event planning is like chaperoning a high school dance."

Knowing the night was likely to be busy and long, Sophie grabbed several crackers and some olives off the charcuterie tray. "It can be a lot of herding cats, but when everything goes well, and the client is happy, it's worth the effort to share in their joy. At the end of the day, aside from the very practical aspect of needing to make a living, that's why we do this."

"That's lovely. It's that sense that y'all really care that made Alyssa decide to use your company. So keep doing what you're doing."

Kyla grinned. "We'll take that praise. Thank you. And please, eat. Frequently, we don't get a chance once things get rolling."

They finished reviewing the list of assignments about the time the caterer's van pulled up. Ciara disappeared to direct them where to set up.

"Just one more thing before we split." Swayze reached beneath the table to produce a bottle of champagne. "I get we should probably wait on this until the night is done, but I just wanted to bring this by to toast to Connor's official successful launch of Ardinmuir Ironworks on social media. People are absolutely loving his work."

"Oh, that's—well, thank you," Connor mumbled.

Sophie reached for his hand. She hadn't checked in on how all that was going because she hadn't wanted to pressure him, and she'd been a little afraid that he'd pull back on everything because he was feeling overwhelmed. "That's amazing. I'm so proud of you."

Kyla leaned over to squeeze his shoulders. "Truly, that's grand, Con. I'm glad to hear it's working out."

Flags of color rose in Connor's cheeks. "Well, people are following. We'll see how much actual business comes from it. I have had a couple of inquiries about possible commissions, so we'll see how everything goes." He flashed a smile at Swayze. "Thanks for your help and bullying me into going ahead and setting it up."

"I love introducing worthwhile people to all my people. What you do with it after that is up to you."

"Fair enough." Grabbing the last of the salami and cheese, he rose and pocketed the keys. "I'm off to pick up guests."

Then he was out the door, leaving them alone.

"And the reluctant artist makes his escape," Swayze intoned. "It's cute how he's so confident in some areas and so shy about others."

At the clear affection in her tone, Sophie studied the other woman. "I suppose we're all more ill at ease when it's about something that really matters to us."

"True story. But he's hella talented, so he's got nothing to worry about." She shoved back from the table. "Shall we go greet some guests?"

Though she'd known this was the plan from the beginning, Sophie still felt a beat of trepidation at being paired with the other woman. Every single time they interacted, she had to get over that knee-jerk wariness. And that wasn't fair. Swayze had acknowledged her history with Connor and done everything possible to put Sophie at ease about the situation. Maybe eventually being around her would stop feeling like a Thing.

Leaving Kyla to oversee the final details related to the music and the setup off the bar, Sophie and Swayze took their positions at the entrance just in time to greet the bride- and groom-to-be. Like Kyla, Swayze was a natural with people, and Sophie was grateful to leave the heavy lifting on that front to her as she led individual and groups of guests back to the party.

She'd just made it back to the door from delivering Connor's first van-full of guests, when she overheard a woman ask Swayze, "Is this Connor MacKean's place?"

Going on alert, Sophie stepped in, professional mode dialed

to eleven. "Good evening. Welcome to Ardinmuir Castle, which has, indeed, been home to the MacKean clan for centuries. Are you a friend of the family?"

The woman's gaze was over-bright with avid interest. "Of Connor's, yes. I'm Blair Pearson. Is he here tonight?"

And suddenly Sophie knew. This was yet another of Connor's former lovers. The cheese and crackers she'd scarfed down during their pre-event meeting turned to lead in her stomach, and her mouth went dry, every word evaporating from her brain.

Swayze stepped in. "As a matter of fact, he is. Such a sweet thing, helping his fiancée out with her event." She grabbed Sophie's left hand and lifted it in an old-fashioned courtly gesture that showed off the engagement ring. "This is her, by the way. Sophie Cameron."

The other woman blinked in shock and actually took a step back. "Oh, I didn't realize—" Color flooded her cheeks. "I'm sorry. Um... Congratulations."

"It's wonderful, isn't it? You enjoy the party now, you hear?" With smooth efficiency, Swayze gave perfect directions to the great hall and nudged Blair on her way.

Through it all, Sophie said nothing, too stunned to react.

As soon as the woman was out of earshot, Swayze moved in close, laying a hand on her arm. "You okay?"

"I... That was masterfully handled. Thank you."

"Just a little Southern girl training on how to put somebody in their place with a smile. Bless her heart. Seriously, though. Do you need a minute? That's gotta be a bit of a shock. You at least had some warning about me."

"I am feeling a little weird." Not the least about how Swayze had so readily come to her defense.

At the sound of footsteps, Swayze's gaze slid to the hall. "Connor!"

"I had to drop off the extra keg to Ewan before I headed out for the next round." He drew even with them and Sophie didn't manage to school her features before he saw her face. "Soph? What's wrong?"

"Blair Pearson," Swayze said flatly.

Connor's expression froze for two long seconds before he closed his eyes. "Fuck."

Well. That was as much confirmation as she needed.

Swayze squeezed Sophie's arm, then nudged her toward Connor. "Why don't y'all go take five? I've got this."

Sophie desperately needed to regain some equilibrium, so she didn't argue when he placed his hand on her lower back and steered her into the family space.

The moment they were alone, he turned to her. "Sophie, I canna apologize enough. I had no idea she'd be here. I dinna even ken what she said, but I'm just... sorry. You shouldn't have to come face-to-face with my past."

He looked so perfectly miserable, she couldn't help but step into him, framing that beloved face. "No, it's—well, I canna exactly say it's fine. I don't love running into any of your former... dalliances. I guess, bringing strangers in for events here, it's inevitable that it could happen from time to time. But I don't blame you for the past you had before we were together."

And she didn't. She knew this man. He was loyal as the day was long. Just because other women continued to find him attractive and want more of whatever they'd had with him, didn't mean *he* was interested.

His arms closed around her as he dropped his temple to hers. "I'm still sorry that it's happening and that it upsets you. You ken you're the only one for me, aye? No matter who came before you, you're the one I'm with now. You're the one who matters."

Here in his arms, she believed it. And if she had the occasional moment of doubt when they were apart, wondering what he saw in her? Well, that was her issue. She'd work on it.

On a sigh, Sophie relaxed into him. "Aye, I do know that. But maybe you could keep reminding me?"

"Every day. As often as you like." One hand trailed down her spine to cup her backside. "I've got several suggestions for how to bring home the point later, when we've got time alone."

Because she knew he wanted her to, she chuckled and pressed her hips against the arousal she could already feel behind his fly. "I'll definitely not say no, Mr. MacKean. But, for now, we both have work to do."

When she stepped back, he kept hold of her hands, lifting them to his lips. "Until tonight."

And as he disappeared to go pick up the next wave of guests, Sophie knew she'd be thinking of the erotic promise in his eyes.

No matter who else she ran into, Connor MacKean was hers.

Seventeen

Alyssa and Ryan's wedding was just over two weeks away, and it was all hands on deck for Ardinmuir Event Planning. Connor stuck his head into the room designated as command central and immediately regretted it as four harried women turned their gazes in his direction. Clearly, no one appreciated his interruption.

Kyla lifted one brow in the way she'd been doing basically since puberty that told him she was annoyed. "Did you need something, Connor?"

"Uh... I was just headed out to Inverness. Did any of you need anything since I'll be in the city?"

"We're good. But thank you." She turned back to whatever list she was obsessing over.

Sophie rose. "Two minutes."

His sister opened her mouth as if she wanted to protest, but Swayze intervened. "Oh, come on, Kyla. Give the lovebirds a moment. It's cute. Besides, Angus texted to say he's got a fresh batch of shortbread about to come out of the oven. I say we need some with a pot of tea to fuel the rest of our efforts."

Ciara piled on. "I'm for that!"

With a rueful smile, Kyla sat back. "Fine. I know when I'm overruled. I could do with a snack."

"Then you should come with to make sure that I, as the resident Yank, don't mess up the tea."

There was a flurry of motion, and suddenly Connor found himself alone with Sophie. "Well, that isnae what I was aiming for, but I willnae be complaining."

She slid into his arms. "Her Mission Mode has gotten worse since pregnancy. All the reading she's done has made her paranoid the business will suffer from the preggo brain forgetfulness."

"Do you need to talk to Raleigh?"

"No, we're handling her. And she's not wrong. Everything's coming together, so there *is* a lot happening right now. I just wanted to steal a kiss before you left."

"As you wish." He lifted her mouth to meet his and fought not to sink too deep into the taste of her. She had work, and so did he. But he'd never get tired of her trust and sweetness. He'd never stop trying to earn it.

With a hum of pleasure, Sophie dropped back to her feet. "What are you headed to Inverness for?"

"Hmm? Oh, I'm making a sweep of my salvage suppliers."

That's not the only reason you're going. Tell her the rest.

But as Connor looked down into her relaxed, happy face, he couldn't do it. "I should be back by dinner. You're sure there are no ingredients I need to grab for you from the international market?"

"I'm pretty sure I bought them out on my last trip. But thanks."

Because his conscience was making him feel squirrelly, Connor released her and stepped back. "I should get on the road so you can get back to work."

"Drive safe. I'll see you when you get home."

With one last stroke of her cheek, Connor tore himself away.

Eejit. Coward.

He continued the litany of insults all the way to his 4x4. Because while he was checking with some of his suppliers to see about getting additional materials, that wasn't his primary reason for the trip. He'd been contacted about a prospective commission job.

By one of his former lovers.

That part didn't bother him so much. He had no issue telling Gabriella he wasn't interested, should this meeting trend in any direction but the professional. But after seeing Sophie's face in the wake of meeting Blair Pearson, Connor just couldn't do that to her. For all she claimed not to hold it against him—and God bless her for that—she certainly didn't deserve to keep having his past thrown in her face. Especially not while she was busy trying to pull off Alyssa and Ryan's wedding. He knew what a big deal it was, and he didn't want to do anything to distract her.

He'd tell her about the job if it turned into a job. With everything going on, he wouldn't be starting on a new project until after the wedding, anyway. And if the job didn't happen, then he'd avoid needlessly upsetting her.

Connor was early to the restaurant Gabriella had chosen. The moment he walked in, he felt underdressed in his kilt and leather jacket. The leather, low-lighting, and white tablecloths screamed a higher-end establishment than he'd been prepared for. But it was too late now. Putting on his best confident smile, he approached the hostess.

"Reservation for Hendry? I believe I'm a wee bit early."

"You are, sir. Your companion hasn't yet arrived. Would you like to wait at the bar?"

"That'll be fine."

He wandered into the hush of the restaurant. The lunch rush was past, with only a half-dozen patrons still lingering over food. The bar itself was separated from the restaurant proper by an atrium. He got distracted from his destination by a metalwork sculpture that looked a hell of a lot like a smaller version of Andy Scott's Heavy Horse sculpture in Glasgow. Bending close, he admired the workmanship, examining how the sculpture was constructed. He hadn't tried his hand at anything purely artistic, but this made him want to try.

"Connor MacKean." At the smooth voice with just a hint of Italy, he turned.

She hadn't changed a bit, still dripping with every bit of the class she'd displayed when she'd booked him for a private tour a few years before. Though he knew her to be closer to forty, her face held that utterly timeless quality chased by artists through the ages.

"Gabriella." Knowing his role here, he strode to greet her, gripping her by the shoulders and leaning in to buss her cheek.

But at the last moment, she turned to brush her mouth to his.

Connor jerked back. "No."

One dark brow arched up. "No? What's wrong, darling?"

Not wanting to make a public spectacle, he kept his voice low. "I'm engaged. If you canna respect that, then this conversation is over before it's started."

Unruffled, she patted his chest. "Of course. My apologies. I didn't know. My felicitations."

Maybe he should add his relationship status to his social media profiles. Perhaps that would cut down on the volume of "thirsty" comments from followers. Or at least put the word out that he was no longer available. It wasn't a perfect solution, but it was what he could do for now.

"Shall we eat and discuss the job?"

"Is there really a job?" He was starting to wonder if she'd dragged him all the way up here under false pretenses.

"I'd like there to be. That depends on you."

"Very well."

They were shown to a corner table. She ordered wine and an appetizer. Connor declined both.

With a moue of contrition, she crossed her legs. "I truly am sorry. I made assumptions. That was wrong of me. Please, allow me to make it up to you by buying you a good meal while we discuss your art."

Somewhat mollified, he unbent enough to order a steak. She chose the scallops, and when the server left, she dove right in.

"I've been researching you, Connor. Searching out the work you've done. It's an interesting blend of architectural pieces and weaponry. Which do you prefer?"

He wondered how she'd managed to track down his clients, but didn't ask. She was a woman who found a way to get what she wanted. He'd liked that about her, once upon a time.

"I can and do enjoy both, but I tend to prefer the projects where I get to experiment with design. So far, that's largely been with blades."

"How do you feel about a chandelier?"

"You want me to design a light fixture?"

"Nothing so pedestrian, darling. I mean a truly grand, unique chandelier. A statement piece that would hang in a room with soaring twenty-foot ceilings and make an impression."

Intrigued despite himself, Connor leaned in.

Over the meal, they discussed the scope, the materials, and the style. What she wanted was a massive undertaking, and it sparked his artist's heart in a way few of his commissions had. More, it was a big job. A job that would command a hell of a price.

"I'd need dimensions and to actually see the site, confirm the structural stability of where you want to hang it before I could even mock something up."

"Yes, of course, but can't you give an estimate? Just a general one, with the understanding that it might change once you get into it?"

He pulled out his phone and began to run some numbers. "Looking at the cost of materials, the amount of time and labor... this is a very expensive proposition. And I'm not just making that up as some means of getting you back for the kiss."

"If you can produce what I actually want, I'm more than willing to pay for it. Money's no issue."

Of course it wasn't. What must it be like to live life like that?

"What you're describing is going to be months in the making and into five figures."

"Done."

Connor stared at her. "That's it?"

"Unless you require something further?"

He thought of Sophie and Kyla, and all their professionalism and contracts. "I'd need to work up a design for your approval, and prepare a proper estimate. Once those are agreed to, I'll need a contract to protect us both."

"Of course. Let's finish up this excellent meal and you can follow me home. Get those measurements and take some pictures of the space. I expect you'll need that to inform your design."

"Now?"

"Why not? There's no time like the present. It's more efficient. Then you can head back home and get to work."

Well, she wasn't wrong. Not having to come back to do those things was a more efficient use of his time. And the prospect of a five-figure commission... That would be a hell of a chunk he could put down on the estate's debt.

Lured by the prospect of finally being able to prove himself to his sister, he extended a hand. "We have a deal."

———

With ten days until Alyssa and Ryan's wedding, Sophie was ensconced at Village Blume, confirming final orders with her distributors and enjoying the relative peace. Everything at Ardinmuir was pure chaos just now. Good chaos, productive chaos, but chaos, nonetheless. She needed the quiet of her flowers and half an hour to update her spreadsheets. They hadn't been top priority since she moved into the castle at the end of January, but she needed to know where she stood.

The news wasn't great. Even with the increased revenues from the event planning business, she wasn't bringing in enough to overcome the hit of the raised shop rent to her bottom line. The more business for Ardinmuir, the less time she had to spend at the shop. So, either they paid for extra help for events, or she had to bring on part-time help at the shop. Either way, it ate into her profits and was steadily eating into her savings, which was a problem, long-term. She'd have to figure something else out regarding the shop. But for better or worse, she'd signed the lease. She could absorb the cost for the year, and it would give her time to make another plan.

The shop bell jingled, and Sophie looked up to find her favorite customer striding in. "Mr. Fraser! How are you today?"

He doffed his tam. "Better now I've seen your shining face."

She straightened from the computer. "You're a wee bit early. I'm afraid I haven't put together Hettie's bouquet just yet."

"That's fine. I can wait. I've nowhere to be just now."

Not wanting him to stay on his feet, hale and hearty though he seemed, Sophie opened the gate that led behind the counter. "Why don't you come on back and have a cuppa with me while I put it together?"

"Well, now, I willnae say no to such good company. These old bones are feeling the cold today."

"It's damp for sure." She gestured him to a chair. "What's your pleasure?"

"You know I love my PG Tips."

"An excellent choice." Once she'd put on the kettle, she moved to the cooler. "Any particular requests this week?"

"Dealer's choice."

It was a standard answer, so she'd already begun plucking flowers for the arrangement. Given the dreary gray weather, she went for bold and colorful, blended with an assortment of greenery. Carrying the lot of it to the worktable, she began trimming stems. "Anything exciting going on with you and the missus?"

"Our grandson Andrew is visiting with his wife Fiona and their wee bairn Rabbie. He's three. Hettie's besotted, she is."

The kettle whistled, so she poured boiling water over the waiting tea bag and set a timer. "Judging from the pride I hear in your voice, she's not the only one. That's so lovely that you not only have grandchildren, you have a great grand!"

"And another on the way, if my Hettie is right. Poor Fiona turned green as Celtics football kit at dinner last night. She blamed it on a stomach bug, but she's got the look."

New life. Expanding families. Hearing such news was Sophie's favorite part of the job. "That's so exciting! Would you like to take a bouquet to her, as well?"

"That's a fine idea."

They continued to chat about his family and the goings on around the village, as he drank his tea, and she made a pair of charming and cheerful bouquets for his ladies. She tied off each with a hot pink bow. "There now. That's sure to brighten their days, despite the grey."

"Those are lovely." He started to rise.

"No, no. Sit. Finish your tea." Sophie leaned back and began to sip at her own. "You and Hettie are such an inspiration to me, Mr. Fraser. Any secrets you want to impart for a long and happy life together?"

William's eyes twinkled. "More for young MacKean than you, I'd wager."

She laughed, willing by now to accept that they had the chance for that kind of future. "I'll have to send him your way."

The bell jangled out front.

"I'll be right back." Setting down her mug, Sophie hurried through the door to greet her customer. Her ready smile died at the sight of her landlord stalking forward, bad temper crackling around him like lightning.

Now what?

Milligan slapped an envelope down on the counter and started to walk away again without a word.

Baffled and annoyed, she called after him, "What's this?"

"Eviction notice."

The words and his flat delivery sent a chill straight down to her bones. "*What?* Why? I signed the new lease. I agreed to your absurd terms. I haven't missed a single payment."

Hand on the door, he glanced back. "You and your stepmother are more trouble than you're worth."

He was piling nonsense on top of nonsense. "What does Lorraine have to do with anything?"

"You went and pissed her off, and now she's not satisfied with simply taking the extra off the top of your rent. Dinna ken what she thinks I'm gonna do about it."

Stupefied, Sophie struggled to process what he'd said. "She's... been getting part of my rent?"

With an uninterested sniff, Milligan jerked a nod. "Aye. For years. Was a convenient way for her to keep you around."

"That's... that's unethical. That's absurd."

"That's business. And it served my purposes for a long time. We had a nice little thing going, Lorraine and I. Devious little minx, and surprisingly good in the sack. But no more. It's no' worth it to me, so I'm washing my hands of both of you. You have until the end of the week to get out."

As the tide of panic rose, she started toward him. "You can't do this!"

Milligan yanked open the door, not even bothering to look back as he called, "Already have."

Then he was gone, leaving Sophie to face the impossibility of the fallout from the disaster he'd just handed her.

Her stepmother and her landlord had been in league together. He'd helped Lorraine torpedo her efforts to move out. The two of them had apparently been having some kind of affair. She thought of all those nights she'd come home to a mess of dishes that seemed far too many for one person. Had it been him?

"Are you all right, lass?"

Wide-eyed, Sophie looked up at William. His weathered face was set in lines of deep concern.

Realizing he'd heard the whole thing, fresh shame crashed down over her. "I... Well, no. I'm afraid I need to deal with this."

"Of course." He glanced at the shop door, where Milligan had disappeared. "That horse's arse will get what's coming to him one of these days."

"If karma is real, then you're right. Let me ring you up."

As soon as he was gone, she picked up the envelope and ripped it open with fumbling fingers. She skimmed the document inside. Her mind was spinning too much to make sense of it, but it looked pretty damned official to her. *Vacate the premises by the end of the week.* Less than five days to clear out her entire shop, when they had to prep for the biggest event they'd ever done. Not to mention her normal business.

Shit.

She needed to call Hamish. Send him a copy of this. He'd want to see her lease as well. The idea of all of it made her wince, because she knew there'd be I-told-you-sos that she'd signed the bloody thing at all without having him review it. From both the MacKean siblings. Hamish himself was far too restrained for such remarks. He'd simply give that silent look of reproach, then throw himself into seeing what could be done. She'd have to carve out time later to wallow in self-recrimination for her terminal allergy to asking for help. Right now, she had to do the hard thing and call him.

But before she could dial, the door opened again, and Talia Cowan strode in.

It was too much for Sophie to put on her polite mask. "I'm so sorry, but I'm really not in a place where I can handle customers just now."

She'd already stepped out from behind the counter, prepared to nudge the other woman along, when Talia clasped her hands, her brows drawing together in an unmistakable expression of concern and sympathy. "You've heard, then?"

Sophie didn't have time for whatever the latest village disaster was, but she knew she'd at least have to hear it. "What are you talking about?"

The younger woman swallowed, looking unaccountably

nervous. "I wrestled about this for the past several days, but I couldn't *not* tell you."

Under normal circumstances, Sophie liked Talia. She'd been a part of Connor's class in school. She tended toward shy and preferred animals to people. But there was no room for patience over her dithering in this moment. "Tell me what?"

"I was in Inverness last week, and I... well, I saw Connor with another woman."

Sophie shook her head. "That can't be." He had been in Inverness to meet with suppliers, but that was all.

Wincing, Talia pressed. "I took photos." She pulled out her phone and swiped at the screen.

Impatient, Sophie took it, expecting to see a blurry shot of some random blond guy who might or might not be Connor. But as she focused in on the first shot, she recognized the MacKean plaid of the kilt, saw the wearer of it kissing some brunette. She swiped through to the next shot of the two of them sitting at a table, heads bent together in intimate fashion over some fancy meal, Connor's face perfectly clear.

Nausea roiled. "This can't be real."

"I didn't think so either. So I hung around and followed them when they left the restaurant. They had separate vehicles. I recognized Connor's 4x4. He followed her to a house—some private residence behind a gate—and went inside with her. There are pictures of that, too."

Practically paralyzed with dread, Sophie swiped again to the next photo, seeing Connor's 4x4, down to the license plate. And the next, where Connor was, indeed, disappearing into the front door of some grand mansion.

Whoever that woman was, she certainly wasn't a scrap metal supplier. And he certainly had no reason to be kissing her, except that he apparently wanted to.

As a playboy would when he got bored with his current plaything.

It was who he'd been for years. How everyone saw him. Everyone but her.

She'd been warned. Cautioned by even his own sister. Hell, she'd run into *two* of his former lovers herself in just the past few months.

What were the chances that she'd been the only clear-sighted one versus simply a challenge he'd finally had the opportunity to pursue? A challenge he was evidently finished with, if these photos were anything to go by.

Was this karma for breaking her promise to her father? An utter implosion of her life in one fell swoop?

Her voice sounded dim and distant to her own ears. "Can you send me these, please?"

"Of course. I'm so sorry, Sophie. You deserve better than this."

There was nothing left to say. As soon as the pictures were received, she ushered Talia out, locked the door, and turned her sign to *Closed*.

It was time to start sorting through the rubble of her life to figure out what came next.

Eighteen

By the time she drove out to Lochmara, numbness had settled over Sophie like a thin scrim of fog, and she was grateful. It wouldn't last. In short order, the fragile reprieve would fade, and she'd have to deal with all the pain. She just had to hope they could figure out a plan for moving the contents of the shop that wouldn't impact the upcoming wedding. And that she'd hold it together long enough to execute it.

Letting herself in through the kitchen, Sophie headed back toward the lounge, where Kyla usually worked. A volley of barking preceded a blur of black-and-white, as Dugal came racing to investigate, his skinny whip of a tail whirling like a helicopter. His grumbling bark was a clear invitation to play.

She extended one trembling hand to scruff his ears. "Where's your mum, then?"

"Sophie?" Kyla emerged from the lounge. "What are you..." At the sight of her, she trailed off, her cheeks going pale. "What's wrong?"

Sophie cursed herself for coming here. For worrying her pregnant friend when they were less than a year from Angus's heart attack. "I'm sorry. I didn't know where else to go." The words came out almost as a whisper because her throat had closed up with the tears she hadn't let fall.

Kyla closed the distance between them, her hands curling tight around Sophie's shoulders as she visibly inspected her from head to toe, searching for injury. "What happened?"

I was wrong. You were right. He doesn't love me.

They were the words that wanted to spill out in a flood. But she didn't let them fall. Because this was Kyla. Connor's sister. And though she'd warned Sophie about him in the first place, Sophie had no idea how she'd react to this. Family meant everything to her.

Better to bring up the business mess first. That was the part of this with a ticking time clock attached. The part that affected them both.

"Milligan is evicting me." Saying it aloud released a little of the stranglehold on her throat.

"*What?*" Color flooded back into Kyla's cheeks in the form of temper. "On what grounds?"

"He said my stepmother and I were more trouble than we're worth."

"Huh?"

In a halting voice, Sophie explained what Milligan had said about Lorraine.

"That manipulative harpy! So, not only has she been mistreating you, basically since your father died, she's been taking your hard-earned money for *years* in some sick effort to keep you dependent on her?"

"I don't know, exactly, but something like that. The specifics don't really matter. I have until the end of the week to get out of the shop. Hamish is working on it to see if he can buy me more time, but at this point, I think we have to assume there won't be any latitude. We need a plan so that nothing is derailed for the wedding. I don't know where I'm going to move everything."

"Of course we can find a place for it. There's plenty of room at Ardinmuir—"

"Not the castle." God, she couldn't stomach the idea of running into Connor yet. One devastation at a time.

At her vehemence, Kyla blinked, her brows drawing together in concern. "Okay, then somewhere here at Lochmara." She squeezed Sophie's shoulders. "I'll call Raleigh. Come in and sit down."

She let Kyla herd her into the lounge and dropped onto the sofa. Dugal immediately clamored up into her lap and began bathing her face with puppy kisses. Sophie cuddled the dog, taking the wriggling comfort he offered as Kyla made the call.

"He's going to grab Malcolm. They'll discuss the options and figure out the best place to put things."

Swallowing hard, Sophie jerked a nod. "There's more."

"I thought there might be. Tell me." Slowly, Kyla eased down beside her on the sofa. When she didn't immediately speak, Kyla reached out to lay a hand on her knee. "Do you want me to call Connor?"

Just hearing his name shattered whatever control Sophie had cobbled together. She burst into tears and buried her face against Dugal's fur. The puppy whined and struggled to lick her tears away.

"This isn't just about Milligan and your stepmother, is it?"

Because she couldn't get control enough to speak, Sophie shook her head.

Her voice was quiet and gentle. "Sophie, what happened?"

Rather than try to verbalize the whole thing, Sophie pulled out her phone, opened to the photos, and passed it over. Pictures were worth a thousand words, and she had four.

Kyla frowned down at the screen, brows knit with confusion, then anger, as she swiped from one to the next. "Who sent these to you?"

Knowing she had to say something to make sure her friend's ire was aimed in the right direction, Sophie swallowed hard. "Talia Cowan came into the shop right after Milligan left. She was in

Inverness last week. The same day Connor was. She saw... this. And thought I needed to know."

She braced herself for whatever reaction was coming. This was the moment of truth where she found out whether family trumped friendship.

With great deliberation, Kyla lowered the phone to the coffee table. Then she wrapped her arms around Sophie, dog and all. "Oh, love, I'm so sorry. I never would have thought he'd do something like this."

"Neither did I."

Kyla eased back and offered a box of tissues. "Are you sure this is what it looks like?"

"I don't know how to argue with photographic evidence. He lied to me, Kyla. He said he was going to meet with salvage suppliers. Does she look like she deals in scrap metal to you? If there was some innocent explanation, why wouldn't he have just told me?"

Her lips thinned, and her eyes were a storm of sympathy and fury. "What do you want to do?"

"I can't go back there. I can't face him right now." The very idea of it made Sophie wither inside.

"Done. We'll close ranks. He won't be allowed near you." The absolute unwavering conviction in Kyla's tone had some tiny piece of Sophie relaxing. Because this was the totally in-control best friend she adored.

"Thank you."

"Of course you'll stay here. And I'll go pick up your stuff. Pack a bag for a few days or as much as you want, so you don't have to go over there. And I'll bring Cori."

The relief at not having to go back to Ardinmuir yet almost had the tears cranking up again. "Thanks. I know I'll have to deal with this, and that I'll have to be there for the wedding. But I just... I can't yet."

Heavy footsteps sounded from the hall. Raleigh stepped into the room, trailed by Malcolm.

At the first sight of Sophie, the Texan squared his shoulders. "Whose ass are we kicking?"

Sophie managed a watery laugh.

Kyla met her husband's questioning gaze. "Well, if you can find him, John Milligan. But that's just bonus points. I've got first dibs on my brother."

Raleigh frowned. "Connor? Why?"

Kyla scowled and curled a hand around Sophie's. "Because he broke the wrong heart."

———

After a solid day's work at his forge, Connor was filthy, tired, and happier than he'd been for a while. He'd finished the last of the frame pieces for the greenhouse. Now he just needed the chance to install them. The work had been monotonous and exactly what he'd needed to free his brain up to work on the chandelier design for Gabriella. At this point, he wanted a beer, a shower, and a night to relax with Sophie. The first two were easy. The last... well, she was in workaholic mode for this wedding. Getting her to slow down would be a challenge. One he was definitely up for.

He snagged a beer from the fridge and headed upstairs. Twisting the top off the bottle, he took a long pull. He'd clean up, then track her down to see if she'd actually remembered to eat. That went for all of them, though he knew Sophie and Ciara were keeping a pretty close eye on Kyla to make sure she didn't overtax herself. If they were all still working, he could sort out dinner.

Opening the door to his room, he stepped inside and turned on the light.

"Stop."

Connor jolted so hard his beer foamed over the lip of the bottle. "Holy shite, Kyla. What the hell are you doing here, just sitting in the dark?"

"Waiting for you, you selfish, two-timing arsehole."

"What the fuck are you on about?"

Kyla shoved off the bed. His sister had a temper that was rarely roused, but it was clearly at a full rolling boil as she stalked forward. "I am talking about the woman that you met in Inverness for an afternoon shag before coming home to *my best friend.*"

His brain short-circuited. She couldn't mean what she was saying.

"I watched you sleep around for years while you were technically promised to Afton, and I never said a word because that was your right. The two of you weren't formally together, and she seemed fine with it. I didn't give a damn where you sowed your oats because it was never at home. But the moment you got involved with my best friend, that was the moment all that changed. You lost the right to bounce from bed to bed, woman to woman. How *dare* you?"

Righteous indignation stirred to life. "What the fuck are you talking about? I didnae cheat on Sophie!"

Stabbing at her phone, she opened something, then flung it at him.

Connor nearly bobbled both it and his beer. Turning the phone up, he saw a photo of the moment Gabriella had kissed him.

Fuck. Fucking fuckety fuck.

His brain had fully caught up to the situation now, and there was no other word for it. Even though he'd felt weird about it, he'd made the choice not to tell Sophie who he was going to meet with that day. And then Gabriella had been... well, Gabriella, and apparently someone who knew him had been around to take pictures and report back. He knew what it looked like. There was nothing in the shot to indicate he'd immediately pushed her away and set her straight. He swiped over to see that there were more pictures. It wasn't clear from any of them that this was a business meeting. The truth wasn't in these photos.

"Where did you get these?"

"From Sophie," she growled.

Connor's head whipped up. "Someone sent these to her?" But he already had confirmation in his sister's behavior. Panic skittered through him. What she must think after seeing these... He turned to the door. "I have to see her. I have to tell her what actually happened."

Kyla's voice snapped out. "No. You will not be getting near her. You're going to explain to *me*, right now, what the fuck this was. And then I'll consider maybe allowing you to get within fifty feet of her."

He wanted to ignore her. To run out this door and straight to Sophie. She'd likely be at Lochmara. But if Kyla was banning access, she wouldn't hesitate to use her husband, Malcolm, Charlotte, and anyone else she considered hers. And if they all thought this bullshit was true...

No. His sister was the dragon playing gatekeeper, and he was going to have to convince her of the truth before he'd get the chance to grovel and beg for Sophie's forgiveness.

"It wasnae what it looked like."

"Then what was it?"

"I was meeting her for a commission."

"Really? A commission for what?" Though Kyla's sneer made it obvious enough what she was imagining.

He scowled at her. "Gabriella and I used to have a history."

"Of course you did."

"Do you want to hear this or no'?"

She folded her arms and waited.

"We used to have a history. Not for years. When she contacted me about a custom blacksmithing job, it was right after Sophie ran into Blair Pearson at the engagement party."

"What are you talking about?"

"She didn't tell you about that?" At the shake of her head, he continued. "At the risk of digging my hole even deeper, one of my former flings was a guest at the engagement party a couple of weeks ago. They had a very uncomfortable interaction that upset Sophie, and because of that, I didnae tell her I was meeting Gabriella. I didnae want to upset her further."

"Connor, why the hell did you meet with this woman at all? Why not just turn down the job?"

"Because it was a big fucking commission, and I wanted my chance to actually do something to help sustain this estate!"

Some of the temper faded from her face. "What?"

Tunneling a hand through his hair, he began to pace. "Everything fell to you after Mom and Dad died. I figured I was already giving everything I had to give by agreeing to the marriage pact, and I just let you bear the burden of everything else. I had no idea what that meant until I got 'hold of the books last year."

Finally, his sister looked vaguely uncomfortable. "I mean... I didn't tell you."

"I should have pushed. I should have known there was more going on. And now that I do, I just want to do my part. I can help beyond just managing the estate, beyond renovating the cottages. This is a fifteen thousand pound job."

"That much?"

"Aye. That's why I met with her. That's why I agreed. When I saw her, I was just trying to kiss her cheek, as an old friend, but she turned her head. I put a stop to it at once, but you canna see that here. It was her choice where we met for lunch."

"You went to her house, Connor."

He set the beer aside. He no longer had a taste for it. "Aye. I had to measure the space for the chandelier she's having me design. I had to get into the attic and look at the existing supports to figure out what sort of additional structure will need to be added to accommodate the weight of what I'm putting up."

Her shoulders slowly dropped.

"Look, I ken this looks bad. I know that, with my history, neither of you has any reason to believe me. But Kyla, if you've ever trusted anything I have ever told you, trust that I didnae do this. I wouldnae do this. I love her."

With a long sigh, Kyla sank back down on the bed. "I believe you. But I don't know if she will. She got confronted with this at work, Connor, after arguably one of the worst days ever."

"Why? What else happened?"

She waved that away. "None of your concern right now. We're dealing with it."

Connor stalked forward, his hands curling into fists. "What's happened to Sophie?"

"Some shite with Milligan. We're taking care of it. Hamish is on it."

Swearing, he paced back toward the door. "I have to see her. I have to explain. If that bawbag is pulling shite, the last thing she needs is to believe I cheated on her."

"You may not have cheated, Connor, but you did lie. That's the thing she stuck on. You lied to her. You made the decision not to tell her that day before you went. You've had five days since then to come clean about the job, and you didn't do it. Because you wanted to avoid the hard conversation. Just like you wanted to avoid the hard conversation with Swayze that got you into this whole relationship in the first place."

The truth of it struck him like a blow. He'd told himself he'd done it to spare hurt feelings. And that was partly true. But it was just as much about avoiding confrontation. About getting to stay the nice guy.

"Well, I dinna want to avoid it now. I want to have the hard conversation. I want to explain to her what happened."

"She's not ready to see you yet."

"Then you explain."

"I could, but I don't think it needs to come from me."

"Then what the fuck am I supposed to do?"

"I think you're going to have to be patient. Give her a little time to cool down."

A little time to cool down would be plenty of time to convince herself of the truth of all of this and that a relationship with him wasn't worth the stress.

"The longer she sits with this, the harder it's going to be to come back from it. Please, Kyla. I'm begging you. Talk her into giving me five minutes to explain."

"I'll try. But if she says she wants time and space, you're going to give it to her. You'll do this on her schedule."

Though he hated it, he didn't see that he had a choice. "Okay." After another moment's hesitation, he looked at his sister. "Are we okay?"

"Yeah. We should have a more in-depth conversation about the estate and our assorted contributions to it. I think we need to clear the air. But later." Kyla stood. "I've packed her a bag. She'll be staying with me for a bit."

Of course she was. Because she thought he'd betrayed her.

Swallowing down the bile that rose at the thought, Connor moved toward the door. "I'll help you with the demon cat."

Nineteen

Kyla: **She's just not ready yet.**

Connor stared at the message, absorbing the knowledge that he'd have to wait. Despite his sister's warnings, he'd tried calling and texting Sophie himself, but he'd received no response. All that told him how deeply hurt she really was.

He considered driving over to Lochmara and camping out until she gave in. Or possibly forcing his way into the house to tell her the story, whether she was ready or not. But he suspected his brother-in-law wouldn't take kindly to that. As Raleigh and Malcolm outweighed him collectively by a damned lot, he didn't really want to do anything to rile them. It seemed he really would have to wait.

As sleep sure as hell wasn't happening, he did the only thing he could: Threw himself into finishing the greenhouse. It had been his labor of love for years. If anything might convince Sophie of how he truly felt about her, it would be this.

He hauled out halogen work lights and a generator, along with the welding equipment necessary to finish rebuilding the final wall. Temperatures weren't ideal, but there were ways to ensure a solid weld, even in the cold. He'd manage. The greenhouse was far enough from the castle proper and all the cottages that the rumble of the generator shouldn't be noticed. Then he retrieved the last of the supports he'd forged and got to work.

Hours passed. Night bled into dawn, but he barely noticed other than to shed the coat he'd worn against the cold. His world had narrowed down to the torch, the frame, and an endless cycle of self-recrimination.

But this was the final piece of the north wall. The last thing needed for completion, other than new glass. It felt strange to be this close to the end of a project that had consumed him for so many years. There'd been a part of him that hadn't really thought he'd manage it. But here it was... one step from done. He'd long ago cleared the interior of the choking flora that had taken it over. There were still dead leaves and other detritus that had drifted in through the missing panes with the change of seasons. But it was nearly ready to be pressed into service again.

Would she want that?

Would she unbend enough to even consider it?

Better not to think that far ahead. Just take the next step. Finish the job.

Flipping down his face shield, Connor set the brace in place.

"Holy crap!"

The accent gave Swayze away. Behind his mask, Connor closed his eyes. He didn't want company. But she'd been given free run of the estate the whole time she'd been here. He was a little surprised she hadn't stumbled upon the greenhouse sooner.

"What is this place?"

Knowing he'd have to engage, he shoved the shield back up. "It's a Victorian era greenhouse. The MacKean at the time— James—made a lot of money in shipping. He was the one who expanded the castle to what you see today. He had this place built for his daughter, Persephone, who was reputed to have loved green, growing things."

"Did she actually or was that something that just got attributed to her because of her name?"

"I dinna ken for sure. It might have been a self-fulfilling prophecy."

Swayze stepped through the open doors and into the greenhouse, tipping her head back to take in the patterned designs around the edges of the frame. "You're restoring it."

"Aye. This is actually why I got into blacksmithing in the first place. Because paying someone would be an enormous expenditure we simply canna afford."

Her hazel eyes slid to him. "You did this for Sophie."

Though his shoulders wanted to bunch, he kept them level. "Aye."

That mega-watt smile spread wide. "Oh, that's awesome!" The grin dimmed as she continued to study him. "Why don't you seem more pleased about that?"

"I dinna know if she'll accept it."

Sucking in a breath, she nodded. "I wondered if something had happened."

"She hasnae said anything?"

"I haven't actually seen her. Which I found kind of odd, considering Alyssa is arriving tomorrow. But everything is well in hand for the wedding, so I had no reason to push. She hasn't responded to my texts, so I just assumed she was busy." Picking her way over to one of the stone benches, she brushed off the debris and sat. "What happened?"

He didn't have to tell her. He didn't owe her an explanation. But he found himself opening his mouth, anyway. "I fucked up. But not in the way she thinks."

"Well, that's gonna take some explanation."

"I'm dying to give it to her, but right now, she's no' speaking to me."

Swayze crossed her arms. "I think you're gonna have to explain to me in more detail."

Connor thought of what Kyla had said about his avoidance of difficult conversations. All of this had started because he'd avoided one with this woman. Maybe he did owe her something after all.

"We're no' engaged."

"You broke up? That's terrible!"

His laugh was bitter. "No, we were never engaged at all."

"What?"

He explained how everything had gone down in Edinburgh. How he hadn't wanted to hurt her feelings and had blurted out about the engagement. "Then, when you showed up as a client here, I panicked. Sophie rolled with it. And after Alyssa and Ryan elected to use Ardinmuir for the wedding, and you were going to be around for two months, we panicked again and decided to stick with the fake engagement." He hesitated, then admitted the rest. "I might have implied you could cause problems for them if we didnae to sort of nudge her into it."

"Wow. That's... incredibly insulting. But overlooking all that for the moment, I'll concede to appreciating your attempt to spare my feelings. It wasn't necessary. Because I'm a big girl who can handle rejection. I'm even choosing to overlook the fact that you totally threw me under the bus to manipulate your way into a relationship with Sophie. Because no matter how you got there, the truth is, you two are in love with each other. That was very, *very* obvious over the past couple of months. You didn't fake that."

"It turned real," he murmured.

That she'd seen it—more, that she didn't question it—gave him hope that maybe what he and Sophie had could survive this.

"So what actually happened?"

"You and Blair Pearson are not the only women from my past who've crossed Sophie's path, as it were." He told her about Gabriella and the photos that had made their way to Sophie. How it looked, despite what was actually going on.

"Oh, damn, Connor. That's bad."

"I know it. It's a simple explanation. I just want the chance to give it to her. But she's no' ready to see me, and I'm afraid the longer she sits with this untruth, the more likely she is to just cut me loose entirely. Because even though it's no' truth, even if she elects to believe me, she's had too much time of feeling like it is true. And that kind of thing leaves permanent damage."

"So, what's your plan?"

He looked around the greenhouse. At all the work he'd done to bring this place back to life. "I dinna have one, exactly. I canna do anything unless she'll talk to me. Kyla tried, but she's no' willing to push."

"Well, then I think you need a little southern girl subterfuge. I'll help you."

Connor frowned at her. "You will?"

"I will."

"Why?"

"Because I've come to think of Sophie as a friend. I'd like to think that you and I are friends. And I know, without a doubt after two months of watching the two of you, regardless of how you got together in the first place, you're meant to be. And I've got enough inherent romanticism to want to help you fix it. So, here's what we're gonna do."

———

Sophie had made a post on the village social media page saying that the shop was temporarily closed due to relocation and stating that she'd notify everyone when she was back up and running, along with a link to sign up for her newsletter. She hadn't checked her email or the comments on that post because she knew there'd be lots of commentary and questions about what had happened, and she wasn't prepared to deal with any of that. She could only focus on one thing at a time. That one thing had necessarily been dealing with the move.

As of last night, Village Blume had been entirely cleared out. Raleigh, Malcolm, and Ewan had done the bulk of the heavy lifting, moving her coolers, worktables, tools, existing stock, and other supplies to a section of the big stone stable at Lochmara. It wasn't ideal or permanent, but there was power for her coolers and space to work so that the preparations for Alyssa and Ryan's wedding could still take place.

Given the bride was arriving today, Sophie's focus had to remain there. At least, that was what she'd been telling herself the whole way over to Ardinmuir and throughout the initial part of this meeting with Swayze to go over last-minute details. She'd been dreading coming here. She still hadn't spoken to Connor. Kyla had confronted him and reported back that whatever had happened wasn't what it looked like. She'd encouraged Sophie to speak to him. Sophie knew she had to at some point, but she just wasn't ready yet. Regardless of what the whole situation was actually about, it didn't erase the fact that he'd lied to her. She was so tired of lies. The ones she'd been told and the ones she'd been party to maintaining. After everything that had happened, she didn't have the bandwidth to parse out whether whatever he told her was the truth.

"Okay, come on."

Sophie blinked Swayze's face back into focus. "What?"

"We're going for a little walk. It'll help clear the cobwebs from your head. Up." Without giving her a chance to protest, Swayze linked an arm through hers and tugged.

Reluctantly, Sophie stood, thinking how very much she truly liked this woman. She wasn't at all how Sophie had imagined, and over the past couple of months, she truly had tried to be a friend. Sophie wondered what would have happened if she'd really let her.

They gathered their coats and stepped outside, following one of the many paths that led into the forest around the castle.

"Okay, what's wrong?" Swayze demanded. "I get you may not want to talk about it at all, but as an uninvolved third party, who doesn't live here and won't be here for that much longer, I'm available for you to dump on, should you wish." When Sophie said nothing, she continued. "Look, I know something is going on, because you haven't been around the castle, and that's just not normal."

Looking into her earnest face, Sophie considered. Maybe it would be easier to talk to Swayze about Connor than Kyla. He wasn't *her* brother, and she didn't have any reason to be anything other than more or less objective.

"Connor and I broke up."

No exclamations. Just acceptance. "Why?"

She thought of the photo. The other woman. No matter what that looked like, Kyla had said it was something else. Sophie couldn't fathom what, but she didn't know for sure that he'd cheated. So instead she said, "It wasn't real."

"What wasn't?"

"Us. The whole thing was fake."

When Swayze just arched a perfectly plucked brow, Sophie let it all spill out. The whole fake engagement they'd put on for her benefit. It felt good to give voice to all of it because she hated lying. Hated the deception she'd been putting on with Connor for the past two months. Getting it out was cleansing, in a way.

At the end of it, Swayze just tucked her tongue in cheek. "Well, I suppose props to him for committing to the story. Though I'm rather insulted either of you thought I'd be the kind of person who'd have such a hissy fit over rejection."

"Some people would have. And, in my defense, I didn't know you then."

"Fair enough. But you know what I know now? That you and Connor MacKean are in love with each other. That wasn't fake. Maybe how you got into it was, but the feelings are real."

"I don't think they are for him."

"Why?"

Because it was easier than trying to explain herself, Sophie pulled out her phone, opened to the offending picture of him kissing the other woman.

Swayze studied it, then used her fingers to zoom in. "Look at his body language here. He's angled like he was bending past her. Her head is turned toward him. His isn't turned toward hers. And his shoulders are bowed a little forward, like he was jerking back."

Sophie frowned at the image. Was she right? At this point, Sophie couldn't tell. She'd stared at this photo until she was sick.

She swiped over to the other damning shot of him following this woman into the house.

"There's no evidence of what happened in that house. Going into it isn't a crime. Hell, for all you know, he stopped to use the bathroom before he got back on the road." At Sophie's bland stare, Swayze waved a hand. "Okay, probably not that. But going inside doesn't mean he slept with her."

"Why are you defending him?"

"First, because going to someone's home was not his M.O. All those years before, he kept things casual and easy. Hotels. B and Bs. Because he deliberately chose people who didn't have connections locally." She pointed to herself. "Case in point. And second, I'm telling you all this because I believe he loves you. Because everything I've observed over the past couple of months tells me so. Because, in the heat of the moment, when he didn't want to offend me, *you* are the name he pulled out of thin air. And I think you owe it to both of you to give him the chance to explain."

She stopped at the head of another path and made an after-you gesture.

And there was Connor, standing twenty feet away, hands shoved into the pockets of his coat. It was the first time Sophie had seen him in person since this whole mess had started and it hurt. She wanted to go to him. To be wrapped up in those familiar, strong arms, because he represented comfort for her. But he was also a source of such pain right now.

It was obvious at a glance that he was in pain, too. Misery and upset painted his features. He didn't look as if he'd slept in days. The scruff of his jaw was thicker, and shadows bruised those bright blue eyes.

Sophie looked back to Swayze. "You shanghaied me?"

Swayze only shrugged. "Sorry, not sorry. You two need to talk." With a quick wave to Connor, she disappeared back down the trail.

The forest seemed too quiet around them.

"Will you walk with me? Please, just give me a chance to explain."

Sophie figured she owed him that, and for all that she'd been avoiding it, she wanted to get this over with. "Okay."

He waited for her to reach him, then fell into step beside her.

"I went to Inverness to meet with someone about a prospective commission. And I didnae tell you because it's for somebody that I used to be involved with. After what happened with Blair, I didnae want to upset you."

It was a pattern with him. Trying to avoid upsetting women. But that didn't explain everything.

"Do you kiss all your prospective clients?" She knew it was petty, but she couldn't quite hold it back.

"No. And I didnae kiss her. She kissed me. Which I cut off immediately, explaining to her about you. She apologized, and we had our meeting over lunch. After which, I went to her home to take measurements of the room she wants me to design a custom chandelier for."

Here was the rational explanation she'd wanted. Something simple. Plausible. And she had to decide if she believed him. Because everyone said that he was a playboy with a short attention span. That he could never be faithful. She was the one who'd seen something different. Did she trust herself more than everyone else?

"I ken you dinna have any reason to believe any of this, given my reputation. The truth is, I've loved you for a long time. And I ken you have no reason to believe me about that either. But maybe this will help convince you."

Before she could process his declaration, they stepped out into a clearing, and Sophie gasped.

She hadn't been paying attention to where they were. Hadn't realized where they'd been going. It had been more than fifteen years since she'd seen the greenhouse. Then it had been a crumbling wreck, a victim of time and rust, with cracked or missing panes of glass and a veritable jungle of overgrown flora. Connor and Kyla's parents had banned them all out of fear for their safety.

This greenhouse had been rescued from ruin, restored to its former glory, with all the Neoclassical and Victorian detail remade like new. The interior had been cleared out. Fresh glass had been installed. Not everywhere, but enough to give the impression of what it would look like fully complete. It was beautiful and awe-inspiring. She understood in a moment that Connor had done this. She recognized his hand in some of the style. She understood, too, that this wasn't an apology because it had to have taken so much time and effort.

"This is why I got into blacksmithing to start. Because I wanted to restore it for you. Not only because you always loved it, but because I thought you could use it for your business. It's been a labor of years. A labor of love. For you."

Sophie's heart squeezed as he turned to face her again.

"I'm sorry I didnae tell you. I'm sorry I didnae trust you to be okay with the truth. I'm sorry about anything that I've ever done to hurt you. But please, please, give me another chance. I swear I can do better."

She'd been right. All along, she'd been right. She was the one who'd seen the truth of him, flaws and all, in a way others hadn't. She knew the real man. Loved the real man. And that man would never betray her.

Tears spilled over again, a blend of relief and grief. "I couldn't believe it. I knew, deep down, that you could never do something like that. But I couldn't find another explanation, and I wasn't ready to find out that everything I believed about you was absolutely wrong. I'm so sorry I doubted you. I'm sorry I didn't let you talk to me sooner. I'd just gotten evicted from the shop—"

"You *what?*"

"—and I found out that Milligan and Lorraine were colluding together, and it's just been a really shitty couple of days."

"Colluding how?"

She gave him the overview.

His hands balled into fists, and temper hardened his eyes. "That wanker. He'll not get away with this. I'll—"

Because she could tell he was spoiling for a fight and liable to go off half-cocked, she laid a hand on his arm. "No. Stop. Hamish is handling it. We've already moved all my stuff out. I need to find a new shop location, anyway, so I'll be done with Milligan and better for it. The only thing I need from you is the thing I've been taking for granted." Closing the distance between them, she framed his face, relishing the roughness of his stubble against her palms and the way his arms came instantly around her.

"What's that?"

"I just need you to love me, as I love you."

"I do. God, I do. Always." He pressed his brow to hers. "Say it again."

"I love you, Connor."

She kissed him then, hauling him close and pouring out all her relief and feeling his answering joy in return. The world that had tipped so far off its axis was finally back to rights. She might have gone on kissing him for hours, but the phone in her coat pocket began to vibrate.

"Do you need to get that?" he gasped.

"I probably should."

Sophie pulled back, only far enough to grab the phone. It was Swayze.

"Hello?"

"Hey, I'm really sorry to interrupt what I hope was heading toward incredible makeup sex, but Alyssa's here early and excited, and I can only put her off so long."

Sophie choked out a laugh. "I'll be along shortly."

"Great."

"And Swayze?"

"Yeah?"

She looked up at Connor and smiled. "Thanks."

"You can toast me at your wedding."

TWENTY

The bridal party had fully arrived and had taken over the private room in The Stag's Head for an informal getting-the-band-back-together sort of dinner before the commencement of all the formal wedding activities tomorrow night. If Connor had gotten his way, he'd have kept Sophie in and spoiled her with a bubble bath, a rom com, and all her favorite movie snacks, before taking her to bed for an early night. After everything that had happened, she was exhausted. But his woman was a consummate professional. So was his sister. The pair of them had elected to have their semi-down time at the pub, to be on hand "just in case." In case of what, Connor had no idea, but they were taking no chances that anything would go awry with this wedding.

He'd been a little surprised Sophie had so readily agreed. Tonight was the first time she'd been out in public since her eviction from Village Blume—news that had gotten out, despite her efforts to keep it on the down low—and villagers had been stopping by in a steady trickle to ask after her.

"When will the shop be open again?"

Sophie smiled at Flora McGowan. "I'm not sure just yet. I'm still looking for a new space. But I'm not closed entirely. You can still make online orders from my website and have something delivered or picked up. And if you sign up for my newsletter, you'll be first to find out when a plan is in place."

"I'll do that."

As the pub door opened, they all compulsively glanced in that direction. John Milligan stepped inside, his face set in furious lines. Connor went on alert. Beside him, Sophie stiffened. And though he didn't look, he knew Hamish and Raleigh were both ready to intercede if necessary. Everyone in the pub was watching.

Flora sniffed and muttered an insult that had Connor arching a brow in surprise. He'd never heard such language come out of the mouth of a granny before. She patted Sophie's hand. "Best of luck to you, dearie."

Tucked as they were at their usual table in a little alcove to the left of the bar, Milligan hadn't seen them yet. He stalked up to the bar and ordered a pint. Without a word, Ewan filled the glass. A few keystrokes on the register, and the total was displayed. Milligan fished out his wallet and offered a credit card.

Ewan swiped it, waiting a few moments before lifting cold eyes. "Declined."

Milligan's face reddened. "Try it again."

He did, to the same result. Milligan pulled out another. Again, declined.

"Do you have cash?"

Evidently not, because the older man swore and turned on his heel. Only then did he seem to realize he was the center of everyone's attention. His ruddy face deepened to more of a purple, and he hurried away.

Almost as soon as the door closed behind him, Toby Byrne, the village mechanic, sidled up. "Bad luck, that. He's been having a streak of it."

"Oh?" Ewan prompted.

"Aye. He asked for a tow today. It was the damnedest thing. His whole bloody engine had disappeared. Like it was beamed up by little green men. He wasnae pleased when I told him it'll take some time to find a replacement. There are the issues with the insurance, and the fact that my preferred supplier has that model on back order."

Laura propped her tray against her generous hip. "Can't you use a different supplier?"

"Aye, I could. But that this one has it on back order makes them my favorite." He winked at Sophie.

Theo Gordon scooted over from the far side of the pub, where he'd been watching a football match. "Milligan's having a whole streak of bad luck. Did you hear a tree fell on his house?"

"Really?" Kyla asked. "We haven't had any storms this week."

"I know. It's the damnedest thing. That big bastard of an oak tree in his yard keeled right on over. And wouldn't you know? There's no' a contractor in the area who can get to him for a solid six months."

Hamish lifted his whisky and sipped. "He's having a bad run of it. The village council has been taking a deeper look at all his properties. They were all out of compliance with code, and interviews with various tenants make it clear that they have been for a verra long time. He's getting slapped with fines going back for years. That'll cost him a pretty penny."

Connor exchanged a look with all of them, allowing just a hint of satisfaction to curl his mouth. They all nodded.

Toby tapped the bar. "Take that beer off your hands, Ewan?"

"On the house."

"Much obliged." He took the glass and strode away.

Theo lifted his beer in a silent toast and went back to watching his match.

Sophie's gaze raked over their table, up to Ewan, and finally settled on Connor. "What did you do?"

He popped a chip into his mouth. "Let's just say I filed a complaint with karma."

She didn't need to know that "karma" was what he'd titled the group text he'd used to call together everyone he knew for a meeting about the dispensation of a little necessary justice.

Turned out Ewan's special forces training was exceptionally handy at keeping them from getting caught.

Sophie was staring at him in a way that told him she didn't believe a word of it. She knew he'd had something to do with all of it, and Connor wasn't entirely sure how she'd feel about it. He understood she valued her independence and prided herself on being able to take care of things on her own.

"You know what? I'm not going to ask." She lifted her glass. "To karma. It couldn't have happened to a bigger arsehole."

The entire pub answered her toast. "To karma!"

The door opened again, and Talia Cowan stepped inside. Connor had been dreading this. But he had things to say to his former classmate, and in keeping with his new policy of not avoiding the hard conversations, he rose. "I'll be right back."

She flushed as he intercepted her halfway to the dart boards. "C... Connor."

Wanting to put her at ease, he lifted both hands. "No. I'm no' here to confront you or tell you off. I just wanted to thank you."

Talia blinked, her big brown eyes confused. "Thank me?"

"The situation you happened upon wasnae what you thought. I love Sophie, and I'd never be unfaithful to her. Something I immediately told my companion that day to set her straight. We had history, and she wasnae aware I was in a relationship."

She winced. "Oh God. I'm sorry. I saw you, and I thought—"

"You drew a logical conclusion based on my past behavior. You weren't the only one. Anyway, Sophie and I have talked about it, and we're okay. But I appreciate the fact that you respect her enough that you'd tell her something improper was happening in order to protect her. A lot of people would have looked the other way."

"If it was me, I'd want to be told."

"Understandably. I also wanted to thank you for not turning around and spreading the story to others. Beyond the fact that it wasnae true, it would have hurt and embarrassed

Sophie. And me. You didnae have to stay quiet, but I'm grateful you did."

"I didnae want to trash anyone's reputation. I just didnae want her taken advantage of. I'm glad I was mistaken. You always seemed like a nice lad in school. I didnae want to be wrong about you."

Connor quirked a smile. "Are we good?"

"We're good. And Connor?"

"Aye?"

"I'm glad for you and Sophie."

"So am I."

Sophie was watching him when he came back to the table. He could see the exhaustion weighing on her, along with a simmering warmth in her eyes that he recognized as pride. Damn if that didn't make him feel fantastic. And that made him want to make *her* feel fantastic.

It must've showed in his face, because she pushed back from the table before he could sit again. "It's been a very long week, and will be an even longer weekend before it's through. I'm calling it."

Connor held her coat. She slipped into it, continuing the momentum to curl around him in a hug. "Let's go home."

Home.

His fingers reflexively dug into her hips as that soaked into him. Before, it had always been "the castle" or "Ardinmuir". This was the first time she'd called it what he'd wanted to be for her.

Oh yeah, things were definitely finally right in his world.

The courtly sweep of his arm toward the door was exaggerated and goofy as hell. "After you, milady. Your chariot awaits."

But her smile, as she put her hand into his, was everything.

———

Alyssa and Ryan's wedding was tomorrow, so it was all hands on deck for everyone at Ardinmuir Event Planning, all the way down to the part-timers and volunteers who were helping out of the goodness of their hearts and bribes of Angus's sweets. While Kyla, Ciara, and the rest of their crew were already on-hand at the estate handling final details for the rehearsal and rehearsal dinner festivities happening later that night, Sophie was ensconced at Lochmara, finishing final bouquets and preparing to transfer arrangements to the van for transport over to Ardinmuir—a process that would've gone far quicker and smoother had it been someone other than Connor who'd volunteered to drive.

He kept invading her space, boxing her in against worktables to take a long, lingering nibble of her neck or brush his fingers along the back of her hand. It was distracting and arousing, and brought back last night with far too much clarity and longing. But she didn't tell him to stop.

Her fingers fumbled with the ribbon she was trying to tie into a proper bow, because his whole body was pressed warm against her back, and his big broad palm had settled low on her belly. The weight of it was giving her ideas she absolutely did not have time to give into.

"Connor, love, I appreciate you volunteering to be delivery boy, but your help is not currently helping."

He nipped at the juncture of her neck and shoulders. "Just giving you some suggestions for how my fee could be paid."

"In kisses?" she suggested.

"Mmm, I do love those. But I'm no' sure it'll cover all the tax."

His hand slid an inch lower, and she sucked in a breath. She was seconds away from saying damn it all and letting him have exactly what he wanted, no matter who might walk into this barn, but the sound of tires on gravel saved her.

Reluctantly, Connor stepped back, promptly picking up a nearby arrangement to hide the evidence of his advances. "To be continued."

"Why don't you take that to the van and take a minute?"

"Aye. Right." He dutifully marched out.

She heard him greet the newcomer and point them in her

direction, so she had time to brush her hair back into place and compose herself.

"Good day to you, lass."

"Mr. Fraser! What a pleasant surprise."

"I apologize for showing up unannounced, but I didnae quite understand the online ordering thing, and I was hoping I might be able to stop by and pick something up. Just something simple. I ken you're in the middle of a big to-do up at the castle."

Sweet, steady man. He wasn't gonna let a little thing like her shop being closed stop him from getting Hettie her weekly flowers.

"Absolutely. Of course. If you'll wait just a few minutes, I can pull something together for you."

She was poking around in her cooler, grabbing blooms and greenery, when Connor returned.

"Flowers for the missus?"

"Aye. Every week for the past sixty-three years. It's part of how I wooed her to begin with. I'm no' about to stop the thing that worked!"

Connor nodded. "Sensible. Consistency is key."

Sophie brought the components to her worktable and began to trim stems. "How did the visit with your grandson and his wife and great-grandson go?"

"Oh, it was grand. We got confirmation that Fiona is expecting another bairn."

"That's wonderful!"

"We're verra excited. The pair of them loved their flowers. Fiona took hers home when she and Rabbie left on Sunday."

"Oh, is Andrew still here?"

William took off his cap and used the bill to scratch at his thinning white hair. "Oh, aye. He extended his trip because he ended up having some business in the area."

"What does he do? I don't think I've ever asked."

"He's actually an investigator for the government. Looks into claims of benefits fraud and the like. He's building quite a case against Lorraine Cameron."

Sophie's hands fumbled again. "My stepmother?"

William grunted in confirmation. "Turns out she's in a lot of trouble."

Wide-eyed, Sophie looked at Connor, thinking this was somehow his doing, but he shook his head slightly before turning avid attention to William.

"What are the penalties for benefits fraud?"

"Fines certainly. And up to five years in prison. And she'll be expected to pay back everything she essentially stole." William folded his arms and grinned. "Couldnae have happened to a more unpleasant woman."

Sophie stared at him for a long moment before finally breaking her paralysis to offer the bouquet.

"This is lovely, lass."

When he started to reach for his wallet, she clasped his hand. "No. No, this is on the house."

"Thank you." With a wink and a lift of the flowers, he said, "I'll see you next week, lass."

They stayed silent until a car engine cranked up.

"Do you think he told his grandson to investigate my stepmother?"

Connor pulled her into his arms, lacing his hands at the small of her back. "I think you are a kind and wonderful person, and that everyone around you kens that has taken it upon themselves to make some... readjustments to the alignment of the universe. So that the people who dinna appreciate that essentially get what's coming to them."

She'd spent so long feeling alone, determined to handle everything by herself. That so many people would act on her behalf left her feeling humbled and warm. She snuggled into Connor. "I'm not sure how I feel about the idea of her doing time."

"Well, if she does, she does. She's the one who committed fraud. I certainly willnae shed a tear over it. You shouldn't either."

"No. I'm done shedding tears."

For a long moment, in the comfort of his embrace, she absorbed the fact that everyone who'd wronged her was finally having to pay for being terrible. Not just because of how they'd treated her, but how they'd treated others. There was a balance to that she couldn't help but appreciate, no matter how it came about.

Linking her arms around his neck, she looked into Connor's beloved face. "I don't quite know what to do now."

"Oh, I ken the end of this fairy tale."

"What's that?"

"You and I, my lovely Cinderella, are meant to live happily ever after."

Full of joy, she beamed up at him. "I can work with that."

Epilogue

"This baby is never coming. She's never giving me my body back. I'm going to be pregnant until the end of time. Why did I think this was a good idea?" Connor's very pregnant, very under-slept, very grumpy sister glared down at her belly.

Raleigh promptly leapt up from the table and began rubbing Kyla's shoulders. "You know Angus totally made a deal with her in the womb not to come before he was home from filming."

Much to Angus's surprise—and to no one else's—he'd made it through all the endless rounds of auditions to be part of this season's lineup of competitors. He'd left at the start of May for filming.

"*I* didn't agree to that." When her belly bulged with a sudden kick, Kyla poked back at it. "You're grounded as soon as you come out, young lady."

The belly bulged again.

Raleigh laughed. "I think she's gonna be stubborn like her mama."

"Gets it honest, going back many generations," Connor added. Even from in utero, it was clear his niece was going to be a ball-buster. He couldn't wait.

Beside him, Sophie dipped a chunk of naan into the last dregs of her curry. "It is weirdly quiet around here with Angus in Berkshire. I'm used to having him and Munro around."

"But, I mean, the longer he's gone, the further he's advanced in the competition, right?" Gavin asked. "Next week should be the quarter final, aye?"

Ciara sighed. "I can't believe we have to wait so long for the season to actually air."

"No matter how far he gets, we're having the biggest party ever when he gets home to celebrate." When Malcolm winced, Charlotte pointed at him. "And you're even going to attend for half an hour before you find a cave to hide in."

"Yes'm."

Ciara glanced at her phone. "Not to change the subject, but have any of you heard from Ewan?"

"Should we have?" Connor checked his own phone, though he hadn't noticed any text notifications. "I thought he was still at that two-week remote hill-walking thing with his mates from his old unit."

"He is. But that whole area is under severe storm warnings. It's going to get really nasty."

"If anyone's going to be fine in that sort of weather, it's Ewan," Kyla assured her. "Anything happens, he certainly knows how to handle himself. As do the rest of his team. I'm sure they saw far worse when they were deployed."

Raleigh and Charlotte exchanged a look, and she began to gather up dishes, the silent signal the evening was drawing to a close.

"I'm gonna get you home, so you can put your feet up."

Kyla linked her hand with his over her shoulder and tipped her head back to look up at him. "With ice cream?"

"Absolutely."

In less than twenty minutes, the dishes had been cleared, the dishwasher loaded, and all their guests departed. There were still pots and pans to wash, but when Sophie moved toward the sink,

Connor snagged her hand. "Let them soak. Let's go take a walk. We've time yet before the rain rolls in, and it's a fine night."

Hand in hand, they strolled out the kitchen door and around to the formal gardens. They still had a long way to go, but since Sophie had taken up permanent residence at the castle, she'd been working her way through reclaiming them. She'd also fully embraced her new greenhouse. The last of the glass had been installed. He'd built her custom tables, and she'd already filled the space with plants.

In anticipation of tonight, he'd filled it with more, kitting the whole place out for romance. Given that everyone had departed, there was no reason to think they'd be interrupted, so he was finally giving them both the fantasy he'd dreamed up so long ago. As they wound their way from the formal gardens into the woods, they talked easily of anything and everything. When they neared the greenhouse, he hit the button on the remote in his pocket and watched the lights come on. Given how late the sun set in summer, it wasn't flashy, but she saw it for the ambiance it was.

Slanting a glance at him through lowered lashes, she grinned. "What are you up to?"

"You'll see."

They stepped inside, and Sophie gasped with delight. In addition to the thousands of fairy lights, he'd raided their event supply closet for yards of gauzy fabric. He'd draped it to artistic effect from the ceiling, so the whole place looked like a fairy bower. A bucket of champagne chilled on one of the potting tables, and in the back of the building was the nest of quilts and pillows he'd made.

She broke away from him, hurrying forward to take it all in with wide, delighted eyes. "Oh! This is wonderful!"

Finally nervous, he waited as she darted around like one of the pollinators in her gardens.

"What's the occasion?"

And as she swung around to face him, he dropped to one knee.

Sophie covered her mouth with her hand. "Oh my God."

"I wanted to do this here, in this place I brought back to life for you. A place you love, and I love because you do." Needing to do something with his empty hands, he folded them over his bended knee. "I've loved you nearly all my life. And I never thought I'd be lucky enough to have the chance to be with you. The past several months have been absolutely the best of my life. And I know that, in a sense, this is really fast, because we've only really been together for six months. But we've known each other all our lives, and I spent way too much time waiting. I dinna want to wait anymore. There's a reason I never asked for my mother's ring back. Everybody outside the family still thinks we're engaged. I want to make it official. Absolutely real for us and everyone else. Will you marry me, Sophie? Make a life with me? Make a family with me? Help fill this castle with all the love and laughter it's been missing?"

Those big, beautiful eyes were teary as she nodded. "Yes. Absolutely yes."

Euphoric, Connor bounded up, closing the distance between them. Taking her hands, he hesitated. "This feels a little weird since I already put the ring on your finger. Like we're missing a step or something."

She looped her arms around his neck, her smile brighter than all the fairy lights. "Oh, given this setup, I think you were jumping right on ahead to the celebration portion of the program. Which I fully support, by the way."

Her giggle echoed off the glass as he swept her off her feet. "And that, my dearest Sophie, is only one of the reasons you're the perfect woman for me."

Then he bore them both down to the nest of blankets to prove all the rest.

————

Wind and rain lashed Ewan McBride's 4x4 as he navigated the lonely Highland road, punctuating his efforts with a steady stream of curses. His two-week long, deep trek into the remote wilderness had been cut short by this bitch of a storm. He and his mates, former members of his special forces team, could have toughed it out. Certainly, they had the training. But as Conroy had pointed out, now that they were all civilians, none of them had to endure it. And that's what continuing their trip would have been. This storm was rolling in and squatting over the region for the next couple of days. They'd decided staying wasn't worth it and packed up, hiking out to where they'd left their vehicles and parting ways.

As a particularly stiff gust of wind did its level best to shove him right off the winding mountain road, Ewan considered he probably should've tried to find some kind of accommodation for the night, rather than driving all the way home to Glenlaig from Riggs Moor in Yorkshire. But he was in it now. It was the middle of the bloody night, so he wouldn't find anywhere open, even if he was anywhere close to civilization.

Which he wasn't. He hadn't seen another vehicle for more than an hour.

Didn't matter. Best to push on and get home. The pub was covered until Monday, so he could pass the fuck out and rest whenever he got there.

Lightning split the sky, so close he saw the forks of it disappearing behind the treeline ahead. The boom of the thunder shook the Land Rover. Ewan slowed further, not knowing what damage it might've done. As he rounded the bend, he caught the first glimpse of light. Then he saw the tree. The behemoth trunk had been struck by the lightning. Even in the driving rain, it was still smoking. The whole thing had crashed onto another car. The light he'd seen was the headlights filtering through the thick branches.

Swearing, he wrestled his own vehicle off the road and grabbed a torch. Within seconds of shoving open his door, he was soaked through. He fought his way through the storm and then the tree. The bonnet of the car was buckled, and part of the roof had caved in under the weight. He could just make out the driver slumped over the wheel. There was no way he was getting that door open without removing some limbs first.

Rushing back to the Land Rover, he dug through his gear until he found the pocket chainsaw he used for firewood while out in the field. Back at the tree, he worked his way closer to the car. When he could reach out, he banged on the window, to see if the driver was conscious. The woman bolted upright with a scream he heard even over the roar of the storm. In the beam of his torch, her eyes were wide and disoriented, full of fear. Blood trickled from a cut on her temple.

"I'm going to get you out!" he shouted.

She didn't seem to understand him. Maybe she couldn't hear.

Not wasting anymore time, Ewan unfolded the chain and looped it around the branch that had to go before he could get to the woman inside. His muscles burned with effort as he dragged the blade back and forth in a smooth, familiar rhythm. This was much harder than sawing through the deadwood they favored for firewood. Water streamed down his face and his clothes clung to every inch. He kept looking back at the driver, but she seemed to be nodding in and out of consciousness. At last, the blade cut through. He wrestled the branch out of the way and reached for the car door, expecting to find it locked.

It wasn't.

Ewan dragged the door open, and the woman jolted awake again, jerking sideways at the sight of him. Aware he was an intimidating bulk, he crouched, trying to use himself to shield her from the storm without looming.

"Are you okay?" he shouted.

She stared at him, a tiny woman with shadows under her eyes and blood down her cheek. Her blonde hair was pulled back into a tail that had come loose in the crash. She might've been anywhere from eighteen to thirty. He couldn't tell.

When she didn't respond, he shouted again. "Can you move? Is anything broken?"

He had to repeat himself a couple of times before she seemed to register what was going on.

"I... I don't think so?" Her words were slurred, and there was still a definite sense of confusion.

He reached forward to release her seatbelt. "I'm going to get you to a hospital."

Her hand shot out and clamped around his wrist in a vise grip. "No hospital."

Ewan took in her wide, dark eyes and the ghostly hue of her face. "You have a head injury."

She squeezed impossibly tighter, each finger seeming to dig into his flesh like a talon. Her tremulous voice was full of urgency. "No hospital. Promise me."

He looked down at her tiny hand, squeezing his wrist with more strength than it seemed like she should possess. In the next flash of lightning, he saw the bruise there in the shape of fingers, a malignant shadow against her fair skin.

Someone had laid had hands on her.

Every protective instinct he had stood up and roared. No one had a right to lay hands on a woman.

Gently settling his hand over hers, where she had his wrist in a stranglehold, he met her gaze. "I promise. No hospital."

They stared at each other for a long moment before all the fight seemed to drain out of her, and her head slumped forward. She'd passed out again.

Wasting no more time, he released the seatbelt and eased her out of the car, carrying her back to his own vehicle. As he transferred her into the passenger seat, he made a vow to himself and to her.

He didn't know what she was running from, but it sure as fuck wouldn't get to her through him.

———

Choose Your Next Romance

So *obviously* we get to see the badass former Royal Marine in action in *Protector in a Kilt*. Who is this mystery woman? You'll just have to order to find out! ;)

Meanwhile, if you'd like more of Connor and Sophie's happily ever after, you can grab their bonus epilogue here: https://kaitnolan.com/playboy-in-a-kilt-bonus-epilogue-download/

Meanwhile, if you're looking for more fake relationship goodness, have you checked out *Until We Meet Again?* This novella is the first part of a two-fer story about Samantha Ferguson and Griffin Powell and it's full of all the Vegas wedding, fake relationship shenanigans you're dying for more of. The rest of their story concludes in *Come A Little Closer*, Book 4 in the Men of the Misfit Inn series (which can totally be read as a standalone).

Other Books By Kait Nolan

A complete and up-to-date list of all my books can be found at https://kaitnolan.com.

Kilted Hearts
Small Town Contemporary Scottish Romance

- *Jilting The Kilt* (prequel)
- *Cowboy in a Kilt* (Raleigh and Kyla)
- *Grump in a Kilt* (Malcolm and Charlotte)
- *Playboy in a Kilt* (Connor and Sophie)
- *Protector in a Kilt* (Ewan and Isobel)
- *Single Dad in a Kilt* (Hamish and Afton)

Bad Boy Bakers
Small Town Military Romance

- *Rescued By a Bad Boy* (Brax and Mia prequel)
- *Mixed Up With a Marine* (Brax and Mia)
- *Wrapped Up with a Ranger* (Holt and Cayla)
- *Stirred Up by a SEAL* (Jonah and Rachel)

- *Hung Up on the Hacker* (Cash and Hadley)
- *Caught Up with the Captain* (Grey and Rebecca)

RESCUE MY HEART SERIES
SMALL TOWN MILITARY ROMANCE

- *Baby It's Cold Outside* (Ivy and Harrison)
- *What I Like About You* (Laurel and Sebastian)
- *Bad Case of Loving You* (Paisley and Ty prequel)
- *Made For Loving You* (Paisley and Ty)

THE MISFIT INN SERIES
SMALL TOWN FAMILY ROMANCE

- *When You Got A Good Thing* (Kennedy and Xander)
- *Til There Was You* (Misty and Denver)
- *Those Sweet Words* (Pru and Flynn)
- *Stay A Little Longer* (Athena and Logan)
- *Bring It On Home* (Maggie and Porter)

MEN OF THE MISFIT INN
SMALL TOWN SOUTHERN ROMANCE

- *Let It Be Me* (Emerson and Caleb)
- *Our Kind of Love* (Abbey and Kyle)
- *Don't You Wanna Stay* (Deanna and Wyatt)
- *Until We Meet Again* (Samantha and Griffin prequel)
- *Come A Little Closer* (Samantha and Griffin)
- *Just Wanted You To Know* (Livia and Declan):
  April 14

WISHFUL ROMANCE SERIES
SMALL TOWN SOUTHERN ROMANCE

- *Once Upon A Coffee* (Avery and Dillon)

- *To Get Me To You* (Cam and Norah)
- *Know Me Well* (Liam and Riley)
- *Be Careful, It's My Heart* (Brody and Tyler)
- *Just For This Moment* (Myles and Piper)
- *Wish I Might* (Reed and Cecily)
- *Turn My World Around* (Tucker and Corinne)
- *Dance Me A Dream* (Jace and Tara)
- *See You Again* (Trey and Sandy)
- *The Christmas Fountain* (Chad and Mary Alice)
- *You Were Meant For Me* (Mitch and Tess)
- *A Lot Like Christmas* (Ryan and Hannah)
- *Dancing Away With My Heart* (Zach and Lexi)

WISHING FOR A HERO SERIES (A WISHFUL SPINOFF SERIES)
SMALL TOWN ROMANTIC SUSPENSE

- *Make You Feel My Love* (Judd and Autumn)
- *Watch Over Me* (Nash and Rowan)
- *Can't Take My Eyes Off You* (Ethan and Miranda)
- *Burn For You* (Sean and Delaney)

MEET CUTE ROMANCE
SMALL TOWN SHORT ROMANCE

- *Once Upon A Snow Day*
- *Once Upon A New Year's Eve*
- *Once Upon An Heirloom*
- *Once Upon A Coffee*
- *Once Upon A Campfire*
- *Once Upon A Rescue*

SUMMER CAMP
CONTEMPORARY ROMANCE

- *Once Upon A Campfire*
- *Second Chance Summer*

About Kait

Kait is a Mississippi native, who often swears like a sailor, calls everyone sugar, honey, or darlin', and can wield a bless your heart like a saber or a Snuggie, depending on requirements.

You can find more information on this *USA Today* best selling and RITA ® Award-winning author and her books on her website http://kaitnolan.com.

Do you need more small town sass and spark? Sign up for <u>her newsletter</u> to hear about new releases, book deals, and exclusive content!

www.ingramcontent.com/pod-product-compliance
Lightning Source LLC
Chambersburg PA
CBHW070524100726

47907CB00004B/969